Jeptha Root Simms

Trappers of New York

A Biography of Nicholas Stoner and Nathaniel Foster

Jeptha Root Simms

Trappers of New York
A Biography of Nicholas Stoner and Nathaniel Foster

ISBN/EAN: 9783337408848

Printed in Europe, USA, Canada, Australia, Japan

Cover: Foto ©Raphael Reischuk / pixelio.de

More available books at **www.hansebooks.com**

TRAPPERS OF NEW YORK,

OR A BIOGRAPHY OF

NICHOLAS STONER & NATHANIEL FOSTER;

TOGETHER WITH

ANECDOTES OF OTHER CELEBRATED HUNTERS,

AND SOME ACCOUNT OF

SIR WILLIAM JOHNSON,

AND HIS STYLE OF LIVING.

BY JEPTHA R. SIMMS,

AUTHOR OF THE HISTORY OF SCHOHARIE COUNTY,
AND BORDER WARS OF NEW YORK.

He lifts the tube, and levels with his eye;
Straight a short thunder breaks the frozen sky.—*Pope.*

ALBANY:
J. MUNSELL, 78 STATE STREET,
1860.

PREFACE.

―――

" To be ignorant of all antiquity," says a popular writer (I. D'Israeli), " is a mutilation of the human mind; it is early associations and local circumstances which give bent to the mind of a people from their infancy, and insensibly constitute the nationality of genius." This is a truism which can not be contra-travened, and although the world is now full of books for good or ill, yet I venture to add another. Well, as this is only a duodecimo, may I not bespeak for it a little share of public favor ? For if it is but a small volume, it has nevertheless required considera-ble time and care to collect and arrange its minutiæ. the author does not claim for it a place among classic works, which sparkle with literary gems; but he does claim for it the merit of candor. In a work purporting to be one of truth, he would not impose upon the credulity of others, what he could not be-lieve himself.

This book has been written with the view of giving the reader some knowledge of the peril-environed life of a hunter; in connection with the early and topo-graphical history of a portion of northern New York. As the forests disappear, the country is settled and wild game exterminated; that hardy race of indi-viduals which followed the chase for a living will have become extinct; indeed, those who would have been called professional hunters, have now nearly or quite all left the remaining woods of New York, and most of them sleep with their fathers. Many of the names with their daring adventures are now forgotten.

How important is it, therefore, to place on record what can still be gathered respecting them, to live in future story; when some American Scott shall have arisen to connect their names and deeds forever, with the rifle-mimicking mountains, the awe-inspiring glens, the hill-encompassed lakes, and the zigzag-coursing rivulets—upon, within, around, and along which they sought with noiseless footstep the bounty-paying wolf, the timid deer, and fur-clad beaver.

I may remark, that one motive in producing this book has been, to contribute materials for the future history of the state. Says an American scholar (W. A. Whitehead), "The general historian must gather his facts from the details of local annals, and in proportion as they are wanting must his labors be imperfect." A small budget of antiquarian matter, and some interesting incidents of the American Revolution are here introduced; and in connection with this subject, I will take occasion to say, that I am collecting original matter of an historical character, with the intention of publishing it at a future, not distant day. There are yet unpublished, many reminiscences either of, or growing out of our war for independence, both thrilling and instructive.

Not a few such are now in the writer's possession. They are generally of a personal and anecdotal nature, and many of them were noted down from the lips of men whose heads are whitened by the frosts of time, or are now laid beneath the valley-clods.

If such an anecdote should still linger in the mind of a reader of this page, or any old paper of interest remain in his or her keeping, that individual would confer a favor by communicating the same to my address. Our Revolution is destined, in its fullness of benefit, to emancipate the world from tyranny; and every minute incident relating to that great struggle is not only worthy of record, but highly important, for the proper understanding of its cost to the young, to whose guardianship its principles and advantages must soon be confided.

The difficulty of preparing a work for the press where much of the matter is to be obtained by conversational notes, is only known to those who have experienced the task; and such best know its liability to contain error. The biography of Major Stoner has nearly all been read over to him since it was written out, and corrected; I can with confidence, therefore, promise the reader, as few errors in this as he will find in any work similarly got up. In conclusion, I would fain express my grateful thanks to those individuals who have in any manner contributed towards making this volume.

Fultonville, N. Y.   J. R. SIMMS.

INTRODUCTORY NOTE

TO THIRD EDITION.

An impression seems to have stolen upon the credulity of many persons, that a full account of Maj. Stoner's eventful life had not been given in this work; but that after his death, the reader would be startled by the narrative of a score of tragic scenes, vieing with each other in horrid detail. Desirous of making the work as authentic as possible, before the first edition of it was published, the matter relating to Mr. Stoner was read over, not only to him, but to Jacob Shew, a compatriot in arms, and after as well as before the war, a resident of the same county. At its conclusion the latter observed that my Leatherstocking had been very candid with me, and as he believed, had told me of all the fatal rencontres he had ever had with Indian hunters, which were much talked of at the time of their occurrence. Mr. Blakeman, a hunter whose name appears in the book, thought Mr. Stoner had killed one Indian whose death I had not recorded, but the senior hunter at a later interview explained the whole matter. The Indian, as he said, did not wait to be killed, and the blood seen near the deserted cabin, which confirmed Blakeman's suspicions, was that of a deer. And here let me add, I never conversed with a more candid and seemingly conscientious man than Nicholas Stoner. He died Nov. 24th, 1853, and was buried at Kingsborough. As some credulous people are looking for what is never to appear, unless in a work of *fiction*, the reader is assured, that after each of the preceding editions of this work were issued, Mr. Stoner, who had read it himself, informed the writer in all candor, that although he had frightened very many Indians, this book contained a true account of all that he had actually killed. He good-humoredly added, that some knowing ones told stories about him which had no foundation in truth, and appearing desirous to make him a very bad man.

1857.   J. R. S.

CONTENTS.

―

Chapter I.

Chapter II.

Chapter VI.

Chapter VII.

Chapter VIII.

Chapter IX.

Chapter X.

Chapter XI.

Chapter XII.

Chapter XIII.

Chapter XIV.

Chapter XV.

Chapter XVI.

Chapter XVII.

CHAPTER XVIII.

TRAPPERS OF NEW YORK.

CHAPTER I.

Incidents of greater or less interest occur in the lives of almost every member of the human family, which only need be known to be justly appreciated, or subserve some good and wise purpose; but occasionally an individual crosses the broad landscape of life, whose career may be said to consist of a bundle of incidents—the greater part of whose existence is in fact so full of novelty as to claim, for at least a portion of it, a record for the benefit or amusement of mankind. Of the latter class is Major Nicholas Stoner, some of the most romantic and daring of whose adventures are presented in the following pages.

To say that a man lived through the American Revolution and participated in its perils, is alone sufficient guaranty that he can, if at all intelligent, recount unique and thrilling scenes as yet untold in history; but when we meet with one who has not only been exposed to the perils of an eight years' war, but has shared in the dangers and hardships of a second war—one, in truth, whose life has been chequered with a thousand hazardous exposures between and subsequent to those wars; we may expect, almost as a matter of course, to learn from him not a little that will prove acceptable to the general reader, nourishing

"The seeds of happiness, and powers of thought."

The facts here given of this celebrated warrior, were noted down by the writer from his own lips at personal interviews; not a few of which have been corroborated by the testimony of others. It is the fortune of very few individuals to pass through a long life surrounded by such a variety of perils, without receiving more personal injury.

Henry Stoner, the father of Nicholas, emigrated from Germany to the American colonies, as is believed, nearly twenty years before their emancipation from British tyranny. He landed at New York, and after a short residence in that city removed to the colony of Maryland, where he married Catharine Barnes, by whom he had two sons, Nicholas and John.

Nicholas Stoner, who was about a year the senior of his brother, was born Dec. 15, 1762 or '63; which year is not now known with certainty, the family record having been burned with his father's dwelling in the Revolution. He is five feet eleven inches high, of slender but sinewy form; and though his light brown hair is now (1848) silvered by the frosts of fourscore winters, and his body is a little bent, yet his step is still firm without a cane, and his intellect vigorous. He has from boyhood worn a pair of small rings in his ears. His complexion, owing to his mode of life, is now swarthy. In his younger days he must have been a man of uncommonly prepossessing personal appearance; for his acquaintances of forty years' standing, speak of him " as one of the likeliest looking men they have ever known." His walk—indeed,almost every motion, betrays his forest life, for he moves with the caution of a trapper and the stillness of a panther; added to which he becomes impatient and vexed at restraint.

The frontispiece, which gives a good likeness of him at the age of about eighty-three, exhibits him accou tred as a trapper. He usually wore a fur cap when hunting, and a short coat, or cloth roundabout. A belt encircled his waist, at the foot of which was fastened a bullet pouch, and beneath which upon the left side were thrust a hatchet and knife; while under his right arm hung a powder horn of no mean capacity. When trapping for beaver, he was often loaded with a bundle of double-spring steel traps; which were suspended beneath the left arm. The frontispiece was engraved from two daguerreotype likenesses, one of which was taken in the village of Johnstown, on the 10th of Sept., 1846; and as there was a militia general training in the village on that day, the old hero was not only accoutred with little trouble to visit the artist, but was greeted at every turn by numerous friends and acquaintances, all eager once more to grasp his hand and give him a friendly salutation. The other miniature, although it does not exhibit the old trapper in his forest garb, was taken subsequently at his place of residence, and is by far the best likeness. A borrowed cap seen in the picture, conceals much of his intelligent brow.

New York city again became the residence of Henry Stoner while his children were quite young, during which Nicholas went to school and learned to read. He was sent to school by John Binkus (if I have the orthography correct), a man of wealth, who had married Miss Hannah Stoner, a sister of the young student's father. During the Revolution, this Binkus became a refugee officer in the famous corps of Gen. De Lancey. Henry Stoner, who had been a kind of trafficker or speculator in a small way since his arrival in the colonies, after a second residence in New York of a few years, resolved to become a pioneer settler, and removed with his family to Fonda's Bush, a place in the Johnstown settlements, so called after Major Jelles Fonda, who took a patent for the lands. The place is situated about ten miles north of east from the village of Johnstown, and the same distance west of north from Amsterdam.

Fonda's Bush signifies the same as if it were called Fonda's Woods, a dense forest covering the soil at that early period—bush being the usual term for woods on the frontiers of New York. Indeed, the Sugar Bush is the present appellation given to woods from which maple sugar is made. At the time of Stoner's arrival, Johnstown, though but a small village, was becoming known abroad, as it was the residence of the baronet, Sir William Johnson (after whom it was called), who as Indian agent for the Six Nations, and as a military man of repute, was notorious in what was *then* Western New York.

As Stoner was the first settler at Fonda's Bush, he left his family in Philadelphia Bush, while he was erecting a log dwelling four miles distant. The last mentioned place, now in the town of Mayfield, obtained its name from the fact, that one or more of its first inhabitants were from Philadelphia, or the vicinity of that city. Some two years after Stoner fixed his residence in the wilderness, Joseph Scott, and about the same time Benjamin De Line, also located in his neighborhood. I say neighborhood because they were the nearest neighbors of the Stoner family, although from one to two miles distant. His residence was still on the wild-wood side of his pioneer brethren. The next man who fixed his residence in the vicinity of Stoner, was Philip Helmer, who drove the wild beasts from their haunts and broke ground two miles to the eastward of him. Andrew Bowman, Herman Salisbury, John Putnam, Charles Cady, and possibly one or two others, also settled in and about Fonda's Bush before the Revolution. Cady, who married a daughter of Philip Helmer, was one of the first settlers at the west village. He is believed to have gone to Canada with Sir John Johnson.

It must have been about the time of Stoner's location in Fonda's Bush, that Godfrey Shew, a German, made the first permanent location near Sir William

Johnson's fishing lodge, denominated the *Fish House*, and situated on the Sacondaga river, eight miles north-east of Stoner's dwelling. Before Shew planted himself at the Fish House, several families of squatters had been there, who had gone " to parts unknown," and desirous of getting a wholesome citizen to remain there, the baronet held out liberal inducements to Mr. Shew, of which he accepted.

In my *History of Schoharie County*, etc.,, I have given some account of Sir William Johnson, with several anecdotes of him—described his stately mansions, and told the manner of his death, &c., &c.; but at the time of publishing that work, I was not aware that he had a more celebrated *summer residence* in the latter part of his life, than that denominated the Fish House. From conversations held within the past year (1849) with the aged patriot *Jacob Shew*, who is a son of Godfrey Shew named above, I am enabled to garner up some more incidents in the life of this nobleman, and authentic memoranda of the classic grounds under consideration, which can not fail to prove interesting to future generations, even though they are little appreciated by the present.

Sir William Johnson, after establishing himself at his Hall in Johnstown, no doubt lived in greater affluence, or more in the style of a European nobleman of that day, than ever did any other citizen of New York. His household was quite numerous at all times, and not unfrequently was much increased by

distinguished guests. He had a *secretary* named
Lafferty, who was a good lawyer and did all his legal
business. He had a *bouw-master*, an Irishman named
Flood. Bouw is a Low Dutch word signifying *harvest*—or as here used, an overseer or manager of the
laborers of the Hall farm. From ten to fifteen slaves
usually performed the labor on the farm, and they were
under the immediate direction of the bouw-master.
The slaves, some of whom had families, lived across
the Cayadutta creek from the Hall, in small dwellings erected for them. They drest much as did their
Indian neighbors, except that a kind of coat was
made of their blankets by the Hall tailor.

He had a family *physician* named Daly, who practiced but little out of his own household. Doct. Daly
was a very companionable man, and often accompanied Sir William in his pleasure excursions. He had
a *musician*, a dwarf some thirty years old, who answered to the name of Billy. He played a violin
well, and was always on hand to entertain guests.
He had a *gardener*, who cultivated a large garden,
and kept that and the grounds about the Hall as neat
as a pin. He had a *butler*, named Frank, an active
young German, who was with him a number of years,
and who made himself very useful to his master.
Frank remained about the Hall until the Revolution
began, when he went to Albany county. He had a
waiter named Pontioch, a sprightly, well disposed lad
of mixed blood, negro and Indian, who was generally

with him when from home.   He had a pair of white,
dwarfish-looking *waiters,* who catered to his own and
his guests' comfort: their surname was Bartholomew,
and they are believed to have been brothers.

   The secretary, physician, bouw-master, and all the
waiters remained, after the death of Sir William, with
his son, Sir John Johnson, until the Revolution began,
and then followed his fortunes to Canada.   The Baronet had also his own mechanics.   His *blacksmith*
and his *tailor,* had each a shop just across the road
from the Hall.   They did very little work for any one
out of the *royal* household.   Sir William was a large,
well-looking and full-favored man.   "Laugh and
grow fat," is an old maxim, of which his neighbors
were reminded, when they beheld this fun-loving man.
He was well read for the times, and uncommonly well
versed in the study of human nature.   Near the Hall
he erected two detached wings of stone, the west one
of which was used by his attorney Lafferty, for an
office, and the other contained a *philosophical apparatus,* of which he died possessed.   The room in which
the apparatus was kept, was called his own *private
study.*   On seeing him enter it, Pontioch used to say:
" *Now massa gone into his study to tink ob somesin
me know not what.*"

   Sir William erected a school-house in Johnstown
soon after he located there.   It was an oblong building
with a desk at one end, and stood on the diagonal
corner of the streets from the county clerk's office—

JOHNSON HALL,

THE FORMER RESIDENCE OF SIR WILLIAM JOHNSON,

AT JOHNSTOWN, NEW YORK.

on the present site of Lucus I. Smith's store. To begin a village, he also erected at the same time six dwelling-houses in the vicinity of the school-house. They were each some 30 feet long fronting the street, by 18 or 20 feet deep, were one and a half stories high, with two square rooms on the floor. Those dwellings and the school-house were all painted yellow. One of the earliest if not in fact the first teacher of this school, was an arbitrary Irishman named *Wall*, who taught only the common English branches. An Episcopal church was also erected in Johnstown under the patronage of Sir William, several years before his death.

In the street in front of the school-house, public stocks and a whipping-post were placed, the former of which were a terror to truant boys, whose feet not unfrequently graced them. Before Godfrey Shew removed to the Fish House, he resided a mile west of the Hall, at which time his children, with those of a neighbor or two, went to school. In the vicinity of the Hall were usually to be seen a dozen or more Indians, of whom the children were afraid; and the fact coming to the knowledge of Sir William, he spoke to a chief in their behalf, and then assured the little urchins, with whom he liked to chat, *that they need borrow no more trouble about their red neighbors.*

He had six children at that time by his handsome brown housekeeper, Molly Brant; and the three oldest, Peter, Betsey and Lana, went to school—George and two little girls being thought too young to send.
3

Wall was very severe with most of his pupils, but the
Baronet's children were made an exception to his
clemency—they ever being treated with kind partial-
ity and pointed indulgence. He observed the most
rigid formality in teaching his scholars *manners ;* a
very important branch of education, and quite too
much neglected in modern times. He required his
pupils, however, not so much to respect age and intellect in others as in himself. If a child wished to go
out, it must go before him with a complaisant—*please
master may I go out ?* accompanied with a bow, a
backward motion of the right hand, and drawing back
upon the floor the right foot. On returning to the
school-room, the pupil had again to parade before the
master, with another three-motioned bow, and a very
grateful—*thank you, sir !*

The lad Jacob Shew, on becoming initiated into
the out-and-in ceremony, accompanied his first bow
with a scrape of the left foot. *Tak the other fut, you
rascal !* was roared with such a brogue and emphasis
by old Pedagogue, as to confuse him, and he flourished the left foot again. *Tak the other fut, I tell ye !*
came louder than before, attended with a stamp that
carried terror to the boy's heart. Comprehending the
requirement, he shifted his balance—scraped with *the
right fut*—heard a surly *that'll doh !* and went on
his way rejoicing though trembling.

In nearly every school of New England and New
York twenty-five years ago, the scholars on entering
and on leaving the school-room during the hours of

school, had to make their manners—the boys to bow, gracefully if they could, but at all events to bow, and the girls to courtesy, genteely, of course. Nor were the manners of the children confined to the school-room; for on meeting any sober person in the street, they had to make their obeisance, and learned to take pleasure and pride in so doing. It was then a very pretty spectacle to pass a country school-house at noon, or when the children were out at play, and see them parade as if by military intuition, and give the traveler a united evidence of good breeding. This sight is occasionally seen at the present day, where female teachers are employed.

Traversing the forest in the French war, from Ticonderoga to Fort Johnson, his then residence, no doubt first made Sir William Johnson familiar with the make of the country adjoining the Sacondaga river; and soon after the close of that war he erected a lodge for his convenience, while hunting and fishing, on the south side of the river, nearly eighteen miles distant from his own dwelling. The lodge was ever after called *The Fish House.* It was an oblong square framed building, with two rooms below, and walls sufficiently high (one and a half stories) to have afforded pleasant chambers. Its site was on a knoll within the present garden of Dr. Langdon I. Marvin, and about thirty rods from the river. It fronted the south. Only one room in the building was ever fin-ished; that was in the west end, and had a chimney

and fire place. The house was never painted, and in
the Revolution it was burnt down, but by whom or
whose authority, is unknown. The ground from where
the building stood, slopes very prettily to the river.
No visible trace of this building remains.

A village has grown up at this place, containing
several hundred inhabitants, and bearing the historic
name of Fish House, although the post office is im-
properly called Northampton, the village lying mostly
in one corner of that town.   The village is built upon
gentle elevations, and a degree of neatness and thrift
pervades it, that agreeably disappoints the visitor.
Among its early influential inhabitants, were Asahel
Parkes, John Trumbull, John Rosevelt, Alexander
St. John, and John Fay.   The last one named located
here in 1803, and the others a few years before.

Where the Stoner family settled in Fonda's Bush,
a pretty village has also sprung up.   It is built mostly
upon level sandy land, and contains double the population of Fish House.   It is situated in the town of
Broadalbin, and like its sister village, has the misfortune to have its post-office called after the town
instead of itself, a discrepancy that should never exist
where it can be avoided.   A plank road went into
operation in 1849, from Fish House to Fonda's Bush,
a distance of eight miles; and another from the latter
place to Amsterdam, a further distance of ten miles,
bringing the three places within a few hours' ride of
each other.

The villages of Fish House and Fonda's Bush must grow in importance with their improved facilities for business—indeed, the travel to those places has been on the increase for several years. From Edinburgh, a little hamlet in Saratoga county, six miles down the river from Fish House, a stage runs twice week to Ballston Spa, stopping at Fish House; and another runs through the place three times a week, from Northville to Amsterdam. Both are mail routes. Northville deserves a passing notice in this place: it is a charming inland village in the town of Northampton, containing two or three hundred inhabitants, romantically embowered among the hills on the north bank of the Sacondaga, six miles above the Fish House, and is fast increasing in importance. The first settlers at this place were Abraham Van Aernam, Paul Hammond, John Shoecraft, Daniel Lobdell and Daniel Bryant. It is now in contemplation to build a plank road from Northville to connect at Johnstown with the one from that place to Fultonville, on the Erie canal.

At a little place about equidistant between Fish House and Northville, on the south bank of the river, with a post-office called Denton's Corners, settled Garret Van Ness, Abel Scribner and John Brown. They located there soon after the war of the Revolution closed; and as they had all three been participators in its perils, they must often have met of a long winter evening and fought their battles over. There is at this place, a bridge across the Sacondaga.

CHAPTER II.

Sir William Johnson was no doubt induced to locate in Johnstown, partly on account of the greater facilities it would afford him for hunting and fishing about the Sacondaga river, over a residence in the Mohawk valley, and partly to obtain more favorable grounds to accommodate the numerous Indians, who at times came to receive presents from the royal bounty. North of the Hall was a forest in which those visitors were occasionally encamped in great numbers.

The Sacondaga and Mohawk rivers are about twenty miles apart, from the Fish House westward, for some distance. The Mayfield mountain stretches across from the former river south-easterly to the latter, and there forms what is called The Nose, while on the north side of the Sacondaga, mountain ranges of hills towering one above the other, bound the view. The lands, on gaining the summit level, a few miles north of the Mohawk, are not mountainous between the rivers, but gently rolling from the Mayfield mountain, some twenty miles to the eastward, until they strike what is denominated the Maxon hill; the northern termination of which at the river the Indians called *Scow-a-rock-a.* The scenery, therefore, to the northward of Johnstown and Fonda's Bush, is very fine.

From the residence of Col. John I Shew, situated on an eminence one and a half miles from Fonda's Bush, and on the plank road to Fish House, is afforded the lover of natural science, in a clear day, one of the richest landscapes in this part of the state. Here the eye, looking north, seems to scan rather more than one-half of an amphitheatre, an hundred miles iu circuit, with rich and varied scenery. Within the view is overlooked the *Sacondaga vlaie*, a body of from ten to thirteen thousand acres of drowned lands. This immense marsh extends east and west about six miles. A strip at the west end, nearly two miles long, lies in Mayfield, and the eastern part extends into Northampton; but the greatest proportion is in Broadalbin, where it is the widest, being perhaps a mile or more in width.

A fine mill stream, called Vlaie creek, because it courses through the great marsh, rises in Lake Desolation, near the Maxon mountain in Greenfield, Saratoga county, and making a grand circuit of Broadalbin, passing in its route through the village of Fonda's Bush, it enters the Sacondaga at Fish House, not more than two or three miles from its source; although some twenty by its sinuous route. The stream is sometimes called the Little Sacondaga. The Indians called it *Ken-ny-ett-o*, says *Isaac R. Rosa*, of Fonda's Bush, who saw an intelligent Indian, many years ago, write the name with red chalk on the door of a grist mill. The signification of this pretty aboriginal name, after which the village and post-office should have been called, is now unknown.

The origin of this marsh is thus given by Lardner Vanuxem, in his volume of the Geology of New York: "The vlie, or natural meadow and swamp which extends along the creek of that name, to near the Fish House, are the remains of a lake, and show the pre-existent state of that country; the drainage of which happened at successive periods, as is beautifully shown, and the extent of alluvial action also, near where the upper and lower roads unite, which lead from Cranberry post-office to the river, near the hill or mountain side. There four well defined alluvial banks exist, resembling great steps or benches ranging by the mountain side, which form a semi-amphitheatre, changing by a curve from a north-east to a south-south-east direction. The upper bank of alluvion rises about a hundred feet above the river; the next below, about eighty feet; the third, from thirty to forty feet; and the lowest, from ten to twelve feet. The upper one is of sand, the second of bluish clay covered with sand, and the two lower ones of sand and gravel.

"The vlie, or natural meadows, are numerous in many parts of the [geological] district: they are the prairies of the west upon a small scale. Their soil, being composed of minutely divided parts of fine earth, is favorable for grass, the rapid growth of which smothers the germinating tree. This is the primary cause why trees do not exist where grass is rank; the others are but subordinate ones.   One and all in the district show the same origin, having been ponds or lakes receiving the wash of the country which they drained, the finer particles of which being diffused through their waters, have by subsidence formed their level bottom, and their highly productive soil for grass."

It is by no means an uncommon occurrence for a pond or lake to become filled up by alluvial deposits, so as to form dry and tillable land; and at times upon the surface of a body of water, a soil is formed that is cultivated without its ever being known to the husbandman, that he is toiling over the bosom of a lake. In confirmation of this I would instance a singular occurrence of recent date.   On the Michigan Central Railway it became necessary to carry an embankment some fifteen feet thick across a piece of low ground, containing nearly one hundred acres dry enough to plow. The workmen had progressed with the grading some distance, when it became too heavy for the soil to support it, and it sank down into *seventy-nine feet of water.* It then became apparent that the low ground had been a small lake, upon the surface of which, in process of time, a soil had collected, composed of roots, peat, muck, &c., to the depth of from ten to fifteen feet thick; the surface of which had become dry.   Had it not been deemed necessary to carry so heavy an embankment over this miniature prairie of now rich arable land, it would probably never have been known that it rested on the bosom of a lake.

On the northerly side of the vlaie and to the west-ward of the centre, are two strips of hard land bearing timber. They are called *stacking-ridges*, from the fact that many tons of hay cut annually on the low grounds contiguous, are stacked upon them to be drawn off in the winter. *Blue-joint grass* used to grow, and perhaps does to this day on the dryest bogs. Formerly immense quantities of cranberries were gathered on the north side of the marsh east of the lower stacking-ridge, on what is called *Cranberry point*. A kind of shovel with fine teeth was some-times used to scoop them up, and nearly a quart could thus be gathered at once. This mode of picking in-jured the vines however. Cranberries are not as plenty here as formerly. Opposite Cranberry point the water in Vlaie creek is said to be very deep.

One of the most interesting features about the vlaie is the fact, that a little knoll or table of hard land elevated some ten or twelve feet, extends into it toward the upper or western end. It is oblong in shape, level upon the top and gently sloping all round. It lies about north-west and south-east, the summit being some 600 feet long by 150 in breadth; and containing in the whole say ten or fifteen acres of very good land. This tongue of land is called *Summer-house point*, from the fact that Sir William Johnson erected a beautiful cottage in the centre of it in 1772, and there spent much of his time in the summer for several seasons. From Johnstown to this point, which is just fourteen miles, the Baronet opened a carriage road. While the road was surveying, a large tree was marked at the end of every mile, and numbered from the Hall. The one denominated *Nine-mile tree*, a large pine, was standing within twenty-five years, and was by the late Gen. Henry Fonda designated to several persons, who have kept vigilance of its locality. The stump of this tree, which has for seventy years been a landmark, is still standing a little east of James Lasher's dwelling in the town of Mayfield.

Summer-house point is approached from the westerly end, upon a strip of arable land, which in very high water is covered, making an island of the point. The Sacondaga patent embraced all or very nearly all of the vlaie. The point which lies in Broadalbin, was embraced in the Sacondaga patent, which conveyed 28,000 acres of land, Dec. 2, 1742, to Lendert Gansevoort, Cornelius Ten Broek, Douw Fonda, Anna J. Wendell and ten others. Of some of the original patentees or then owners, Sir William not only bought the point, but many of the lands in and contiguous to Fish House, in which village the Northampton and Sacondaga patents unite.

The cottage erected on Summer-house point stood precisely in its centre. It was a tasty one story building, fronting the south, upon which side was its front entrance. The roof sloped north and south. A piazza supported by square columns extended around the sides and east end, with a promenade upon the top nearly as high as the eaves. It had a gable window at each end on the first floor, and two windows at each end on the second. A hall ran across the building in the centre, with a square room upon each side of it, handsomely finished, well furnished, and each room lighted by two front windows. It had a nice cellar kitchen, the entrance to which was on the west end which room was always occupied in the summer season by *Nicholas* and *Flora,* a pair of the Baronet's slaves, who were there to keep every thing in order, and minister to his comfort during his visits. The cottage was painted white, with the corners, doors, widow casings and columns painted green, as was the English taste of the times—the whole contrasting beautifully with the wild scenery around.

A large garden was cultivated on the point, two cows kept there, and when the Baronet was there two horses also; as he usually rode there in a carriage. He planted fruit trees there, and two antiquated apple trees of a dozen or more are still standing. The stone of which the cellar and well were made, were brought from Fish House in a boat, and as stone were scarce on the sandy lands contiguous, early settlers with sacrilegious propensity have carried off and converted them to other uses. The plow has removed all traces of the well, which was on the verge of the knoll south of the house, and has nearly filled the cellar, a small cavity only remaining. A log house and well were built on the south side of the point toward the western end just after the revolution, but the dwelling is now gone, and most of the stone which were used in that cellar. The nearest house now to the point, is that known as the Brown place, where Samuel Brown, an old pensioner, lived and died.

I have said that the Kennyetto coursed through the vlaie. It enters a narrow strip of it south-west of the point, and runs along the latter upon its southerly side, where it is some two rods wide, and usually three or four feet deep. The Mayfield creek, a mill-stream about two-thirds as large as the Kennyetto, runs through that part of the marsh in Mayfield, and sweeping its north margin, unites with the latter stream at the extremity of the point. The Brown farm lies betweeg the two strips of the marsh named, and near where they approximate. Besides those named, several other streams enter the marsh. On the north side at Cranberry point, a mile from Summer-house point, Cranberry creek runs in, and nearly loses itself before reaching Vlaie creek, as the stream is called after it receives Mayfield creek. On the south side two mill streams run in, in Broadalbin, one nearly opposite Cranberry creek, called formerly Frenchman's creek, and the other a mile below called Han's creek; and yet so great is the natural process of absorption and evaporation constantly going on

4

here, that the creek, where it issues from the vlaie and
enters the Sacondaga at Fish House, discharges but
little if any more water than passes Summer-house
point, in the Kennyetto; indeed, it is said by some
of the observing citizens near its mouth, that less
water issues from the marsh than did formerly.

Frenchman's creek is so called, because a Frenchman named Joseph DeGolier located at an early day
upon its shores about two miles from its mouth.   It
has since been called McMartin's creek, after Duncan
McMartin, Esq., who established himself and erected
mills upon it many years ago.   McMartin was a surveyor and laid out most of the roads in and around
Broadalbin.   He was a man of wealth and respect-
ability, and was appointed a judge of the common
pleas in 1818—was a master in chancery, &c., &c.;
and as an evidence of his enterprise, erected a substantial brick edifice upon his farm, some few years
before his death.   This same stream has also been
called Factory creek, from the fact that a woolen
manufactory was established upon it near the residence of Mr. McMartin, as early as 1812 or 1814.
It is still in operation.   Han's creek got its name
from the following circumstance: Some few years
before his death, Sir William Johnson and John
Conyne were fishing for trout in the mouth of this
stream, when as Conyne was standing up, an unexpected lurch of the boat sent him out floundering in
the water.   He shipped a sea or two, as the sailor

would say, before he was rescued by the helping hand of his companion from a watery grave. My informant heard the Baronet relate the circumstance at Johnson Hall to a large circle of friends soon after, with his usual gusto for such adventures. He not not only had a hearty laugh over it then, but often afterwards when telling *how Conyne plunged into the water to seek for trout.* Hans being the Dutch of John, and the familiar name by which Sir William called his companion in relating the incident; hence the name for the stream.

There is now along the sides and lower end of Summer house point, a stunted growth of alder and swamp willow, but when occupied by Sir William Johnson, the bushes were all cut off, and the margin of the stream kept clean. He had a beautiful boat there, in which he used to go down to the Fish House, four miles distant, sometimes with company, for he entertained numerous distinguished guests, and at other times attended only by a few servants, or possibly by his faithful Pontioch, who rowed the boat while he sat in the stern and steered it. His greatest time for hunting and fishing was in the spring and fall. When the marsh was flooded, a boat would pass over it any where, the water rising at Summer-house point, from six to eight feet above low water mark. At such times the prospect was grand from the promenade of his cottage, access to which was gained by an outside stairway, near the hall door. Thousands upon thousands of ducks and wild geese were then floating upon the waters, at which time his double-barreled gun was in almost constant requisition. Some twenty five years ago, ducks used to breed about the vlaie. They are sometimes caught in nets there, and taken to market.

In company with Dr. William Chambers, Marcellus Weston, Esq., my patriotic old friend Jacob Shew, Col. John I. Shew his son, and little Haydn Shew, I visited Summer-house point on the 29th day of August, 1849, and well was I compensated for the journey. It is a most delightful place, divested of all historic associations, but clothed with them, it is one of the most interesting spots imaginable Recreating in fancy the white cottage with green facings, I could almost hear the notes of Billy's old fiddle, as his greatest skill was taxed to please the ear of some fastidious city guest; and at some witticism of the happy host, I seemed to hear peal after peal of merry laughter, and now and then an Indian whoop, as in former days they rang out upon the gentle breeze. The fairy craft of some forest son seemed once more to be gliding along the grass-hidden stream with its blanket-clad navigator standing erect as of yore, and bound for Sacondaga. Imagination pictured Pontioch caressing his favorite steeds, and calling on Nicholas to aid a black driver in rubbing them dry; and as I passed the entrance to Flora's department, to look at the noble animals, I seemed to see upon one side of it scores of pigeons and wild ducks, with the saddle of a deer; and on the other a large heap of golden trout, to supply the cottage larder and feed its guests.

But I find I am growing visionary, and will dismiss this subject, with my grateful thanks to the gentlemen who conducted me to Summer-house point, where I trust I may again light up " the council fires" of imagination—again be surrounded by intelligent friends—again see some little Haydn hooking perch or sun-fish—again see the happy hay makers near the upper stacking-ridge—and again seek for some relic of the point's first occupancy, if only to be rewarded by the limb of an old apple tree.

CHAPTER III.

Sa-con-da-ga is an aboriginal word, which signifies, as the Indians assured Godfrey Shew, *much water*, Capt. Gill, an Indian hunter, said it meant *sunken* or *drowned lands.* It no doubt has particular reference to the flooding of the vlaie. The Sacondaga shooting out from the mountains in Northampton, enters the semi-amphitheatre in a south-eastern course, and continues that direction in what seems a great basin, until it gets to Fish House, where, receiving the Vlaie creek, and striking spurs of the Maxon mountain, its course is changed to a north-eastern one, thus making two equal sides of a triangle some twenty miles in circuit. The vlaie is about as low as the bed of the river, and when the latter rises suddenly, it sets back up the creek with a heavy current, so as not unfrequently to carry bridges *up stream,* that were over the streams in the marsh. The Sacondaga continues a north-easterly course, until it enters the Hudson some thirty miles from the Fish House. A small steam boat has been plying for two seasons between Fish House and Barber's Dam, a distance of about twenty miles. This dam is situated at the head of what is usually denominated the Horse race, or rapid water, which extends from thence to the Hudson. Conklinville, a

small hamlet, with several mills and a leather manufactory, has recently grown up at the dam.

Daly's creek, a stream running into the Sacondaga
on the east side, and near Barber's dam, got its name
from the following circumstance. Dr. Daly, the
family physician of Sir William Johnson, was at the
mouth of this stream with the latter on a fishing excursion, as in days gone by it was a great place for
trout. A little eddy in the water had caught up a
bed of leaves, and the top ones were so curled and
dry, as to lead the doctor to suppose they were quietly
reposing on the top of a small sand bar. It is not
unlikely that Sir William, to please himself or guests
that may have been with them, humored the joke, if
he did not set it on foot. Catching the painter, the
doctor sprang out to draw the boat upon the bar—
when lo! he went plum up to his arms in the water.
This incident not only added a yarn to the Baronet's
long budget, which he often spun at the doctor's expense, but served to originate a name for the stream.
Some few years after the above incident transpired,
Godfrey Shew, his sons John and Jacob, and Edmund
Pangburn, were fishing at the mouth of Daly's creek,
when a similar little eddy of crisped leaves attracted
the notice of young Jacob, and to get the wrinkles
out of his legs, he concluded to step out of the boat
on the bar. He did so, and down went the leaves,
and still deeper down the boy to get a handsome
ducking, and be laughed at by his comrades when in

the boat.　Query: Should not this stream be called Shew's creek, some part of the time?

Near the mouth of Han's creek, and about half-way from Summer-house point to Fish House, dwelt before the Revolution the family of Henry Worm-wood.　He had three daughters and two sons.　The oldest daughter, whose name is now forgotten, married and went to Schoharie; the other two, Susannah and Elizabeth, lived at home.　Susannah, the eldest of the two, was a beautiful girl, of middling stature, charmingly formed, with a complexion fair as a water lily—contrasting with which she had a melting dark eye and raven hair.　Elizabeth much resembled her sister, but was not quite as fair.　An Irishman named Robert or Alexander Dunbar, a good looking fellow, paid his addresses to Susannah, and soon after married her.　The match was in some manner brought about by the Baronet—was an unhappy one, and they soon after parted.　She however retained as her stock in trade a young Dunbar.　What became of Dunbar is unknown.

Sir William was on very intimate terms with both the Wormwood girls, but the most so with Susannah, after she became a grass-widow—at which time she was about twenty years old.　Those girls were often at the cottage on the point, and not unfrequently at the Fish-house.　As the latter place was not furnished, when Sir William went down there intending to stay over night, he took down a bed from the point,

which, " as the evening shades prevailed," was
made up on the floor. In passing Wormwood's
dwelling, some half a mile distant from his boat at
the nearest point, if he desired an agreeable companion for the night, he discharged his double-barreled
gun, and the two shots in quick succession, was a
signal that never failed to bring him a temporary
housekeeper. Susannah was his favorite, and so
pleased was she with his attentions, that she often
arrived on foot at the fish house before he did,
especially if he lingered to fish by the way.

Wormwood and his wife sometimes accompaaied
one of their daughters to the fish-house, where they
occasionally remained over night. The old man had
the misfortune to break an arm, and by imprudence
he kept it lame for a long time. Early one morning
he called in at Shew's dwelling, situated over a knoll
and perhaps one-fourth of a mile from the fish-house.
Rubbing his arm he began to give a sorry picture of
its lameness, in which he was suddenly interrupted
by Mrs Shew. " Poh!" said she, " you have made
it lame by sleeping on the floor again at the fish-
house."

" No I haven't," said he, " I slept on a good bed; for
Sir William brought down from the point a very nice
wide one, which was plenty large enough for four"—

" *Four?*" quickly interrogated Mrs. Shew, greatly
surprised at the reply of Wormwood, " pray how did
you manage to sleep *four* in a bed?"

"O, easy enough. Susannah made it up very
nicely on the floor, and then Sir William told us how
to lay. He first directed the women to get in the
middle, and now, said he to me, you get on that side
and take care of your old woman next to you, and
I'll get in on this side and try to take care of Susannah. No, I didn't make my arm lame by sleeping
on the floor *last* night." It is unnecessary to add,
Mrs. S. did not question her neighbor any farther.

To dispose of this family in a few words, which
catered for years to pamper the baser passions of an
influential man, liberally endowed with Solomondic
lust; the two sons went to Canada with Sir John
Johnson; Elizabeth married *somebody* and moved to
—*somewhere;* and Susannah, with an heir to the
Sacondaga vlaie—sex unknown—remained about
Johnstown with her parents until the Revolution was
over and then went to Canada. Old Wormwood
was seen at Amsterdam after the war by a former
neighbor, who enquired *where he lived?* "Any
where," he replied, "where I can find a house."
Poor weak man, he has beyond a doubt parted with
his "mortal coil" long since; but his old bones, we
hazard a conjecture, more than once felt the need
of Sir William's 'wide bed,' or some other, before
that solemn event.

About the fish-house, Sir William Johnson reserved one hundred acres of land, which was confis-

cated with his son's estate in the Revolution. When
sold by the sequestrating committee, it was purchased
by Major Nicholas Fish (he was adjutant-general of
militia after the war), for one hundred pounds. Maj.
Fish sold it at the close of the war to Asahel Parkes,
of Shaftsbury, Vermont, who resided several years
upon it. He built a dwelling upon the low ground a
few rods from the mouth of Vlaie creek, and the following spring he was driven out of it by some four
feet of water. Traces of this building are still to be
seen west of the road, just above the river bridge.
Parkes sold the Fish-house farm to Alexander St.
John. The village has since been built upon it.

The bridge just alluded to crosses the river where
it makes its great angle, and only a few rods below
the mouth of Vlaie creek. The Sacondaga at this
place is about two-thirds as large as the Mohawk is
at Fultonville. The cost of this bridge, a covered
one, in Barber & Howe's *Historical Collections of
New York*, is erroneously stated to have been sixty
thousand dollars. It cost about *six thousand dollars*,
and was built by the state's munificence in 1818, at
which time Jacob Shew was in the legislature and
advocated the measure with success. It was supposed the state would soon realize the funds again,
by the sale of her lands on the north side of the river,
a market for which would be more readily found by
improving the way to them. How profitable the in-
vestment has proved for the state we are unable to

say, but the convenience of a free bridge to the public is invaluable.

Among the unwise measures adopted in the early part of our struggle for liberty, was that of fortifying Summe-house point; it being supposed by some that an enemy from the north, would be likely to approach the point by water. Part of a regiment of continental troops under Col. Nicholson was stationed here much of the summer of 1776. An intrenchment six feet wide and several feet deep was cut across the eastern end of the point; while the cottage in green livery, as we may suppose, assumed a warlike aspect. The point as a military post was abandoned at the end of the summer. The summer-house shared the same fate as the fish-house, in the Revolution; as they were both burnt about the year 1781. We suppose that, from the fact that this cottage had been occupied by the Americans as a military post, and that the repossession of it by Sir John Johnson was now placed almost beyond a doubt among the impossibilities, he gave instructions to some hostile invaders to burn that and the fish-house, that they should fall to the ownership and occupancy of no one else. All traces of the fortifications on the point have disappeared, the ditch having become entirely filled up by deposits from the marsh.

Just before Summer-house point was garrisoned, a scout of several men was sent from Johnstown to reconnoitre in its vicinity. From the point they crossed

the marsh to the bank of the Sacondaga, and not finding any trace of an enemy's approach, they returned
to the point. When ready to retrace their steps to
Johnstown, they found the boat had been left by some
person on the opposite shore of the Kennyetto. In
attempting to cross the stream and get it, one of the
men, named Willie Boiles, a continental soldier, was
drowned. His body was recovered and buried on the
northerly end of the point, a few rods southerly from
the fence toward the road, and not far distant from the
Mayfield creek. No stone or stake indicates the spot.

Summer-house point was sold by Jeremiah Van
Rensselaer, one of the committee for sequestrations,
to James Caldwell of Albany. Who now owns this
delightful spot I am unable to say. Formerly, when
it became the rallying spot for hay-makers, cranberry-
pickers and fishermen, temporary bridges were made
across the creeks upon its sides, by throwing over
stringers and covering them with brush and hay. The
timber was drawn upon the point in the winter, to be
restored in the summer.

A settlement was begun in Mayfield, some ten miles
to the northward of Johnson Hall, under the patronage
of Sir William Johnson, about as early as Stoner's
location at Fonda's Bush. The first settlers who obtained a title from the Baronet to *one hundred acres*
of land each, were two brothers named Solomon and
Seely Woodworth, Simeon Christie, two brothers
named Reynolds, Jacob Dunham, ——Cadman, Jona.

Canfield, Capt. —— Flock, a captain when in New England; and possibly one or two others. Christie was a Scotchman; the rest of the settlers, or nearly all of them were enterprising Yankees. The Woodworths were from Salisbury, Connecticut; Seely settled near the present site of Mayfield Corners, and his brother about a mile to the westward of him. The rest of the pioneers were scattered about the woodman's neighborhood. Perhaps the only descendant of this early settlement now living upon the homestead, is Simon, a son of Simeon Christie.

Solomon Woodworth was killed by the Indians in the Revolution, as I have elsewhere published. The circumstances attending his death, as related by an eye-witness, I design to give the public at some future day, as also the captivity of several of the settlers at Fish House and Fonda's Bush, and fate of Eikler and young Shew. Old Mr. Dunham was murdered by the Indians in the war, as related on page 294 of my *History of Schoharie County, etc.*, where the name is inaccurately printed Durham. His wife was not murdered at the time, as there stated. The house was plundered, but from motives of policy not then burned. Dunham had a son, a young officer under Capt. Solomon Woodworth, who shared the fate of his brave commander, as will be shown hereafter.

After Shew located at Fish House, and before the Revolution, John Eikler, Lent and Nicholas Lewis, brothers, Robert Martin, Zebulon Algar, a family of

Ketchums and one of Chadwicks, also settled in that neighborhood. All of them left at the beginning of difficulties, except Shew, Martin and Algar. These pioneers at first had to go to Johnstown for their milling. To accommodate them and the Mayfield settle ment, Sir William Johnson erected a small grist mill at the latter place, in 1773 or '74, and had the avails of it during the remainder of his life. It was either burnt in the war, or rendered nearly valueless by neglect. The mill property having been confiscated, it was purchased at the close of the war by Abraham Romeyn, the oldest son of the Rev. Dr. Romeyn, who had been an artificer in the Revolution. He rebuilt the mill again, and put it in operation.

Soon after Romeyn got his mill in operation, Thomas Shankland—who had been a prisoner among the Indians—erected a grist mill on the Kennyetto, in the present town of Providence, to which the Fish House settlers repaired, as it was a mile or two nearer than the Mayfield mill, with no intervening marsh. This mill is now owned by Jonathan Haggidorn. The bolts in those mills to separate the flour from the bran, were turned by hand. It was the usual practice for customers to turn the bolt for their own grist—a task they were by no means pleased with. After the country became more settled, and probably as early as 1800, one Van Hoesen erected a mill also in Providence, situated about half a mile east of Fish House, on a stream which rises on the Maxon mountain.

Speaking of mills, we are reminded of the following anecdote of Sir William Johnson. While he was living at Fort Johnson, he made some alteration in his grist-mill near by—putting in a new pair of millstones. A German named Francis Salts, who was erecting a mill for Messrs. Philip and Jacob Frederick, situated on the Schoharie river, some five or six miles above its mouth, called on the Baronet to purchase the old grinders. The price was stipulated, and after some little conversation about the terms of payment, the quondam owner told his customer to take them home, get his mill in operation, and if he would sing a song when the debt was due, that pleased him, he would exact no other pay.

It was not long ere the buzzing and clitter clatter evinced the new mill in successful motion. When pay day for the millstones arrived, Mr. Salts went to Fort Johnson to cancel the debt. He was quite a song singer, and had possibly prepared himself with something new, expressly for the fastidious ear of his creditor. In the presence of several of the Baronet's friends, who were, no doubt, invited in expressly to hear them, song after song was sung, to the evident amusement of all save the one he desired to please; but his features remained uncommonly rigid. Having exhausted his catalogue of German songs, without discovering any expression of delight on the countenance of his creditor, the millwright thrust his hands into a deep pocket, and drew forth a long pouch of the **ready,** singing in no very good humor as he did so:

𝔊𝔢𝔩𝔡𝔰𝔞𝔠𝔨, 𝔊𝔢𝔩𝔡𝔰𝔞𝔠𝔨, 𝔡𝔲 𝔪𝔲𝔰𝔰𝔱 𝔥𝔢𝔯𝔞𝔲𝔰,
𝔇𝔢𝔯 𝔐𝔞𝔫𝔫 𝔴𝔦𝔩𝔩 𝔟𝔢𝔷𝔞𝔥𝔩𝔱 𝔰𝔢𝔦𝔫.*

" That will do—now put up your money," said Sir William, at the end of a burst of laughter.

"And are you paid? " asked Salts, with evident surprise, as he returned the purse to his pocket.

" Yes, yes," said the now delighted lover of fun, " that will do—that's the best of the whole." The songster went home rejoicing, and left the Baronet and his guests to discuss the merit of his songs over a bottle of wine, when he was far away.—*Col. Peter Young and Volkert Voorhees.*

If Sir William Johnson enjoyed a joke at the expense of some friend, they occasionally got the rig upon him, as the following anecdote will show. Just after the close of the French war, in which he had acted so conspicuous a part, and for which he was placed on the baronial list, Sir William had occasion to go to Albany. At that period there were only two or three dwellings in the whole distance between Albany and Schenectada, and they were little if any better than squatter's lodges of more modern times. There were numerous little swamps and marshes along the road, and the Baronet returning to Schenectada on horseback, passed a little marsh, in which he heard,

* Money bag! money bag! you must come out!
The man he will be paid!
5*

as he believed, the voice of a new animal. Nearing a house just after, he inquired, *What animals were making such a strange noise?* He was answered with a grin, that they were *bull frogs!* He spurred up his horse, not a little mortified to think he had but just learned, as his countrymen would say, " *what a toad a frog was.*"

The family of which he inquired knew him (indeed that family which did not know him in Western New York, was behind the times), and soon the nature of his inquiry reached the ears of his most intimate friends, who bored him so unmercifully about it, that he was obliged to own up. He admitted that he never was so ashamed of having asked a question in his life, as he was of that about the *new animals* on the pine plains below Dorp.—*James Frazier.*

After the preceding pages were stereotyped, I learned that the given name of Dunham, mentioned on page 49, was Jacob: that when he was murdered, as stated on page 50, which took place April 11, 1779, a son named Samuel met the same fate. Zebulon, another son, was made prisoner, but escaped from his captors while they were engaged in plundering the house. John, a third son of Jacob Dunham, fell with Capt. Woodworth, in Fairfield.—*Hon. John Dunham,* of Wells, N. Y., a son of Ebenezer Dunham, and grandson of Jacob Dunham, above named.

CHAPTER IV.

Very little is known of Nicholas Stoner's boyhood, but from his propensity in riper years we may suppose, that if he did not play off some wild pranks, it was only for the want of a butt. With perceptions naturally quick, his city life afforded him a fine school for the study of human nature as developed in the actions of men; but the transition at so early an age to sylvan shades, where, instead of artificial objects he might behold nature by the pencil of God adorned, was genial to his untamed spirit, and he was soon fitted to enjoy to the fullest extent the life of a woodman: finding music in the scream of the panther, growl of the bear and bay of the wolf.

When a cry from the Boston *Cradle* announced that the infant *Liberty* was about to be strangled by its pretended nurse; the *Gray Forest Eagle,*

" An emblem of freedom, stern, haughty and high,"

having plumed his broad wing for a heliocentric flight, was up—

" And away like a spirit wreathed in light,"

he fluttered over the land of his choice, until he aroused the patriotism not only of the indweller of city and village, but of him, who, though isolated his home, could appreciate untrammeled thought and act.

The first two years of the war of Independence, the pioneer inhabitants of New York enjoyed comparative tranquillity; for the swift-footed Indian had not fully determined to raise the hatchet of death against unoffending innocence, in a quarrel that did not directly concern him, and crimson the altar of domestic happiness for the golden calf royalty had set up: but as the portending storm lowered, and it became known that the red man, having sharpened his scalping knife and participated in the war dance of his nation, was then on his way to the frontiers; exposed settlers who were inclined to look with favor on the acts of those who were raising an arm of rebellion along the seaboard, found it necessary to remove to thickly peopled neighborhoods.   Accordingly, the families making up the small and scattered settlement of Fonda's Bush, except that of Helmer and Putman, removed early in the summer of 1777, to Johnstown : soon after which Nicholas Stoner went to reside with the Fisher brothers in the Mohawk valley.*   Living with patriots,

* John and Harmanus Fisher. They resided at that period where the Hon. Jesse D. DeGroff now resides, between the villages of Fonda and Amsterdam, and were both killed and scalped by the Indians and tories in the summer of 1780; at which time the former was a captain and the latter a lieutenant of militia. Col. Frederick Fisher (or Visscher, as he wrote his name in the latter part of his life), a third brother, chanced to be there at the time, and was scalped and left for dead, but recovered and lived many years. For a more particular account of the Fisher family and their sufferings, see my *Border Wars of New York*.

although a lad of only 14 or 15 summers, it is not surprising that young Stoner, who had been properly
schooled at home as the removal of the family indicates,
should have imbibed the spirit which throbbed in older
hearts, and been ready to stand or fall with the common cause of his country.

Visiting his friends in Johnstown in the summer of
1777, at which time it had become a military post,
Nicholas, for whose ear martial music had peculiar
charms, needed but little persuasion to become a soldier, and enlisted as a fifer into a company of New
York troops, commanded by captain Timothy Hughes.
Not long after his brother John, a mere boy, enlisted
under Capt. Wright. Captain W. had been a British
drum-major previous to the Revolution, and being
pleased with John, undertook to perfect him in the
art of *flammadiddles* and *paddadiddles*—in other words,
in the ability to make a world of noise in a scientific
manner. Henry Stoner, imitating the example of his
boys, soon after enlisted under Capt. Robersham for a
term of three years. The father and sons were all in
the same regiment, so that they not only saw each
other almost daily, but the former could to some little
extent, still exercise the duties of a parent. The regiment alluded to was commanded by Col. James
Livingston, of which Richard Livingston was lieutenant-colonel, and Abraham Livingston captain; the
three Livingstons being brothers. In August 1777,
the troops under Col. Livingston joined the army of

Gen. Arnold, while on its way up the Mohawk valley, to succor Col. Gansevoort at Fort Stanwix. Among the patriotic rangers who left Johnstown at this time was Jacob Shew, who is still living.

Nicholas Stoner saw the spy, Han Yost Schuyler, who was captured at Shoemaker's place (where Spencer now lives, at the upper end of Mohawk village), set out on his mission to excite the fears of the enemy, and thus save his own neck from a halter.* Boats

* This Han Yost (John Joseph) Schuyler and Walter Butler were fortunately made prisoners near Fort Dayton, about the time of Arnold's arrival at that post. Butler was sent down to Albany as a prisoner. Schuyler had entered the Mohawk valley as a *spy*—was tried by court-martial and sentenced to be hung, his coffin being made ready to receive his remains. Gen. Arnold thought to turn his life to more profitable account than his death, and agreed to spare him on condition that he would enter the camp of St. Ledger, and by an exaggerated account of the forces advancing under his command, thus contribute towards raising the siege of Fort Stanwix, then called Fort Schuyler. Schuyler accepted the terms for his life; and his brother Nicholas was retained as a hostage, to suffer in his stead in case of a noncompliance. Han Yost entered the enemy's lines, and his known fidelity to their cause gave his representation of Arnold's forces no little weight. Probably Schuyler had been sent below to learn whether American troops were approaching. The camp was thrown into confusion, and it was resolved to raise the siege. Several shrewd Oneidas friendly to the American cause were in the secret, and ere St. Ledger began his retrograde movement, one of them dropped into the camp as if by chance. He was interrogated as to his knowledge of the approaching Yankees, and replied mysteriously, but in a manner to inspire awe. " Are the Yankees numerous?" inquired a tory officer. The Indian pointing to the surrounding

laden with provisions were taken up the Mohawk, guarded by troops along the shore. As they drew near the theatre of the brave Herkimer's disasters, evidences of the terrible onslaught at Oriskany met them. Near the mouth of the Oriskany creek, a gun was found standing against a tree with a pair of boots hanging on it; while in the creek near, in a state bordering on putrefaction, lay their supposed owner. In the grass a little way from the shore, lay a genteely dressed man without coat or hat, who it was supposed had made his way there to obtain drink. A black silk handkerchief encircled his once aching head. John Clark, a sergeant, loosened it, but the hair ad-

---

forest replied by asking—" Can Oneida count the leaves? Can white man count the stars?" The siege was precipitately abandoned, and agreeably to arrangement another and another Oneida entered the ranks of the foe to add their enigmatic testimony to that of the first. The stratagem succeeded to a charm; and finding opportunity to return to the army of Arnold, and thence to Fort Dayton, Schuyler saw his brother set free and went back to Canada. Subsequent to the war, Schuyler returned to Herkimer county where he died. Facts from *John Roof*, who was on duty at Fort Dayton, and saw the coffin made for Schuyler, and who was familiar with the circumstances which led to his arrest and novel liberation; corroborated by *John Dockstader*, of Herkimer. Says the latter, this Schuyler had a brother and two sisters who were carried captive to Canada in the French war, and were retained there until it closed. Herkimer, then called the Palatine's village, was invaded by the French and Indians in November, 1757, its dwellings, grain, mills, etc., destroyed by fire, and its inhabitants mostly slain or carried into captivity; as we may show at some future day.

hered to it on its removal, and he left the prize. He took from his feet a pair of silver shoe-buckles. His legs were so swollen, that his deer-skin breeches were rent from top to bottom. Nine dead bodies lay across the road, disposed in regular order, as was imagined, by the Indians after their death. The stench was so great that the Americans could not discharge the last debt due their heroic countrymen, and their bones were soon after bleaching upon the ground. A little farther on an Indian was seen hanging to the limb of a tree by the heels. He was suspended with the traces of a harness from a baggage wagon by the Americans, as believed, after death. Col. St. Ledger having made a flying retreat towards Canada, Gen. Arnold, after giving his troops time to rest, left Fort Stanwix and returned with his command to the army of Gen. Gates near Stillwater.

At some period subsequent to the action of September 19th, in which Gen. Arnold was by many thought the master spirit of the American officers engaged, an altercation took place between him and Gen. Gates, supposed by some on account of envy entertained towards the former, either by Gen. Wilkinson or Gen. Gates, and possibly both,* which resulted in his being deprived of his command. Consequently, in the sanguinary battle which took place on Bemis's Heights, October 7th, Gen. Arnold had no authority for the glorious deeds he there performed. Towards evening

* See Neilson's *Burgoyne's Campaign*, page 150.

of that day, that daring chief led a body of troops into the very heart of the Hessian camp; carrying dismay along the whole British line.   In this impetuous onset he was shot through the leg,* and would to God the ball had passed through his heart; and that that fearless and reckless leader, who, up to that hour had been one of LIBERTY's boldest champions, could have sealed with his life-blood his former deeds of glory! Yes, would to God that that brave general, who had faced his country's foes on the snow-clad plains of Abraham, and been a companion in peril of the gallant, warm-hearted Montgomery, could now have found a grave on those heights, where his own blood had mingled with that of the foeman!   But alas! alas! a sombre destiny awaited him.

Among the death-daring spirits who followed Arnold to the Hessian camp, was Nicholas Stoner, and near the enemy's works he was wounded in a singular manner.   A cannon shot from the breastwork killed a soldier near Stoner, named Tyrrell.   The ball demolished his head, sending its fragments into the face of Stoner, which was literally covered with brains, hair and fragments of the skull.   He fell senseless, with the right of his head about the ear severely cut

---

* A wounded Hessian fired on Arnold, and John Redman, a volunteer, ran up to bayonet him, but was prevented by his general, who exclaimed, " *He's a fine fellow—don't hurt him!*" The Hessians continued to fight after they were down, because they had been told by their employers that the Americans would give no· quarters.—*Stoner.*

by portions of the skull bone, which injury still affects
his hearing in that ear.   Shortly after, as the young
fifer was missing, one Sweeney, an Irish soldier, was
sent to seek out and bear him from the field; but a
cannon shot whizzed so near his own head, that he
soon returned without the object of his search.   Col.
Livingston asked Sweeney where the lad Stoner was?
" Ja—s! colonel," replied the soldier, " a goose has
laid an egg there, and you don't catch me to stay
there!"   Lieut. William Wallace then proceeded to the
spot indicated by the Irishman, and found our hero
with his head reclining upon Tyrrell's thigh, and taking
him in his arms, bore him to the American camp.
When young Stoner was found, a portion of the brim
of his hat, say about one-fourth the size of a nine-pound
shot, was observed to have been cut off very smoothly,
the rest of it was covered with the ruins of the head
of Tyrrell, who, to use the words of Stoner, *did not
know what hurt him.*

Peter Graff, from Switzer Hill, and Peter Conyne
also from the vicinity of Caughnawaga, were at the
American camp as teamsters on the day of this battle, and served as volunteers among the troops led on
by Arnold.   Conyne having raised a gun to fire on
the enemy, received a bullet in his arm and breast.
Young Stoner and Conyne were taken from Stillwater
to Albany in a boat with other wounded Americans.
Col. Frederick Fisher chanced to be in that city when
they arrived, and took Stoner home with him, from

whence he carried him to Johnstown. He was under the care of Dr. Thomas Reed, a surgeon in Livingston's regiment, and was cured. Conyne also recovered.

In the summer of 1778, the three Stoners were all on duty in Rhode Island. In an engagement with the enemy while there, the father was wounded by a musket ball, which lodged in his head. He was sent to Providence, where he was trepanned, and recovered. A piece of silver placed over the wound, it was believed, the Indians who afterwards killed and scalped him, obtained with their plunder. The relic (an ounce ball), was preserved by the wounded man, but was lost when his dwelling was burnt by the hirelings of Britain.

While the Stoners were serving in Rhode Island, the following incident occurred in the American camp. Two soldiers, Williams a Yankee, and Cumming an Irishman, had a quarrel, in which the former gave the latter a severe flogging. To revenge his chagrin, the worsted combatant took a shirt from his own knapsack, and placed it in that of Williams, to give it the appearance of having been stolen, in the hope of · seeing the latter punished. The officers found it necessary to use severe measures for petty theft, as it was of very frequent occurrence. The missing garment of Cumming having been found in Williams's possession, the latter was tied up with his coat off to be whipped. The son of Erin, conscience stricken, then advanced into the ring, and drew off his coat to

take the lash.   He said he had received one licking
from Williams, and although he had used stratagem
to get him publicly flogged, he would rather receive
the *scorpion-tailed cat* himself, than see a man punished for a crime of which he was not guilty.   So
manly a confession on the part of Cumming, excited
the admiration of the Rev. John Greenough, a baptist
minister, and chaplain of the regiment, who interceded
with Col. Livingston, and he readily forgave them
both.

The Americans had several skirmishes with the
enemy in Rhode Island, in the summer and autumn of
1778, in two of which Nicholas Stoner was engaged.
Capt. Hughes was out one night with his command
as a piquet guard on Poppasquash point, opposite
Bristol.   The troops having been observed before dark
by a British vessel in the vicinity, a body of marines
and grenadiers landed and made them prisoners.   The
enemy having gained the beach in boats, came round
a salt marsh which was separated from a corn field by
a stone wall.   Capt. Hughes and his men were on the
marsh side of the wall, and fired on the marines as
they approached.   The latter called to them not to
fire, saying, " we are your own men."   As they drew
near, their white belts betrayed them however, and
the Americans attempted their retreat.   In endeavoring
to leap the wall, our hero missed his footing and fell
back, at which instant he was seized by the collar by
a British grenadier named John McGaffee.   At this

instant another soldier raised his musket to strike him down, but was prevented by McGaffee, who exclaimed, "Vast, shipmate, it is only a child." Daniel Basin, a Frenchman, who was leaping the wall near Stoner, was bayoneted and killed. Capt. Hughes and all his men were made prisoners, except the one killed, and two who were missing, supposed to have scaled the fence and escaped; and as the American army was near, they were hurried into the boats and taken to Conanicut island. While crossing the marsh to the boats, the young fifer thought it was best to secure the rum in his canteen, and accordingly took a long gurgling swig, which was broken off by McGaffee, who claimed a share, as being his by the fortune of war, and he gave the finishing guzzle. As they neared the beach, Stoner threw the empty casket away. An officer hearing it strike the water, raised his sword to punish, as he supposed, an act of treachery, thinking a prisoner had cast a cartridge-box from him, but McGaffee, with his tongue now oiled, again interposed, and observed that the boy had only thrown away an empty and valueless canteen.

At daylight the prisoners were paraded and lodged in the enemy's prison on the island. When aroused by the morning roll-call, young Stoner, who had been wofully drunk, from his attempt to swallow the contents of his own flask the evening before, and whose brain was still broiling from the effects of the potation, started up, supposing at first he was required to play the re-

6*

veille in the American camp, but he was soon brought
to his senses, and to a situation in which he could
get sober at his leisure; in other words, he learned
that others were to pipe while he danced. John Stoner
was at this time a drummer in the American camp,
not far distant from where his brother was a prisoner;
indeed, the spangled banner was floating in sight.*

Gen. Prescott,* the British commander on that station, was captured the summer before Capt. Hughes
was taken. He had gone to pay his devoirs to a
buxom widow, at a little distance from his own camp,
and a slave of the lady found means to communicate
the fact to the Americans. Lieut.-Col. Barton, of the
Providence militia, an officer of spirit, at once conceived the bold project of his capture. At dead of
night, in a barge, well manned by stout-hearted volunteers with muffled oars, he landed and approached
the house in which the general was so happily quar-
tered. Feeling quite secure, he had accepted the kind
lady's hospitality, and resolved to tarry all night.
Possibly his arrest was set on foot by the fair hostess,
for woman often proved the champion of freedom.

The general was nabbed in a bed-chamber; and
without allowing the drowsy hero time to collect his

---

*At the time Gen. Prescott's capture was noted, it had escaped
the writer's recollection that an account of it had ever been published; and Stoner's narrative of the event was adopted in the
first edition, making it a year later than its occurrence. It took
place July 10, 1777—five miles from Newport. Col. Barton left
Warwick Neck with 38 men in two boats, surprised the general
in bed, and returned with him in safety (*Holmes's Annals*).

scattered thoughts, or the war-god to chase the dreams of love from his mind—or, indeed, what was far more uncharitable, time to put on his breeches, he was hurried off to the rebel barge. Passing through a piece of standing barley, his legs were tickled, as we may suppose, not in the most agreeable manner. So silently had the Americans arrived, and so brief had been their stay, that they were even bending their oars for their own camp before the general's guard could be mustered. Great was the surprise among the British next day, when it became known that their general had been spirited away. On being apprised of the fact, some of the soldiers were heard to say, " The rebels have got the old rascal, and I hope they'll kill him!" He was a man some sixty years of age, was a severe disciplinarian, and not very popular. He was exchanged for Gen. Lee—for which object he was possibly captured—in April preceding the surprise of Capt. Hughes. After several months imprisonment, Capt. Hughes and his command were exchanged.

In the fall of 1778, the several regiments of New York state troops having become much reduced, a new organization took place, their number being lessened, at which time Nicholas Stoner joined the company of Capt. Samuel T. Pell, attached to Col. Cortlandt's regiment, which marched to Schenectada. The state troops were sent, during the winter months, to different frontier stations, and Capt. Pell proceeded to Johnstown for winter quarters.

Small parties of the enemy kept the inhabitants along the frontier of New York, in a state of almost constant alarm.   While stationed at Johnstown Nicholas Stoner often went hunting and fishing with other lads, to provide a dainty morsel for some officer, who thought more of his palate than of his purse; and consequently paid liberally for their success.   Young Stoner, in company with three others, one Charlesworth, Charles Darby and John Foliard, all nearly of the same age, went out with guns and fishing tackle, in the vicinity of Johnson Hall.   After they had become busily engaged along the Cayadutta,* all at once Darby, without uttering a word, was seen to start as if terribly frightened, and run off in the direction of the Hall.   His comrades soon learned the cause of his alarm, by seeing a small party of Indians emerge from a patch of hemp not far distant from them, and near the Hall barn.   One of them fired on Charlesworth, but the boys scattered, fled and all effected their escape.   These Indians, or, as probably some of them were, tories disguised, had no doubt visited the settlement as spies, and were anxious to take back a prisoner as a proof of having accomplished their mission. They were sure of their reward, if they could return

* *Ca-ya-dut-ta* signifies *muddy creek*, says the Hon. John Dunham, of Hamilton county, who had the signification from Indian hunters.   The creek courses in Johnstown through a soil which gives to the water at most seasons of the year a dirty appearance; hence the aboriginal name.

with occular evidence of having visited the place designated by some British or refugee officer in Canada.

Thomas Harter, an inoffensive man, nearly *seventy* years old, who resided in Scotch Bush, a few miles from Johnson Hall, went to his field, bridle in hand, to catch a horse, and was made prisoner and taken to Canada, by a small party of the enemy (in the fall of 1778, or spring of 1779), that did not wish to harm him, but were anxious to prove they had been to Johnstown. His unaccountable absence from home greatly alarmed his family, but their apprehensions were softened by a tory neighbor, who assured them he was alive, but had been taken prisoner as a matter of necessity, and would be kindly used. His treatment was not as cruel as that meted to most prisoners, and he lived to return home, to the great joy of his friends.

CHAPTER V

Conrad Reed, a baker in New York city, married Miss Barbary Stoner, a second sister of Henry Stoner, and removed to Johnstown just before the Revolution. He dwelt some distance from the fort, but was employed to bake for the garrison. When on duty at Johnstown, the Stoner boys not unfrequently took occasion to visit their uncle's family, but those visits were not approved by their father; who knew that his kinsman was tinctured with royalty, and he often cautioned them against going there. Nicholas called there one evening, and had been but a short time in the house, when he heard a slight tap upon a window. Mr. Reed instantly disappeared through a trap-door into the cellar without a candle, and his wife went out of the house. There seemed a sprinkling of mystery in the affair, but it did not excite Stoner's fears, and he awaited in silence the issue. After a few minutes' absence, his aunt came in having in her hand several gaudy handkerchiefs. She appeared rather more reserved after the singular interruption of the family, and he soon returned to the fort.

Stoner learned subsequently, that a small party of the enemy, one of whom was John Howell, who dwelt between Johnstown and Sacondaga, had visited the settlement as spies: that they had seen him through the window, and by a tap on a pane of glass, a signal she well understood, had called out Mrs. Reed, to consult her about making him a prisoner. She told them that if he was captured there, it would be the ruin of their family; for her husband would certainly lose his employ as baker for the garrison, if in fact he was not imprisoned. They reluctantly withdrew, although Howell could hardly consent to let so favorable an opportunity pass for securing certain evidence of having accomplished their mission. The young fifer did not know until long after, how near he had been to a Canadian prison. The handkerchiefs left with Mrs. Reed were presents, to adorn the necks of several tory ladies, whose husbands or lovers were in Canada.

About a mile from the Johnstown fort (the jail inclosed by strong palisades), dwelt Jeremiah Mason, whose family was numbered among those in the vicinity, as friendly to the cause of liberty. This Mason had a daughter named Anna, about the same age as our hero; who was a maiden very fair to look upon. Nature had given her charming proportions; a stature seemly, gracefully jutting out where swellings were most becoming, and bewitchingly tapering where diminution is sought in female form. Her skin was clear and fair, and her hair and eyes black, the latter shaded by raven lashes under the control of muscle, that gave to the organs of love a most melting expression.

Some distance farther from the fort, and on the same road as Mason, dwelt a family named Browse; the male members of which were in the camp of the enemy. At home were Mrs. Browse and two beautiful daughters. They, too, were in their teens, and like Anna Mason, they had sparkling black eyes, ruby lips and cherry cheeks. The war of the Revolution soon rendered neighboring families distant and formal, where they looked with diverse favor upon the acts of the contending parties, even though they had been intimate before. The resolutions of vigilance committees often tended to such a result.

I have remarked elsewhere, that young Stoner, when on duty at Johnstown, went hunting in the proper season. His *pigeon hunting* often gave him an interview with the young ladies named, and not unfrequently did Anna, as the hunter was about to proceed farther from the garrison, with some anxiety and a reproving look, cast a caution in his path from her father's door, such as " Nicholas, you'll be surprised yet at that tory house and taken off to Canada: you had better not go there." If the maiden had not conceived some attachment for the young fifer, the reader will agree with me, that she was possessed of *sisterly feelings.* He was then *quite partial* to Anna, as he admits, and we think he must have promised her to limit his future excursions to a nearer range, else why the caution observed in another visit.

As the young musician usually hunted in the same

direction, it was suspected by more than one at the station that he went sky-larking, and James Dunn, who was possibly in the secret of his destination, one day told Capt. Pell that " if he did not look out he would lose his fifer, as he not only went upon danger-ous grounds, *but hunted two kinds of pigeons.*" The captain, whose inclinations led him to follow all the fortunes of war, took occasion secretly to catechise the young hunter; and the latter, with his usual can-dor, owned up. The consequence was, the commander of the garrison concluded the hunting of *pigeons* must be rare sport, especially if they were not too lean, and soon obtained a promise from young Nimrod to take him where he could find one nestled.

Arrangements having been made for a hunt, secretly of course, a garment was thrown over the back of an old white mare belonging to the widow Shutting, which sought its living around the fort; and selecting a propitious evening, the hunter and his pupil—under cover of a cluster of trees a little distance from the garrison, mounted their Rozinante and set off. The reader may be surprised that they started on a *pigeon* hunt in the *evening*, and still more when informed that they left their shooting-irons behind; but this is all owing to his ignorance of the policy of war, for he should know that game is easier taken on the roost than on the wing.

It was the wish of the master hunter to avoid pass-ing on their way the house of Jeremiah Mason, and

7

why, possibly the reader may infer; he says himself, however, it was from fear a watch-dog might betray the nature of their errand and thus startle the *best* game : consequently a blind and circuitous route was chosen, some distance from the public highway. Whether the animal was too heavily loaded or not, we can not judge any better than the reader (sin is said to be weighty), but sure it is that in threading an intricate footpath carpeted by a web of briars and underbrush along a ravine, the mare stumbled and went heels over head, sending her riders far from her, if not pell-mell, certainly Pell and Nick. Bestowing some harsh epithets upon the poor beast, which probably had the worst of the bargain, they did not attempt to remount; but leaving the old mare to her fate, they proceeded on foot.

On arriving near the hunting-grounds, Stoner went forward to reconnoitre, and finding the coast clear, returned and conducted his captain into a neat little cottage, with two rooms below, and possibly as many above.   The ceremony of an introduction once passed, the captain soon found himself quite at home.   The time for retiring to rest at length arrived, and as the old hen roosted in the room they were in, it became necessary for the hunters to leave it: consequently the hunter most familiar with the premises, followed the pullet in its flight to a chamber.   The other bird soon after fluttered past the captain into an adjoining room, whither he pursued possibly to capture it.

I do not consider it important to the present narrative to stop and inquire of an ornithologist,

> " If birds confabulate or no:
> 'Tis clear that they were always able
> To hold discourse, at least in fable;"

and that the genus *columba*,

> Soon are cooing when together
> If they meet in coolish weather,

is a fact so well established, it must be obvious to the reader that *pigeon hunting* may be rare sport. Some time after the beautiful birds under consideration had flown to separate rooms, into which we can not think of introducing the reader, as the cooing was done agreeably to the most approved style then in vogue in western New York, the loud barking of Mason's dog fell upon the ears of the hunter closeted above. His apprehension was in a moment on tiptoe; for to be surprised by a party of the enemy and either slain or captured with his captain in such a place and at such an hour, without their having the least means of defence, he readily saw must bring scandal if not dishonor upon the American arms; and he descended (although his bird attempted with a delicate little claw to prevent) to take a midnight observation.

It turned out that Mason's sentinel was barking at the old mare the hunters had abandoned. Having collected her scattered limbs, she too had concluded to go *browsing*, and was, as the reader will perceive, on the right track. On the return of his pioneer, the captain was gratified to learn that there was no real cause of alarm, and pigeon hunting soon prospered again. Towards the dawn of day the sportsmen returned to the garrison; Capt. Pell exacting from his musician the most solemn assurances of *secresy* respecting his successful and only attempt at fowling among the Browse, *until he should meet with me.*

The female and infant part of many families in the border settlements of New York, whose male members were foes of the country, removed about this period to Canada, among which was this Browse family; and such others as did not go voluntarily, were compelled to by an act of the state legislature soon after.

In the summer and autumn of 1780, Nicholas Stoner was on duty in the valley of the Hudson. He was a fifer of the guard at Tappan, which attended Major Andre from his prison to his gallows; and witnessed the execution of that unfortunate man. The gallows was constructed, as he says, by the erection of two white oak crotches, with a cross-piece of the same kind of timber, all with the bark on. Not far from the gallows was an old woman selling pies, to whom Stoner directed his steps. He met at her stand Elijah Cheadle, then a stranger to him. They paid this huckstress $100 in continental money, for either an apple pie, or pumpkin pie, which at first she declined receiving: she finally concluded to take it, observing as she did so, " My children, the pie is worth more than the money, but I will take it that I may be able to say, I sold a pie for *one hundred dollars.*" Mr. Cheadle settled at Kingsborough after the war, where he resided at the time of his death, Sept. 23, 1849.

While stationed at Snake Hill, near the Hudson, young Stoner's inclination to mischief procured for him a duplicate flogging. There was daily about the camp a boy named Albright, who had been so unfortunate as to lose an eye. Stoner, inclined to be waggish with all, procured the eye of a beef butchered in the neighborhood, and offering it to Albright, said to him, " Here, take this and you will then have two eyes and be somebody." The boy complained to his mother, an Irish woman, who, stating the matter to the commanding officer, had the satisfaction of knowing that he was punished for treating her son so unkindly. Stoner did not relish the interference of the mother, as the boy was about his own age, and began to puzzle his wits for some method of retaliation. A soldier's agent is powder, although he may be a fifer, and loading an ugly looking bone with the dangerous dust, he watched a favorable opportunity when she was near his tent, and applied the match to it. The explosion was greater than he had anticipated, and the scattering fragments not only tore the old woman's petticoats, but severely wounded her arm. Although he had improved a most promising occasion to avoid detection, yet some trivial incident betrayed Stoner as the artillerist, and he was very severely whipped for the act. He was served rightly no doubt.

7*

In the fall of 1781, Nicholas Stoner was on duty at
Yorktown, and when the seige of that place closed, he
saw Gen. O'Hara surrender his sword to Gen. Lincoln.*

A part of the time while at Yorktown, our hero
was a fifer under the noble-hearted Lafayette.   One

* Several errors have crept into history about this ceremony.
The facts were as follows: In May, 1780, Gen. Lincoln, then in
command at Charleston, S. C., was compelled to surrender his
sword to Cornwallis. When his lordship found himself obliged to
yield to the allied army, he knew that Lincoln, who was his
equal in rank, was with the conquerors, and as the terms now
meted to him were precisely like those dictated to Lincoln, he
possibly may have conjectured that that officer would be designated
by the great American commander to receive his own polished
blade. Be that as it may, certain it is that instead of appearing
on the occasion, as a man of real courage and generosity would
have done (for that officer lacks moral courage who can not share
defeat with his men), he feigned illness and sent Gen. O'Hara to
do the disagreeable honors; and that officer very handsomely performed the ceremony of tendering his sword to Gen. Lincoln, who
was appointed by Washington to receive it. *Capt. Eben Williams,** who was present assured the writer, that Lincoln received,
reversed, and again restored the hilt of the weapon to its owner,
*with a dignity and grace of gesture he could never forget, for he
had never seen it equalled.* Several persons who witnessed this
ceremony have corroborated what I have here stated, and an old
soldier (*James Williamson*), who received half the British stand-
ards, to the question, why did not Cornwallis surrender his own
sword? replied, "*I guess he was a little sick at his stomach!*"

In a picture intended to represent this scene, and but recently
got up, Gen. Washington erroneously appears in the act of receiving the resignation from O'Hara, the latter being on foot. The

* This hero died at his residence in Schoharie, July 1, 1847, aged nearly 98
years. He was beloved by all who knew him.

Darby, a fifer, having been killed, Stoner was sent as a substitute to Gen. Lafayette's troops.

Mr. Nicholas Hill, a worthy and intelligent citizen of Florida, N. Y., was also at Yorktown during its seige, as a young musician. He informed the writer, at an interview in the summer of 1846, that the firing on the British works did not take place until the Americans had completed a line of redoubts and bomb batteries, so as to play on the greater part of the enemy's fortifications at once. The allied army had raised a liberty pole, and the signal to commence an assault was given in the evening, by a hand-grenade sent up near the liberty pole, attached to a sky-rocket. The gunners stood ready with linstocks on fire, and as soon as the grenade exploded in the air, they were applied to the cannon. (Dr. Thatcher, in his *Military Journal*, says Gen. Washington applied the first match.) The simultaneous discharge of such an array of ordnance, was perhaps never heard before; and nothing

general officers present, American, French and British, as several witnesses have assured the writer, *were all mounted.* The picture of this scene by Trumbull, a beautiful steel copy of which is made the fontispiece of *Howe's Historical Collections of Virginia,* although painted soon after, presents the British general trudging along on foot, and without side arms; while Dr. Thatcher, in his *Military Journal,* made at the time and published long since, stated that he was elegantly mounted. Col. Abercrombie, who commanded the left wing of the British army on this occasion, was also on horseback. It is to be regretted that more care is not taken in preparing *historical* pictures, lest truth be violated, and the young taught popular errors never to be corrected.

could in the night exceed the sublimity of the concussion. To use the language of Mr. Hill, "*It seemed as though the world was at an end—or that the heavens and the earth were coming together!*" It must have been the most magnificent salute ever before given in America. After the first discharge the firing continued as fast as the pieces could be loaded.

At some period of this seige, Mr. Hill was so fortunate as to obtain *eleven guineas* from the pocket of a dead Briton. "While this money lasted," says Stoner, "we who were so fortunate as to have the pleasure of his acquaintance, lived like fighting cocks."

The British prisoners made at Yorktown, were sent to interior military posts; and Col. Cortlandt's regiment, to which Nicholas Stoner belonged, on its return march took five hundred prisoners, destined for Fredericksburg, in charge for some distance. While the troops were crossing at a ferry, probably York or Rappahannoc river, Stoner saw a French officer drop his purse, and lost no time in restoring it to the owner. The officer grateful for its recovery, although he had not yet missed it, rewarded him with a half doubloon ($8), numerous bows, and not a few expressions of regard, such as—"You pe a *grand* poy! You pe bon honest American! You pe a ver fine soldier, be gar!" and the like. The reception of this money, obtained through the generosity of a kind hearted stranger, for an evidence of commendable integrity, afforded young Stoner more pleasure, as he assured the writer, than could possibly the whole amount the purse contained, had he dishonestly kept it; for to retain that which we know another has lost, is almost as great a crime as to purloin it either by stealth or force; and a "conscience void of offence," allows its possessor to sleep soundly and have pleasant dreams. The young musician had many friends while his eight dollars lasted, for *come easy, go easy,* was the soldier's motto.

Henry Stoner, as elsewhere stated, enlisted for a term of three years, in the American army. At the expiration of that time he received his discharge at Verplanck's point, soon after which he reënlisted at Groton, for three months, to fill another man's place. After the time of his second military engagement was up, he returned home. For about one year he lived on the farm of Col. John Butler, on Switzer hill, from which he went to reside near Tribe's hill, not far distant from Fort Johnson. The farm to which he removed from Butler's, is now in the town of Amsterdam, and was long known as the Dr. Quilhott place: the late John Putman, if we mistake not, was residing or this farm at the time of his death.

In the summer of 1782, a party of seven Indians traversed the forest from Canada to the Mohawk valley, the ostensible object of whose mission was to capture or destroy William Harper, afterwards judge (he resided for some years in Queen Anne's chapel parsonage), John Littel, afterwards sheriff, and such others as chance might throw in their way. Arriving

at the house of Dries* Bowman, to the eastward of
Johnstown, the hostile scout learned that Henry Stoner
was a whig of the times; that he had two sons then
in the American army, and that he was living in a
situation from its retirement, exposed to their mercenary
designs.   Thwarted in their original plan, they directed their steps, piloted by Bowman, to the dwelling of
Stoner, and on their way captured a man by the name
of Palmatier.

Unsuspicious of danger, Mr. Stoner, accompanied
by a nephew named Michael Reed (son of Conrad
Reed), went early one morning to a field to hoe corn;
it was the first hoeing for the season.   Mrs. Stoner
having prepared breakfast, blew a horn to call her
friends, and they were about to leave the corn-field,
as young Reed, a lad then in his teens, discovered
two Indians armed with hatchets approaching them
from adjoining woods, and directed the attention of
his kinsman that way.   The latter, who kept a loaded
gun in his house, attempted to gain it by flight, seeing
which, one of his foes ran so as to cut off his retreat.
While making an angle in the road, the savage headed
him, by crossing a piece of growing flax.

Whether the victim offered to surrender himself a
prisoner to the British scalper, is not known; it is
very probable he did; but the cry of mercy was un-
heeded, and the assassin's keen edged tomahawk descended with a crash, through an old fashioned beaver

* Dries is an abbreviation for Andreas, the German of Andrew.

hat and what resistance the skull offered, and penetrated the brain. The scalping knife was quickly
unsheathed, and several fingers of a hand the stricken
patriot had laid imploringly upon his aching forehead,
were nearly cut off with the scalp lock—*the* merchandise that would then most readily command British
gold. Some of the Indians now ran to the dwelling,
which was soon rifled of its most valuable contents,
and set on fire. As they approached, Mrs. Stoner discovered them near the door, and snatching up a frock,
threw it out of a back window which was open. The
enemy lingered sufficiently long to secure what plunder they desired, and see the house so effectually on
fire as to ensure its destruction, and then directed
their course towards Canada. No personal injury
was offered Mrs. Stoner, and soon after the destructives
had retired, she obtained the dress cast from the window, the only article she was enabled to save, and
went to the house of John Harman, a neighbor, supposing her husband and young Reed were prisoners.

Bowman aided the prisoners in carrying their plunder to a secret hiding place, near the Sacondaga,
where, beside a log, they had concealed food. Palmatier effected his escape on the first night after his
capture, to the great joy of his friends; and the feigned
prisoner, Bowman, was allowed to return home the
night following, From their secret rendezvous, near
the present village of Northville, the party journeyed
with their captive Reed, by the northerly route to

Canada, where he became a drummer in Butler's Rangers and remained until the war closed.

Harman, after the arrival of Mrs. Stoner at his house, suspected Bowman of treachery, and made known his suspicions to some of his neighbors, who went with him to Stoner's premises. Going from the ruins of his house to the corn field, they found him where he had been cut down, in or near the road. He was still alive, and although unable to speak, signified by signs, his desire for water, which was procured in a hat as soon as possible; but on drinking a draught he expired immediately. He was buried beneath a hemlock tree, near which he had been slain. Thus ignobly perished a brave man, who with scores of other citizens on the frontiers, of all ages, sexes, and conditions, found an untimely grave, because the evidence of their destruction would command a liberal price in the camp of the enemy. English freemen, where is thy blush? Where is thy shame for the deeds of hellish cruelty inflicted by thy hirelings, not only on brave men, but on unoffending mothers and smiling infants? LIBERTY purchased at such a price, oh, with what jealousy should it be guarded!

When Palmatier returned and made it known that Bowman had aided the Indians in carrying their stolen goods, the latter was arrested by patriots and confined in the Johnstown jail, then fortified. A party of whigs, among whom were Godfrey Shew and his son Henry, John Harman, James Dunn and Benjamin

DeLine,* assembled, fully determined to make Bowman confess his evil deeds. Among other devices resorted to, to make the tory disclose the information desired, a rope was thrown round some fastening overhead with a noose upon his neck; and he was required to mount a barrel. But he was interrogated and threatened in vain; and after the patience of his accusers was well nigh exhausted, Dunn, who partook largely of the patriotic spirit of the times, swore he should hang; and kicking the barrel from under him he did hang—or rather stood very uncomfortably upon air for a little time; but was finally taken down, and with various warnings about his future conduct, was again allowed his freedom.

At the time of his father's death, Nicholas Stoner was on duty at King's Ferry.

* At the time of Sir John Johnson's invasion of Johnstown and its vicinity in the summer of 1780, DeLine and Joseph Scott were living in Johnson Hall. When Johnson visited there to procure his concealed property, DeLine and Scott were made prisoners and taken to Canada. From his having been a hunter and familiar with the forest, DeLine was tightly bound. This was the second time they were taken to Canada during the war, and how long they remained prisoners there at this time is unknown to the writer. James Jones of Florida composed the following distich, which was often sounded in their ears after the war :

And when they came to the Hall, the house they did surround,
And Ben De Line and Joseph Scott made prisoners on the ground

John, a son of Philip Helmer, named as one of the pioneer settlers in Fonda's Bush, who remained there after his patriotic neighbors had removed to Johnstown, accompanied Sir John Johnson to Canada on his removal from Johnson Hall, early in the Revolution. Returning to the settlement not long after, he became an object of suspicion; was arrested by the patriots, and confined at Johnstown. A sentinel was placed over him who was very green in the service, and improving a favorable opportunity, the prisoner took occasion to praise his gun; and closed his adulation by requesting permission to look at it, which was readily granted. The piece had hardly passed out of the young guard's possession, ere his authority was set at defiance, and its new owner took it to a place of retirement to inspect its merits; which were not fully decided upon until he had safely arrived in Canada.

At a later period of the war, young Helmer again had the audacity to visit the Johnstown settlements. He returned late in the fall, and was concealed at his father's house for some time, intending on the return of spring, if possible, to take back some recruits with him for the British service. The nonintercourse so generally observed between whig and tory families

favored his design, but by some means his place of
refuge became known to three patriotic neighbors,
Benjamin DeLine, Solomon Woodworth and Henry
Shew, who determined on his capture. Well armed,
they proceeded one night to the vicinity of his father's
dwelling, and concealed themselves at a place where
they had reason to suppose he would pass. They had
not been there long when, unsuspicious of danger, he
approached the trio, who poised their fire-arms and he
yielded to their authority, and was lodged in the Johnstown jail. The entrance to the fort through the pick-
eted enclosure, was on the south side.

Helmer had a sister named Magdalene, the Germans
call the name Lana, by this name she was known.
Miss Lana was on intimate terms with a soldier then
on duty at the Johnstown fort; and at an interview
with him after one of several visits to her brother, to
whom she carried such little comforts as a sister can
provide, she got a pledge from him, that when on
sentinel duty he would unlock the prison door and set
the prisoner free. It was in the night time and while
his vigils lasted, that she had found access to the prisoner. True to his promise, Lana's lover did set her
brother at liberty, and, with another soldier, was se-
duced from his duty by the prisoner, when both fled in
his company. When she *wills* it, what can not woman do? A sergeant and five men, Amasa Stevens,
Benjamin DeLine, before named, and three continental
soldiers were soon upon their trail, which they were

enabled to follow by the fall of a light snow, and taking with them a lantern that they might travel by night, they came up with and surprised them in the woods. The two soldiers were fired upon and killed, but Helmer, with a severe bayonet wound in his thigh es-. caped: he was afterwards discovered nearly dead, in some bushes where he had concealed himself, and was taken to the fort: there he was cured of his wounds and again imprisoned. By some unaccountable means he succeeded the third time in effecting his enlargement; fled to Canada, and there remained. He, too, had been a hunter before the war, and was familiar with the forest. A part of the preceding facts were from Jacob Shew. At an interview between Helmer and Nicholas Stoner, which took place in Canada subsequent to the war, he told the latter that he suffered almost incredible hardships in making his last journey to that country.

In the last year of the Revolution, Nicholas Stoner belonged to a band of musicians, which marched into New York with troops under Col. Willett, on its evacuation by the enemy. He played the clarionet, as did also Nicholas Hill. During the stay of Gen. Washington in that city, an exhibition of fire-works took place, on which occasion the band alluded to performed. Stoner also saw Washington enter the barge at Whitehall on his leaving New York; and to use his own words, *was one of the band that played him off.*

Mischief lurked in the veins of young Stoner to the end of the war, and often brought him into difficulty, from which fortune sometimes extricated him quite as easily as he deserved to be.   The summer of 1783, was one of comparative inactivity in the army, as hostilities had nearly ceased that spring.   Stoner was with a body of troops which were encamped back of Newburgh, when a little incident occurred which afforded some momentary amusement.   In the camp was a black soldier, who had frozen off his toes while under Col. Willett the preceding February, in his abortive attack on Fort Oswego.   In consequence, the poor fellow experienced such difficulty in walking, that few could observe his peculiar gait, without having their risible faculties get the mastery.

As he was waddling along near the young musician, the latter called him a *stool-pigeon*.   The words were scarcely uttered, ere the sable patriot, who felt the insult sensibly, pursued the offender, armed with a bayonet, threatening vengeance.   A clarionet was a poor weapon with which to repel an attack, and its possessor fled for dear life, and took refuge in the hut of Lieutenant-Col. Cochrane, who was then entertaining several friends.   So abrupt an entrance started all to their feet, little doubting that the enemy from New York were upon them: but fears of an invasion were soon at an end, as close upon the heels of Stoner came tumbling in the infuriated, frost-bitten hero.   *What's the matter?   What has happened?*   What means this

8*

intrusion? several voices were at once demanding, as the last enterer, almost out of breath, stammered out—"Massa curnil! dis deblish musiker, he 'sult me berry bad; I'm lame, can't help it; froze my feet, like to froze my body too: all under Curnil Will't in de bush; snow knee deep: dis rascal call me *tool pigeon;* I no stand it."

"I comprehend," said Col. Cochrane: "you have been very unfortunate while in the service of your country, and it grieves you, as well it should, to have any one speak lightly of your misfortunes."

"Eez zur!"

"Well, my good fellow, leave the matter to me, and go to your quarters: I'll punish the impudent rascal."

"Dat's wat I want," said the lame soldier, now restored to good humor; "he desarbs it, and I hope you whip him berry hard, massa curnil; yah-yah-yah—"

"That I will," interrupted the officer.

"Tank you, curnil, cause you my friend;" continued the offended warrior, as he turned to go out, and restored a care worn drab and black hat to his bump of pugnacity. While closing the door to leave the presence of his umpire and friends, a smile of satisfaction was seen lurking about his under lip, and he was observed to close his fist and shake it at his offender, as much as to say—"Ha, de curnil gib it to you; you get your hide loosened dis time."

While the dialogue lasted, a frown sat upon the

brow of Col. Cochrance, and the young culprit began
to feel in imagination the whistling lash his unruly
tongue had invoked; but no sooner had the complainant closed the rough door, than, in spite of all his
efforts to the contrary, he found himself obliged to
join his merry companions and laugh heartily. The
figure of the limping negro, who, if he did not wear
cotton, was amazingly outward-bound, seemed still
before him, and turning to the mischief-maker, he
with no little effort gave him a sharp reproof for thus
imprudently wounding the feelings of one who should
exite his sympathy; and then, not daring to venture
a longer speech, lest he should spoil it with a laugh,
he ordered him from his presence with a threat of
terrible vengeance at the end of a rawhide, if he ever
did the like again.

Bowing his thanks for the easy and unexpected
terms meted to him, young Stoner promised to do better in future, and as he left the hut to seek his own,
the walls of the rude dwelling behind him shook with
the boisterous merriment of its inmates, at their very
unique entertainment.

When the war of the Revolution closed and the
dove took the place of the eagle—when the prattling
infant could nestle in its mother's bosom secure from
midnight assassins—when the warrior once more laid
aside his sword and musket to grasp the hoe and spade
of thrift—when commerce again spread her white
wings without fear of the foeman's fire—when art and

science again smiled o'er hill and dale, enriched by
the blood of freemen slain—when LIBERTY, with a
home of her own, invited the oppressed of the earth
to her embrace, extending to the penury-stricken the
horn which needed only his industry to become one of
plenty—then and not till then did our hero, grown to
man's estate, return again to reside in the vicinity of
Johnstown.

Where is the hoary-headed warrior that never felt
the melting influence of woman's smiles? If any such
there are, let them come forth while I tell them a brief
love-story of their own time. I have already informed
the reader, that there dwelt at Johnstown in the Revolution, a soft haired, dark eyed maiden named Anna
Mason; and have shadowed forth the fact, that a little
intimacy existed between her and our hero in their
youthful days. As no matrimonial engagement had
passed between them, not having seen or heard from
the young *pigeon hunter* for several long years; and
not informed whether the glory of a dead warrior or
the triumph of a live one were his; in fact, not knowing if he were alive in a distant colony, but what
some other young heart then beat against his own; it
is not surprising that she looked upon him as lost to
her, however vividly fancy at times may have brought
back his graceful figure.

Among the Johnstown patriots was a young man
named William Scarborough, who answered also to
the name of Crowley. His mother, at the time she

married Jeremiah Crowley, was a widow Scarborough, her husband having been killed in the batteau service, and was already possessed of little Willie, but people did not always stop to consider his true parentage, and after a while he almost ceased to be called Scarborough. On page 477 of my *History of Schoharie County, etc.,* where his death is mentioned, he is called Crowley, as I was then ignorant of his true parentage. William Scarborough, who was in some respects a very worthy young man, paid his addresses to the charming Anna Mason. Now William was a brave youth, and had been in the service of his country, which Anna happened to know, and on which account she the more highly respected him; for the women of that period could and did discriminate between right and wrong; between *liberty* and *oppression.* To cut a long story short, for wooing is full of mazes and phases, and interesting filagree, William found himself enamored with the bewitching Anna, who, on his making tender advances, cast a long sigh on the war-path of a certain *hunter,* blushed deeply and reciprocated ardently his attachment.

Early in the year 1781, but in what month we can not speak with certainty, Anna Mason was led to Hymen's altar, an altar on which have been offered many pure affections, but few more unsullied than hers, and became the bride of her heroic William. Days, weeks, even months passed, and still the young wife was happy; should she ever be otherwise? for she had a kind husband, and was surrounded by those who loved and respected her.

The green summer flew past, and autumn with her russet-clad meadows and golden forests arrived, and still Anna Scarborough was cheerful and happy: but alas! a civil war that had raged for years and stained with life-blood the threshold of many dwellings within a few miles, was still devastating the land; and although the war-cry for a little season was removed to a distance, and no immediate danger was apprehended, yet the midnight alarm *might* again break on the ear, and the most tender ties be sundered in a moment: for

Storms that have been again may be!
The battle-axe if yet on high,
Stained with the blood of martyrs free—
When thought most distant may be nearest by;
And from it fondly cherished may not fly.

On the morning of October 25, 1781, a large body of the enemy under Maj. Ross, entered Johnstown with several prisoners, and not a little plunder; among which were a number of human scalps taken the afternoon and night previous, in settlements in and adjoining the Mohawk valley; to which was added the scalp of Hugh McMonts, a constable, who was surprised and killed as they entered Johnstown. In the course of the day the troops from the garrisons near and the militia from the surrounding country, rallied under the active and daring Willett, and gave the enemy battle on the Hall farm, in which the latter were finally defeated with loss, and made good their retreat to Canada. Young Scarborough was then in the nine months' service, and while the action was going on, himself and one Crosset left the Johnstown fort, where they were on garrison duty, to join in the fight, less than two miles distant. Between the Hall and woods they soon found themselves engaged. Crosset after shooting down one or two, received a bullet through one hand, but winding a handkerchief around it, he continued the fight under cover of a hemlock stump. He was shot down and killed there, and his companion surrounded and made prisoner by a party of Scotch troops commanded by Capt. McDonald. When Scarborough was captured, Capt. McDonald was not present, but the moment he saw him he ordered his men to shoot him down. Several refused; but three, shall I call them men? obeyed the dastardly order, and yet he possibly would have survived his wounds, had not the miscreant in authority cut him down with his own broadsword. The sword was caught in its first descent, and the valiant captain drew it out, cutting the hand nearly in two.

Why this cold-blooded murder? Were those hostile warriors rivals in love? Had the epauletted hero, commissioned at the door of the infernal regions, sought the hand of the blooming Anna and been rejected because his arm was raised against his suffering country? Or must the prisoner be destroyed because in arms

with his countrymen? A more hellish and malignant
act was not perpetrated, even by the sons of the forest,
on the frontiers of New York.* Jeremiah Crowley,
the step-father of Scarborough, was made a prisoner
by the enemy and taken to Canada. Mrs. Scarborough,
who was at her father's on the morning of the action,
fled to the fort with her father, Mrs Mason choosing
to brave the dangers of the day to save her effects.
Mason's house stood a little north of the present site
of John Yost's tavern, and on the edge of the Hall
farm. The action was fought in its vicinity, and thirteen balls were fired into it, which no doubt kept the
old lady from falling asleep. One of McDonald's men,

* Previous to the war, McDonald and Scarborough were neighbors, and in a political quarrel which took place soon after the
commencement of national difficulties and ended in blows, the
loyalist was rather roughly handled. A spirit of revenge no doubt
prompted him to wreak his vengeance on an unarmed prisoner.—
Stoner.

Scarborough was overbearing and at times insolent towards those
who differed with him in politics. On one occasion during the
war, at the gristmill in Johnstown, Scarborough met an old man
upon whom he heaped a deal of abuse. The young miller, a mere
lad, offended at such unkind treatment, jumped into a sleigh then
at the door, rode up to the fort, and informed the garrison of what
he had witnessed. Several soldiers, determined to see fair play,
returned with the miller; and on their reproving Scarborough for
ill treating the poor old man, he turned upon and began a quarrel
with them. The result was he received a severe castigation for
his temerity, which cooled him down. From *James Frazier,*
then a boy, who, if I mistake not, witnessed the whole scene at
the mill.

who had been ordered to fire on young Scarborough and refused to obey, was so disgusted with his captain for the act, that he deserted the same evening and joined the Americans.

On the morning after their death, the remains of Scarborough and Crosset were taken to the fort on a wooden-shod sleigh drawn by horses.* Need I stop to tell the reader how the young bride, Anna Scarborough, was overwhelmed with sorrow on the day succeeding the Johnstown battle? How her keenest sensibilities were on fire, at beholding the mangled remains of her beloved William; and what mental agony she endured? But such sufferings are at all times the attendants of a civil war, in which neighbor is clad in armor against his fellow, and kinsman against those of his own blood. Some time after the death of her husband, and about eleven months after the sealing of the nuptial vow, Mrs. Scarborough was presented with a daughter as a pledge of her early love, which tended in no measured degree to reconcile her to the cruel fate war had meted her. This daughter grew up to woman's estate.

Time and change of circumstances, with the blessings of social intercourse returning at the close of a protracted war, again restored the young widow, who possesed a buoyant disposition, or a spirit to wrestle

---

*Yockum Folluck, a soldier killed in the Johnstown battle, was found with a piece of meat placed at his mouth, as supposed by the Indians in derision. Folluck resided in the vicinity of Johnstown.—*David Zielie.*

successfully with trials, to the enjoyment of society
and the shaded realities of life.

One that has won, again may win;

and soon after the return of Nicholas Stoner to Johnstown, he came within the pale of the young widow's
charms, which in the military camp had often brought
him to his senses, and shortly after sought and obtained
her hand in marriage. Although her affections had
been chastened by the blight of sorrow, her young
heart was still susceptible of an ardent offering to the
one who had inspired the first budding of love there,
and she proved a boon companion and cheerful wife.
The fruit of this connection was four sons and two
daughters. Three of the sons are still living. The
daughters were Mary and Catharine: the former married William Mills, and now (1847) resides in Fulton
county; and the latter died when a young woman.

Nicholas Stoner, the first two years after his marriage, lived near Johnson Hall, and then settled at
Scotch Bush, now known as McEwen's Corners, in
the western part of Johnstown, where he resided many
years. John Stoner, whose temperament did not bring
him into trouble often, continued in the army to the
close of the war; after which he was for several years
employed by Col. Frederick Fisher, who built him a
farm-house nearly on the site of his homestead, and
where he had been scalped by the Indians. To the
location of this dwelling, a substantial brick edifice,
I have already alluded. After John Stoner left the

employ of Col. Fisher, he married Miss Susan Philes, by whom he had a daughter, Catharine Ann, and four sons.

Soon after the Revolution, Nicholas Stoner was for three years a deputy sheriff under John Littel, Esq. He was also a captain of militia, and filled several town offices at different periods. When we again came to blows with England, because of her insolence in searching our ships and impressing our seamen into her service, the Stoner brothers were once more enrolled in the American army; John enlisting in 1812, and Nicholas in 1813. John Stoner, who was a drum-major in this war, was taken sick at Sacket's Harbor and died there. Nicholas enlisted at Johnstown into the 29th New York regiment, of which Melancthon Smith was colonel, G. D. Young lieutenant-colonel,* and John E. Wool, major. He joined the company of Capt. A. P. Spencer, Lieut. Henry Van Antwerp being the recruiting officer under whom he enrolled his name. He proceeded to Utica, and from thence to Sacket's Harbor, where he remained until fall; at which time he went into winter quarters at Greenbush. Early the following spring he joined the army at Plattsburg, going from Whitehall by water.

Lake Champlain and the territory adjoining it, in in September, 1814, became the theatre of some of the most important events which characterized the war

* Lieut.-Col. Young was killed in 1817, in the abortive attempt of Gen. Mina to revolutionize Mexico.

of that period.　The withdrawal of troops from Plattsburg to succor Fort Erie, determined the governor
general of Canada, Sir George Prevost, to attack it
with a force he supposed irresistible; and for that purpose he invaded the territory of the States on the 3d
day of September, with an army some *fourteen thousand*
strong, well equipped and provided with a splendid
train of artillery.　About the same time, so as to make
a clean sweep, Commodore Downie, with a naval
force far superior in number of vessels, guns and men,
made preparations to engage the American flotilla on
Lake Champlain, then under the command of the gallant Commodore Thomas McDonnough, who, ten years
before, had so distinguished himself under Decatur in
a captured Turkish ketch before the walls, and under
the very batteries of the bashaw of Tripoli.

Gen. Macomb, at Plattsburg, had only about fifteen
hundred men at his command when the invasion of
Prevost began, but his call on the patriotic sons of
New York and Vermont was promptly obeyed, and he
was enabled to keep a vastly superior force at bay,
until reinforced sufficiently to cope with his adversary.
From the 3d until the 11th of September, repeated
engagements took place contiguous to Plattsburg, in
several of which Nicholas Stoner, then a fife-major,
was engaged.　He took a musket, however, and performed duty at this time as a sergeant, and as he was
a good marksman, several must have fallen before his
deadly aim.

There was not a little excitement in the American camp at Plattsburg as the British army was advancing on that post, and great exertions were made to put it in a fit state for the enemy's reception. The meritorious young Trojan, Captain Wool, as a reward for his daring conduct in storming Queenston heights, in October, 1812, had been appointed major, of the 29th New York regiment, and in the absence of its colonels, the command of it devolved upon him in September, 1814.

As the enemy were approaching, Major Wool volunteered his services, and repeatedly on the 5th of September, urged General Macomb to allow him to meet the enemy and make at least *a show of resistance;* as nothing more could be expected against such odds. The general met his earnest solicitations with some coolness, and expressed his apprehensions that if he went out he would be captured. On the evening of the 5th, the gallant Wool received a reluctant assent to meet the enemy, but was not allowed to do so until morning. So anxious was he for active service, however, that long before day light on the 6th, the major had mustered his corps and was on the Beekmantown road. Gen. Macomb had assured him Capt. Leonard, with his company of artillery, should accompany him, but the latter declined marching without the express orders of the general, and he moved forward without him. His own regiment then numbered only 200 men, to which were added about 50 from other regiments,

9*

and some 30 volunteer militia: in all nearly 280 men.
Gen. Mooers had been stationed on the Beekmantown
road with a regiment of 700 militia, previous to Maj.
Wool's going there, and the latter was commanded by
Gen. Macomb to set the militia *an example of firm-
ness.*

The enemy on the morning of the 6th were advancing by three roads, the eastern road running
along the western shore of Lake Champlain; the western leading from Chazy to Plattsburg, and called the
Chazy road, and the centre known as the Beekmantown road. Maj. Appling with a body of riflemen
was posted on the eastern or lake road, Maj. Wool on
the centre; while the enemy were allowed to advance
on the Chazy road without opposition. Maj. Appling
directed his attention chiefly to obstructing the road
by falling trees, and fell back in time to join Major
Wool near Plattsburg.

On arriving, just at day light, at Gen. Mooers's camp,
seven miles from Plattsburg, Maj. Wool found the
enemy, 4000 strong, were not far distant on that road,
and already moving. Gen. Mooers made several attempts as the enemy drew near, to form his men for
action, but they broke and fled, most of them without
firing. Maj. Wool told him he had better head his
men if possible, and with them make a stand upon the
road, so as to cover his own retreat.

The unexpected flight of the militia, as may be supposed, created some confusion in the infantry, to re-

cover from which and gain a little time, Maj. Wool
ordered Capt Van Buren with his company to charge
the enemy. The brave captain expressed a doubt
about his ability to do it; fearing his men would de-
sert him. *" Shoot down the first man that attempts to
run, or I will shoot you!"* was the peremptory order
of the enthusiastic major. Van Buren quickly moved
forward to execute the command, but when within a
few rods of the foe, satisfied his handful of men could
hardly be trusted to charge such a billow of animated
matter, he ordered them to halt and fire. The fire
was well directed and told fearfully in the enemy's
ranks, which were sufficiently retarded for Maj. Wool
to dispose of his Spartan band to his mind. That
Capt. Van Buren did good service in his morning salute, is proven by the fact, that *twenty* of the enemy
were carried into the house of a Mr. Howe, living
near by. Maj. Wool formed his men in three several
double platoons; one occupying the road, and the
others the fields or woods a little in rear of the first,
and on either side of the road with out-flankers. The
British in column continued to advance, and in the
order named the Americans kept up a street fight,
firing and retreating before the enemy: the troops in
the street again forming and deploying in the street
after each fire, a little in the rear of the field troops;
and those in turn forming and deploying in rear of the
platoons occupying the street. Thus did this little
detachment of brave men resist the invader's approach

step by step for nearly six miles, doing at times fearful execution in his ranks, and setting truly an example of firmness that would have done credit to veteran troops, with a Buonaparte for a commander.

On an eminence in the road, called Culver's hill, Lieut.-Col. Willington, of the 3d regiment of British Buffs, an officer of gallant bearing, was slain, with a number of his men; while a little farther on, *forty* of the enemy, dead and wounded, were borne into the house of Maj. Platt, among whom was Lieut. Kingsbury, and possibly some other officers. Learning in the morning that Capt. Leonard had not accompanied Maj. Wool, Gen. Macomb ordered him forward to his assistance. At the junction of the Chazy and Beekmantown roads, called Halsey's corners, he joined the infantry with two six-pounders. At this place the militia, having recovered from their panic, were brought into action by Gen. Mooers. They were posted in woods on the right and also in the rear of the artillery; the infantry being mostly behind a stone wall along the Chazy road, to the left of the ordnance. A part of it was stationed so as to conceal the artillery, however, and as the British advanced, unsuspicious of receiving such a salute, the war-dogs were unmasked, and several round shot plowed their bloody furrows the entire length of the enemy's column. At this moment the Americans observed, says an eyewitness, " one of the finest specimens of discipline ever exhibited." The gaps in the British ranks were closed, as if by magic, and steadily onward was their march.

As the enemy neared the field-pieces, they were greeted with grape shot, which caused them to halt, but the British bugles soon sounded a charge, and the Americans were obliged to retreat, which they did in good order to Gallows hill,* at which place they made the last stand on the north side of the Saranac. Adjutant Boynton, a young officer of great merit, and whose services to Maj. Wool were invaluable on this stirring day, was sent by the latter with orders to Maj. Appling to join him. The order was heroically executed though one of great peril, as he was exposed to the fire of many scores of British muskets, and Maj. Appling joined the invincible 29th near Gallows hill. After a brief stand at the latter place, the Americans fell back across the Saranac, and taking up the bridge in their rear they kept the enemy upon the north side of the river. In removing the plank of this bridge, the Americans suffered considerably. Maj. Stoner assisted in taking up this bridge, and also the one over Dead creek. The enemy's loss in this long road fight with the troops under Maj. Wool, in killed and wounded, was about 240, a number nearly equal to his entire command during the greatest part of the action. The American loss was about 45 in killed and wounded. Maj. Wool had a horse shot under him

* On this hill the Americans erected a gallows and hung a British spy upon it.

during the day. For the masterly manner in which he acquitted himself on this occasion, he was breveted lieutenant-colonel; a promotion he could not that day have merited, had he not been surrounded by a band of iron-hearted warriors.

In the action at Gallows hill the following incident took place. William Bosworth, a serjeant-major who had deserted from the British and entered the American service, and on the day in question had greatly distinguished himself, received a musket ball through his thigh which brought him to the ground. It was impossible for the Americans to bring off all their wounded, so closely did the enemy press upon them. Apprised of the fact that Bosworth was down, Major Wool, addressing himself to Adjutant Boynton, exclaimed, " See that the boys throw Bosworth on a horse and remove him to a place of safety, for if he falls into the hands of the enemy they will either hang or shoot him: he is too good a fellow to be used up in that manner; *take him off?*" A horse was quickly provided which Stoner held, while two soldiers placed the wounded sergeant upon his back, his blood running down the animal's side. The wounded man was taken to Plattsburg and afterwards to Burlington, Vermont, where he recovered. The reader may not be surprised to learn, that the generous-hearted major, who was not unmindful of the fate of a poor soldier, even in a fearful shower of iron and lead, is the illustrious Major-General Wool, who has been one of the brightest stars of that heroic band, which has recently covered itself with such a blaze of glory in Mexico.

The army of Prevost was kept on the north side of the Saranac by Macomb until the 11th of September, at which time Downie prepared to engage with Mc-Donough. Undaunted by the superior naval force of his adversary, the latter met him with a firmness and coolness characteristic of the man. It is stated in a newspaper account of his death, that he engaged the enemy at this time with a confident trust in the God of battles for his success. Calling his brave tars around him on the quarter-deck, as the enemy hove in sight, upon his knees he commended his cause to Him who governs the universe. This engagement was witnessed by both armies, it is reasonable to suppose, with intense excitement; as upon its result was suspended the probable fortune of the land forces. At 9 o'clock the contest began, and in less than two hours the Confiance, the enemy's flag-ship, had, with two other vessels, struck her colors to the Americans, and several British galleys had been sunk: the rest of the fleet escaped by flight, the victors being unable to pursue them, as there was not a mast standing in either squadron to which a sail could be raised. Commodore Downie was among the slain.

A pleasing incident attendant on this battle should be given in its connection. In the midst of the fiery contest, a hencoop on the Saratoga, McDonough's flag-ship, was shot away, and a liberated rooster flew into

the rigging overhead and began to crow. The circumstance was ominous, and contributed in no little
degree to inspire the hardy tars with confidence, and
they responded with a round of cheers and renewed
exertions to his Yankee-doodle-do!

The artillery of the land forces was almost constantly in play during the naval engagement, but when
the Confiance struck her colors, the army of Macomb
took time to give a huzzaing, that fell on the ears of
Prevost like the knell of death. The army of the latter was in full retreat, early in the evening, for Canada.
That they might have something to remember their
Yankee neighbors by, as they were about to strike
their tents, Macomb fired a national salute, *with ball
cartridges*, into their camp.

The remains of Commodore Downie, with those of
five of his fellow officers, and the remains of five officers of Commodore McDonough's squadron, were
brought on shore and buried by Gen. Macomb with
the honors of war; on which occasion Maj. Wool was
master of ceremonies and selected the place of burial.
The music which led the procession consisted of some
fifteen fifes and as many drums, the latter all muffled,
and was commanded by Maj. Stoner: the tunes Logan
Water and Roslin Castle, were played during the
ceremony. The bodies were taken to a grove of pines
and arranged side by side in three several rows. Two
stately pines are still standing, one on each side of
Downie's grave. While on that station Maj. Wool

had the remains of the officers which fell on the Beekmantown road, removed and deposited beside those
which fell in the naval service.   After the war Mrs.
Mary Downie, a sister-in-law, erected a tablet to the
memory of her gallant kinsman.

Some weeks after the above incidents transpired,
Major Stoner conducted several British officers to the
grave of Commodore Downie, where some of them
manifested much feeling, mingling their tears of sympathy with the dew-drops of heaven.

When Great Britain became satisfied that her
claims to oceanic rule were not well founded, and the
American army was disbanded, Gen. Macomb offered
Maj. Stoner strong inducements to join the national
army, which he declined.

On the 11th of September, 1842, twenty-nine years
after the event, the Clinton County Military Associa-
tion celebrated the anniversary of the battle of Plattsburg at that place, in a very commendable manner,
on which occasion monuments were erected to the
memory of all the officers which had been buried near
Commodore Downie.   Gen. Wool and his suite were
present by special invitation, to take part in the interesting proceedings.   Appropriate addresses were
delivered by General Skinner, Col. McNeil and Gen.
Wool.   The ceremony of placing a monument at Col.
Willington's grave, was very properly assigned to
Gen. Wool, before whose prowess he had fallen in
battle.

10

How creditable to the enterprise and magnanimity of the citizens of Plattsburg, in so just and appropriate a manner to meet and mingle their sympathies over the remains, not only of their illustrious friends who had fallen in the service of their country, but also over those of their gallant and unfortunate foes, who found a final resting place beneath the pines of a foreign land. Warrior foes, there gently slumber.

CHAPTER VII.

I have chosen, in this narrative, to present Major Stoner's military life connectedly, although some of the incidents which follow, transpired between the wars.

Fond of novelty and adventure, and inured to privations and hardships in the Revolution, which peculiarly fitted him for a life so full of excitement and peril, Maj. Stoner became a celebrated hunter. Nor was he the only gamester who traversed the then wilderness of North-Eastern New York: several of his companions in arms were often by his side, threading their own intricate foot-paths along a score of crystal lakes, the greater part of which are now situated in the present counties of Fulton and Hamilton. There were other Nimrods, or master spirits, in this particular avocation, two of whom were Nathaniel Foster and Green White. The former lived in Salisbury, Herkimer county, and the latter in Wooster, Otsego county. The Johnstown sportsmen not only met Foster, White and other sportsmen associated with them—as they usually went in pairs for the greater security in case of sickness, accident or difficulties with individuals of the craft—but white men and Indians from the shores of the St. Lawrence.

Difficulties sometimes arose between these strangers of like avocation, and in the absence of any other tribunal, *might* made *right*. Trouble seldom originated between the white hunters, however, as the more noted were not only known to each other, but their traps readily recognized by some peculiar mark, were not molested, unless it were to take out game in danger of being lost; in which case some token was left to apprise the owner who had it, and that it would be accounted for at a subsequent meeting. Over-jealous of their rights, the New York and Canadian trappers did not at all times scruple to avenge an injury done them, with the life-blood of the offender, as I shall have on several occasions to show.

The class of men of whom I am speaking, not only entered the forest with their traps, their rifles, and a good supply of ammunition, their hatchet and knife, and often a jug of rum; but what was all important, a pocket compass and some sure means of kindling a fire. Friction matches were then unknown, but fire was soon enkindled with flint, steel and tinder, or touch-wood; and now and then when *they* became wet, by a flash in the pan of a gun. If trappers chanced to visit the water courses alone, they almost invariably took with them a well trained dog. Pack horses were often employed to carry provisions to the hunters' canoes, which were usually moored in some little eddy, contiguous to which the trapping began.

One of the evils if not entailed upon us, at least

greatly augmented by war, is that of wide-spread IN-TEMPERANCE; and few who had been served for years with a daily ration of rum or whiskey, could refrain from its use in after life: indeed soldiers had not only to drink with each other after the Revolution, as a matter of courtesy, but every one esteemed it a privilege, nay a *duty*, to treat a hero who had periled his life for his fellows: hence many of them who could not say NO when invited to drink, had to become a walking slop-bowl, and receive flip, kill devil, punch, or the raw material divested of its lure. Many a scar-honored veteran filled a drunkard's grave, because *custom* compelled him, of all others, to drink; and not a few more of the same band would have found such a grave, had not *temperance* hung her rainbow along Heaven's blue arch, inscribed—My worthy, it shall not only be your privilege, but creditable for you to refrain from the use of that which sets the brain on fire, destroys domestic happiness, and causes premature death.

Vaumane Jean Baptiste De Fonclaiere, a Frenchman who had emigrated to this country in the Revolution, married in New England, and after the close of the war kept a public house in Johnstown for many years. The first house he occupied is still an inn, and is yet standing, a few doors south of the court house.*

* In 1796, De Fonclaiere erected a tavern stand at Johnstown, in the forks of the Fonda's Bush and Tribe's Hill roads, which stand was known for many years as Union Hall, and in which as

The Canadian hunters, who were familiar with the forest between Montreal and Johnstown, from having traversed it repeatedly to obtain American scalps, not unfrequently visited the latter place when peace returned, to sell their furs, where they found a ready market. A party of seven arrived there in the spring of the year soon after the Revolution, with a large quantity of fur, and put up at the inn mentioned; disposing of their wealth to John Grant, then a village merchant. He was enabled to carry on the traffic, through the agency of Lieut. Wallace, who could speak the Indian tongue.

"mine host," he spent the remainder of his days. This Hall building is now owned and occupied by Mr. V. Balch as a private dwelling. The following anecdote of the old Frenchman, who is still remembered around Johnstown for his extra bows and especial regard for the comfort of his customers, was witnessed by the Hon. Aaron Haring.

There stands in Johnstown, on the east side of the street, a few rods to the southward of the first inn kept by De Fonclaiere, an antiquated building with a gambrel roof, owned and occupied before the Revolution by Maj. Gilbert Tice. The latter building after the war, was occupied as a tavern stand by Michael Rollins, a son of the emerald isle. De Fonclaiere kept a span of mettlesome horses, and when a deep snow had spread her white mantle over the bosom of the earth, and the bells and belles began to jingle and smile, the restless steads harnessed to a sleigh to give his ladies an airing, were brought before the door, with their nostrils snuffing up the wind in the direction of the Mohawk.

Left only *un leetle moment* to their own wills, the gay animals of Mons. De Fonclaiere, either of which would have served a Ringgold or a May for a charger, abused the confidence of their

During the stay of these northern hunters in Johns-town, Maj. Stoner, then a deputy sheriff under Littel, was there on professional business. A constable whom he desired to see, he found seated in De Fonclaiere's kitchen, near a table, on which stood several flasks of liquor, furnished at the expense of the Indians. About

master, and dashed off at the top of their speed. In front of the rival inn stood a cow directly in the beaten path, which belonged on the premises. Strange as it may seem, as the sleigh passed the cow, she was thrown upon her haunches, and, as chance would have it, rolled on her back plump into it. The party in-tending to occupy the seat instead of the kine, came to the door in time to see the latter drive off in triumph, urging on the horses by a most doleful bellowing. The horses started in William-street and ran south to Clinton-street, thence east through Clinton to Johnson (now Market) street, south up Market to Montgomery street, west through Montgomery to William street, and down the latter to the place of starting. The best part of the joke was, that on turning into William street from Montgomery, at the next corner above, and only a few rods from where the cow was taken in, she was, sans ceremony, thrown out again. A war of words instantly followed this adventure, between the rival land-lords. Said De Fonclaiere, greatly excited — "*Keep you tam Irish cow out von my sleigh!*" "*You French booger,*" retorted Rollings with an oath, "*do you kape the like of yeer fancy horses away from me cow!*" This novel incident afforded a fine subject for village gossip, as the reader may suppose, long after the excitement it awakened had died away.

Inscriptions from tombstones in Johnstown.— "In memory of John Baptiste Vaumane De Fonclaiere, formerly a captain in the Martinique regiment, in the service of His Most Christian Ma-jesty Louis XVI, and for thirty years past a citizen of the United States, who departed this life 5th January 1811, in the 71st year of his age." "In memory of Achsah, wife of Vaumane De Fonclaiere, who died Aug. 15, 1831, in the 73d year of her age."

the room were several Indians, and perhaps some female members of the family, as they were preparing
dinner for their red customers.   Maj. Stoner, who was
not then altogether free from the maddening influence
of those flasks or some others, observing one of the
strangers near Thompson to be of light complexion,
addressed him in a friendly, perhaps playful manner,
about his origin; and the Indian, not appearing offended in the least, replied that he was part white.
At this juncture, up came another of the party, and in
an insolent manner demanded of Stoner in broken
English, Indian and French, what business he had to
interrogate his comrade.   "Out, you black booger!"
said the major, who never would take an insult from
an Indian with impunity; rolling together threaten-
ingly at the moment the bones of his right hand.

Liquor is brought forward to cement friendship, yet
it often produces an adverse result, for men influenced
by it need little provocation to fight.   Face to face
the two, now foes, grappled to test their physical
powers.   The major was too much for his antagonist,
and in the scuffle which followed, threw him head-
long upon the table, oversetting it and dashing its
quadrangular, half-filled bottles into scores of angles
never heard of in geometry.   Quick as thought, the
red man was upon his feet and leaping the table
had again clenched with his adversary.   Cooking
stoves are an invention of the last forty years, and in
the kitchen where this scuffle took place, yawned a

huge fire-place filled with blazing faggots; while upon the hearth before it stood a platter of fried pork swimming in hot fat, and a dish of wilted sallad, just taken from a bed of coals by some member of the family, who was providing dinner for the fur-sellers. Stoner attempted to cast the Indian into the fire, but falling a little short of the aim, the latter fell plump into the dish of gravy, burning his back adown in a most frightful manner.

The fracas had occupied but a few moments, yet the whoops and loud threats of the combattants, with the whys and wherefores of spectators, and screams of women, had been sufficient to throw the whole house into one of uproar and confusion. The honest landlord entered the kitchen trembling between contending emotions of fear and passion, believing that the character and business of his house would be ruined; and with numerous threats against sheriff Stoner, uttered in broken English, as soon as the storm began to subside, ran off to get a writ of Amaziah Rust, Esq., then a lawyer of the place. Now Squire Rust, as it happened, was a particular friend of our hero, and knowing what an untamed spirit he possessed, and withal how he felt toward the race who had murdered his father, he was probably not much surprised to hear that the major had worsted an Indian; and laying down his pen and assuming a thoughtful mood he gravely inquired, " Do you not know, sir, that Captain Stoner is apt to be deranged with the changes of the moon?" "No, monsieur," replied Fonclaiere, " me did not know that. O! le diable, vat shall I does then? me ruined sartain!" With kind assurances from Mr. Rust (who was less anxious for business than are some professional men), that all would soon be forgotten—that Stoner would no doubt make full reparation for the property destroyed, and that the reputation of his house would not receive any lasting injury on account of the morning's frolic; the landlord was persuaded to go home and overlook the matter.

On returning to his dwelling, how provokingly wrong did the poor Frenchman find things had gone in his absence. Leaving the kitchen after his second encounter with the intrusive Indian, Major Stoner entered the hall where he almost stumbled upon an Indian called Captain John, who was lying upon the floor in a state of beastly drunkenness. Excited by the strong waters of death, and impassioned by what had already transpired, he halted beside the inebriate, in whose ear as it lay up, was suspended a heavy leaden jewel; the weight of which had caused the boring to become much elongated. Placing one foot upon his neck, and thrusting a finger into the slit in the ear, the unpolished ornament was torn out in an instant, and fell upon the floor. Unconscious of the injury done him, the poor Indian turned over with a grunt, and Stoner passed into the bar-room: the place at that period least calculated of all others, to quiet a raging mind.

STONER AVENGING HIS FATHER'S MURDER.

See page 119.

The name of Stoner had doubtless fallen upon the ear of a half-drunk Indian in the bar-room, while the kitchen scene was enacting, and reminded him of his former acts; for he had drawn his scalping-knife to boast to several by-standers (one of whom was Abraham Van Skiver), of the deeds of blood recorded upon its handle. *Nine* marks indicated the number of American scalps he had taken in the late war; " *and this,*" said he, pointing to a notch cut deeper than the rest to indicate a warrior, " *was the scalp of old Stoner!*" Major Stoner entered the room just in time to hear the savage boast of scalping his father, and as the braggart was dancing before the bar with yells and athletic gestures, cutting the air with the blade which had so many times been stained with the crimson torrent of life: stung to madness by the thought of being in the presence of his father's murderer, he sprang to the fire-place, seized an old-fashioned wrought andiron, and with the exclamation, " *You never will scalp another one!*" he hurled it, red-hot as it was, at the head of the warrior. His own hand was burned to a blister, even by the top of the iron, which, striking the object of its aim in the hottest part across the neck with an indellible brand, laid him out at full length upon the floor; the register of death dropping from his hand.

The quarrel having arrived at so dangerous a crisis, some of the friends of Major Stoner succeeded in getting him out of the house; while other individuals ran for a physician, restoratives and the like. The Indians of the party who were not disabled or too drunk to stand up, were boisterous in their threats of revenge; but being advised to leave town, and possibly not feeling very secure in their own persons after what had already happened, they lost no time in preparing for a departure to the wilderness. A German, named Samuel Copeland, was employed to carry them in a wagon to the Sacondaga river, near the fish-house, where they had left most of their rifles, their squaws and canoes. It was the opinion of the physician and others, that the Indian with seared jugular, could not possibly survive; but he was, with his fried companion, taken along by his fellows. It was never satisfactorily known in Johnstown whether this party of hunters all reached Canada alive or not, but it was supposed that at least *one* of the number died on the way.

Fearing this party of red men might return and revenge the injuries done them on the settlement, if no notice was taken of the affair, a person in Johnstown lodged a complaint against him for the part he had acted at De Fonclaiere's, and he was arrested and put in jail.* As soon as it became known abroad that he had been incarcerated, and only a day or two was sufficient to spread the news, a large number of men

* The wood work of this old stone building, which served as a fort in the Revolution, was burned in Sept. 1849. The building has since been repaired, and restored to its former appearance.

of Revolutionary memory, many of whom had been sufferers in person, property, or friends, by the midnight assaults of their country's foes, and who were now disposed to justify the conduct of their former companion in arms, in his attempt to slay the murderer of his father, assembled around the prison and demanded his enlargement. Of those congregated were several of the Sammonses, Fishers, Putmans, Wemples, Fondas, Vroomans, Veeders, Gardiniers, Quackenbosses, and a host of others, whose names can not now be remembered. The jailer was unwilling to liberate the prisoner without a formal demand, and the mob, provided with a piece of scantling, stove in the door and brought him out.

At this period one Throop kept a tavern near the centre of the village, with whom sheriff Littel was then boarding; and thither the party in triumph directed their steps to drink with the liberated hero. After allowing the mob some time to jollify, the jailer went down, and getting Stoner one side, asked him *if he was ready to return!* "Yes," he replid, and at once set out with the turnkey for the jail, some forty or fifty rods distant. He was soon missed, and the *liberators*, learning that he was again on his way to prison, once more set the law at defiance, and rescued him from the custody of the officer; when, to comply with their wishes, he went home to his anxious family, and there quietly remained. Thus ended an eventful scene in the old hero's life.

11

After the incidents above narrated had transpired, and the Indian trappers returned to their wigwams, the prowess and fearless acts of the Johnstown warrior gave him no little celebrity along the water-courses of Canada; and many a red pappoos was taught in swaddles, to lisp with dread the name of Stoner.

CHAPTER VIII.

" Dark green was the spot, mid the brown mountain-heather,
  Where the pilgrim of nature lay stretched in decay,
Like the corpse of an outcast abandoned to weather,
  Till the mountain-winds wasted the tenantless clay."

Walter Scott

We are now to consider a peculiarly exciting portion of our hero's life, and may fail to give the reader
but a faint idea of the countless novel incidents following the footsteps of a master hunter, although in
fancy full

"Oft have we seen him at the peep of dawn,
  Brushing with hasty steps the dews away,
To meet the sun upon the upland lawn,"

and thus followed him on to the wood-entangled glen;
where the growl of an animal caused a startle and
placed the thumb on the fire-lock; the rustle of a leaf
fevered the blood, and the snap of a forest-twig sent
it tingling to his brain.

In trapping, Major Stoner used heavy steel-traps
with two springs for beaver and otter, and occasionally single spring traps for muskrat, when their fur
would pay. He had one trap four feet long made like
the former, and designed expressly for bears. The
jaws of this ugly looking customer, are crossed on the
under side by spikes, which, when an animal is en-

trapped, are driven through the leg and render its escape impossible, unless it gnaw its own limb off above the fastening, and thus gain its liberty. To this trap is attached a chain five feet long, with two grappling hooks at the end, so shaped as to fasten either to a tree or the ground, and *bring up* the game. The trap and chain weigh nearly forty pounds. It required two hand-spikes with this trap beside a log, or in some other favorable position, to set it; on which account the wary hunter, when the jaws parted, used the precaution to place a billet of wood between them while adjusting the pan, lest through accident he might find the spikes boring his own limbs. Nearly thirty bears have been taken in this trap, one-third of them by its owner. On one occasion a bear left its toes in the trap and escaped. For a view of this trap, doing execution, see cover of the book.

If hunting with a partner, each carried three beaver traps, and when traces of game were observed the traps were set in the water, and to them the animals were lured by a peculiar kind of bait called castoreum, or beaver-castor, remarkably odorous and attractive even in the water. That taken from one beaver was often the agent for exterminating several of its fellows. The usual time of hunting began with cool weather in the latter part of September, and lasted about two months, or until the streams and lakes became frost-bound and the hunter's paths obstructed by snow. The avocation was often renewed for several weeks with the breaking up of winter, the hunters at times starting upon snow-shoes.

One of the individuals with whom Major Stoner sometimes hunted, was Capt. William Jackson, a man of courage and great muscular strength. On one occasion they set out for a hunt towards spring, traveling on snow-shoes. Arriving at a place where they had to cross a field of ice, Jackson took off his snow-shoes. With other indispensables he was carrying a sharp axe, and by some misstep he slipped and fell upon it, cutting himself under his chin in a shocking manner. His companion was two days in getting him back to the nearest settlement; which was in Chase's patent, now Bleeker, and about eighteen miles from where the accident happened. Leaving his wounded friend well cared for, Stoner retraced his steps to the wilderness; and Jackson sent James Dunn a few days after, to supply his place.

Finding an inviting prospect for their business on the Sacondaga, they began to set their traps. Hunters erected lodges for their accommodation at suitable distances from each other. They were small huts made of bark, peeled for the purpose, hence the necessity for an axe; besides, it was needed in preparing fuel, and also in making canoes; which they constructed by digging out a suitable log. Stoner and Dunn, after building huts, preparing for each a tree-canoe, and securing the pelts of some six or eight beavers, left their traps set and came out to the settle-

ment on Chase's patent for provisions. They left
their canoes in their absence, in a stream running from
Trout lake into the Sacondaga. Their journey to obtain food, principally bread, as hunters could generally
supply their larder with fish and wild-game, occupied
only a few days; yet on their return they soon discovered that all was not right. The first trap they
looked for was one that had been set by Dunn, on the
outlet a little distance from the lake; it was gone.

Leaving their canoe in an eddy made by a deposit
of drift-wood, they landed and proceeded with caution
up the creek. Arriving near the lake they heard a
loud *halloo!* to which Stoner responded, although his
companion thought it a loon. They now halted and
awaited in silence, to learn what human voices besides their own, broke the general solitude of the forest.
Soon the light dash of a paddle was heard, and immediately after an Indian in a bark canoe rounded a
point of land, and a few strokes from his brawny arm
sent his fairy craft into the outlet of the lake, beside,
and very near the white hunters. Scarcely had the
shoal navigator gained the point named, when another
Indian, on foot, rounded the point also, and stood
within a few paces of the pale-faced strangers. At
the feet of the Indian in the canoe lay a rifle and one
of Stoner's traps. The hunter on shore was armed
with a tomahawk, carrying in one hand the shell of
an immense turtle, which the water had drifted upon
the beach. Both parties evinced surprise at the meet-

ing; but the Canadian trappers, who proved to be St. Regis Indians, appeared least at ease.

Hunters, as a class, are very tenacious of their rights, and priority of occupancy usually establishes a claim to hunting grounds. Some of their traps had been left along the shore of the lake, in the direction from whence the Indians made their appearance; and after a most formal meeting, the Johnstown hunters charged the strangers not only with appropriating their fur to their own use, but also their traps in which it had been taken. This was denied on the part of the accused, notwithstanding one of the traps was in their possession, and a fierce quarrel of words followed, graced by an exchange of harsh epithets, until

" Revenge impatient rose."

The Indian on shore, who was nearest to Stoner, and on whom the latter vented not a few wicked sayings, declared that he had seen the traps alluded to at some distance above, and that they had not been molested. The white hunters insisted upon having the accused go back with them to see if the traps were as they had been left; this the other party attempted with sundry excuses to evade doing. The one on land then endeavored to gain a little distance under some pretext, and the other, saying he would go back as desired after gathering some bark, was observed to grasp his rifle, abandon his canoe and leap from it to the shore opposite Dunn.

At this instant the sharp crack of a rifle was heard, and in the echo sent back by the hills came a yell from the quivering lips of the Indian on the lake shore, not unlike that of a savage in his last moments—the tortoise-shell falling unreclaimed from his hand. Indeed, human bones might have been seen on this spot long after the incident here related had transpired. Dunn was a man of small stature, but made up in nerve and agility what he lacked in physical strength; and seeing the Indian leap from his canoe, he sprung into it in his pursuit, thinking thus to cross the creek dry-shod and detain him. But the frail barque would not withstand his weight, augmented with his descent from the shore, and he went through it plump up to his waist in the water. Observing that his antagonist was fleeing, without waiting to extricate himself from his unpleasant dilemma, he raised his gun and snapped it, but as the priming had been wet by his fall, (percussion locks are an invention of a later date,) the trapper escaped. Had he looked back and observed the plight of his pursuer, he would no doubt have halted long enough to have sent a bullet through his head. Whether these two Canadians were alone on this hunt is not known, but their loud halloo would seem to indicate that they were not.

It was conjectured that the hunter who had just escaped from Dunn had fled directly to the Indians' camp; and with his trusty piece well loaded, Stoner left his companion at their own canoe to get dry as best he could, and being set on the opposite shore, proceeded in search of said camp. To seek this wilderness lodge alone, without knowing its whereabouts or how it might be guarded, was, after what had transpired, one of the most presumptuous and daring feats any individual could perform, as a concealed foe might have detected an approaching footstep and speedily revenged the fall of a friend; but the mission was just suited to the spirit of the trapper who had undertaken it, and onward he went, regardless of peril. In a secluded spot some half a mile or more from its outlet and not far distant from the lake shore, he arrived at the object of search. It was a well built cabin for comfort, constructed principally of bark and set against a bold rock, so as to make that subserve the purpose of one wall. It had evidently been abandoned with precipitation, for it was not only cheered by a blazing fire, but in it had been left a beautiful bark canoe, finished and decorated in the most tasteful Indian style, a trap with one spring, a spear, and a scalping-knife. The latter instrument had no doubt been forgotten in the hot haste, attendant on removing fur, eatables, etc., as so indispensable an article to an Indian's full equipment for the chase would not have been left intentionally, unless it were a duplicate. The articles found in this camp became a lawful prize, according to the custom prevailing at that period among trappers, predicated on the rule of might and right. The Indians' canoe at the outlet of the lake was constructed of spruce bark, and made near there, but the one at their wigwam was of birch or some very light bark, and had doubtless been transported from Canada. Launching his trophied craft on the bosom of the sheen lake, this white forest son returned in it to his anxious companion.

The Johnstown hunters, reclaiming all their own traps but one, after continuing their avocation a while longer with some success undisturbed, indeed

Sole monarchs of those crystal streams,

set their faces towards home, to relieve the solicitude of their families and engage in cultivating the soil.

After another seed-time and harvest had gone by, Maj. Stoner, accompanied by William Mason, his brother-in-law, returned to the same hunting grounds that himself and Dunn had visited the preceding spring. Expecting again to renew the exciting avocation of a trapper, Stoner concealed his traps in the spring in some safe place near Trout lake, after greasing them thoroughly to prevent injury by rust. Loaded with provisions and Mason's traps, having said the necessary good-byes, the trappers buried themselves in the dark forest, the one familiar with the destination acting as pilot,

"Their clock the sun in his unbounded tower."

The Johnstown trappers struck the Sacondaga, where, discovering signs of a beaver, they set one of

Mason's traps, and with a vigilant look-out for other evidences of the desired game, they proceeded on in the direction of Stoner's traps. Next day Stoner sent Mason down several miles, to see if the first trap set did not contain a beaver. He returned with an assurance that the trap was not sprung, and whether it had been or not he could not determine; but that on a log which crossed the river near it, he had noticed the tracks of a bear. Stoner thought it strange that a beaver had not sprung that trap, and still more wonderful that a bear should prowl around it; and the morning after Mason's return they visited it together. The instant the practiced eye of the senior hunter caught a glimpse of the foot-print pointed out by his partner, provoked at his stupidity in not determining more readily what animal had made it, he demanded with a look of surprise, in rather ill humor and possibly at the end of an oath, *if bears wore moccasons?* Mason, who now rightly divined how the tracks came there, was almost as much surprised at his dullness of perception as his companion had been. On examining the trap, the discriminating eye of the master hunter also discovered that it was not in the position in which it had been left two days before, and it was conjectured that a beaver had been taken from it and the trap again set.

Stoner now proposed to Mason that he should remain concealed and await Bruin's return to obtain an interview; but the latter, who was a very strong man,

though timid, refused to remain alone. " Well," said
the former, " then I will lay near the trap and see
what kind of a bear comes to it." He secreted himself, with the young trapper in his rear, and had been
there about half an hour, when he heard on the opposite side of the stream the muffled and cautious tread
of the anticipated bear. At this most exciting moment might have been heard a noise in the morning
stillness, resembling that of one iron slipping suddenly
against another. The delicate ear of the visitant
caught the sound, and listening, with head bent forward, surveyed with scrutiny every surrounding object.
All was again silent as death, save the murmur of the
rippling rivulet; and reassured that he was alone, and
that the click which fell upon his acute organs was
made by the leap of a squirrel, or some small animal
that had suddenly broken a dry twig, Mason's bear,
with an eye oft scanning the direction of the trap
under consideration, stealthily approached the fallen
tree, which served as a bridge to cross the limpid river.

The bear, which, as we have already seen, wore
moccasons, was tall, very erect, with long, black
straight hair, and was clad in a smutty blanket,
strongly girdled at the waist. In one of its huge paws
it carried a dangerous weapon sometimes called a
tomahawk, and beneath the bosom of the blanket
above the girdle, peered out the hairless tail and possibly hind legs of a muskrat. A rifle that seldom
required a second poise at the same object, was steadily

aimed at this old bear from the time of his appearance until he reached the centre of the log over the stream, when it suddenly exploded, and unable longer to retain an upright position, Bruin reeled and fell off with a death-groan, his life-blood crimsoning the pure waters of the Sacondaga.

The traps of the Johnstown hunters were not again disturbed this fall, and at the close of the trapping season they returned home bearing a valuable lot of fur, among which there was at least one muskrat's pelt. The junior trapper, notwithstanding his bear had met with a fate " which," to use the words of his partner, " would let the succotash out of his stomach and the eels in," could not be induced to visit his traps alone in this excursion after the second day.

CHAPTER IX.

While Maj. Stoner was living in Johnstown, and not long after he commenced housekeeping, a large bear came into his wheat-field, doing no little mischief. To destroy this grain destroyer he erected a staging and watched repeatedly for him, but his vigilance was all in vain, and the wheat, when ripe, was harvested. As the corn began to fill in the ear, Bruin again thrust himself upon the hospitality of the major. His bearship soon found, however, as have some more worthy though less courageous, that the charities of the world are granted grudgingly to strangers. For several evenings after his first entrance, the husbandman vainly sought an interview with his unwelcome guest, with malice aforethought rankling in his breast, death intent absorbing all his thoughts, and a rifle loaded with two balls resting in his arms.

At length, in one of his nightly watchings, he heard his dusky visitant testing the quality of the tender ears, and although the night was dark, he approached sufficiently near to gain an indistinct view of him, and instantly leveled and fired. At the report of his rifle, agreeably to concert, a large watch-dog confined in the house was let out by Mrs. Stoner, and as the interloper retreated from the .orn, was soon yelling at his heels. He leaped a fence into a field where a lot of flax had been spread, and after pursuing some distance the dog returned home. In the morning, blood was observed on the fence where the animal had crossed, and it was conjectured that if wounded he would not return. Imagine Stoner's surprise, therefore, the very next day, when a neighboring woman came running to his house, near which he chanced to be at work, to tell him that the bear had come back, and was then in their orchard, but a short distance off.

Leaving the dog confined in his dwelling, to be let out if he fired, armed with his rifle, he ran to the orchard. He was not long in getting a shot, and soon the dog was at his side. The bear, badly wounded, was overtaken by Growler at the roots of a dry tree, and several times, as the former attempted to ascend, the latter pulled him back. Without leaving his tracks after he fired, the sportsman, as was his custom, lodged another charge in his rifle. To his chagrin he found that the stopple to his powder-horn was broken off, and he was obliged to cut a hole in the horn to obtain a charge of powder. This occasioned some delay in loading, and by the time he had finished, his dog was crying most piteously. Not pleased with being so unceremoniously drawn back, the bear turned upon his adversary, and succeeded in getting a paw of the latter in his mouth.

A dog in distress never fails to bring down the

vengeance of its owner upon the object causing it; and hurrying to the tree where was enacting the tug of war, he thrust the muzzle of the piece into Bruin's mouth to pry open his jaws and liberate his canine friend. Not altogether pleased with the interference, the grain and apple-eater struck a blow at the intruder with one of his monstrous paws, tearing off one leg of his pantaloons, and leaving the prints of his nails on the flesh. The end of the gun being still in the animal's mouth, he discharged it and blew out his brains. The yell of the dog attracted the attention of several neighbors, and just as Stoner fired a second time, Lieut. Wallace and his hired man, Hulster, arrived at the scene of action, armed with pitchforks.

The bear proved to be very large, and had one white paw. On examining, to learn the cause, it was found that one of the bullets fired at him in the corn-field, had passed through the centre of a forefoot while in an erect position, and the animal had sucked it until the inner part was white as snow.

Major Stoner was not only a trapper, but in the proper season he indulged frequently in a deer or a fox hunt; in which he was generally successful. On a certain occasion many years ago, accompanied by Benjamin DeLine and Jacob Frederick, he went to hunt deer around the shores of the Canada lake, since by some called Fish lake, and by others Byrn lake. They succeeded in killing two noble deer, and started toward night to cross the lake in the direction of home. Their water-craft, a tree canoe, when they were all in with their game, was loaded almost as heavily as she could float; and the wind causing the waves to roll, made the voyage a dangerous one. Stoner managed the canoe, while his companions, seated on its bottom, used the utmost caution to preserve its equilibrium: but long before the little barque neared her destined landing, she began to dip water. Safety required that his comrades, whose seat became uncomfortable as the water ran round them, should keep quiet, while Stoner renewed his exertions at the paddle to gain the opposite shore. As it became doubtful whether the destined haven could be gained, Stoner steered for the nearest land, which proved to be a projecting point of a small rocky island, which, in the absence of a better name, I shall call Stoner's island.

The farther they sailed, the more the gale increased, and as wave after wave left a portion of its crest in the overloaded canoe; the situation of its inmates became one of the greatest peril. DeLine and Frederick, substituting their hats for basins, used their utmost exertions to keep the boat afloat by bailing, while Stoner, urging upon his friends the necessity of coolness and a uniform position, sent her forward rapidly. Still several rods from the land, and already up to his knees in water, as the canoe was nearly full; DeLine sprang out and found bottom, although the water was several feet deep. Fearing that if their craft foundered they would lose their guns and game, and ob-

12*

serving that DeLine got on so well, Frederick also
jumped into the lake; but a little distance made quite
a difference in the depth of water, for he found no
bottom. He was unable to swim, and seeing him
sinking below the surface, Stoner leaped out to his
rescue. His hair fortunately was done up in a cue,
wound with an eel-skin, and at this his deliverer made
a successful grab and swam to the shore. All having
gained the land, the canoe, which had been guided
along by DeLine, was drawn up on the beach, its
valuables removed to a place of safety, and its water
emptied out. Frederick, whose powers of suction had
gained him one swell too much, soon disgorged the
contents of his stomach; and when he could again
speak, he broke out with an oath in imperfect English,
"*I cross de ocean all safe from Sharmany, and O,
musht I pe trown in dish tam vrog-pont!*"

Stoner's island, although preferable to the bottom
of the lake, was far from affording the weary hunters
a very comfortable night's rest. It had indeed some
trees and wild-wood vines, but nothing like a human
habitation; still, as the gale continued with unabated
violence, and it was now almost night, it was out of
the question to think of proceeding farther that evening: they therefore set about making themselves as
comfortable as circumstances would permit. As not
only their guns and ammunition were wet, but their
materials for kindling a torch, they were obliged to
camp down with their clothes saturated and their

bodies shivering, without one blazing faggot to dry their garments or cheer the midnight hour.

The Sun once more came peering o'er the Earth, sending his light in golden streams through the primitive forest which covered the surrounding hills, to reflect their mellowed rays on the glassy waters of Lake Byrn; in the bosom of which Stoner's island lay reposing, as calmly and as quietly as an infant nestled to sleep in its mother's arms. The deer-hunters rose betimes, and although their study of cause and effect, as we may suppose, had been somewhat limited, still the contrast of nature's dramatic scenes since the previous evening had been so great, that they could not fail to mark the change, and look with an admiring eye on the rich and varied scene Heaven had spread before them. Once more embarked with their treasures, they gained the lake shore in safety, and proceeded home without further adventure. For the kind services rendered him at the lake, said Frederick, on his arriving at his own dwelling, " *Now, Nick, schurst so long ash I has von cent in de vorld, so long you shall never wants for any ting, for bulling me out from dat tam vrog-pont mit mine eel-shkin dail.*"

For saving his life in the manner here related, this worthy German proved the sincere and grateful friend of our hero to the hour of his death, just before which event he urged upon his children as a debt due to himself, that they should never see his lake savior want the comforts of life. It is gratifying to observe that the Fredericks (a very respectable name in Fulton county) have honored their father, even in death, by remaining the warm friends of the *old trapper*, their father's friend; having ever held themselves responsible for the proper fulfilment, if needs be, of their parent's unostentatious wish.

On the eve of our last war with Great Britain, Major Stoner and William Mason entered the wilderness with their traps, and were gone over two months. Their stay was protracted several weeks beyond the time intended, and their anxious friends, who had heard nothing from them, began to consider them as lost forever.

Hunters usually carried fishing tackle, and although they often had to do without bread in long hunts, they could generally procure a supply of fish or wild game. Their food frequently consisted of either deer's or bear's meat, and not unfrequently of squirrels, rabbits, ducks, partridges, and possibly the flesh of beaver. Meats were usually roasted before the fire on a spit of wood, one end of which was planted in the ground.

If the reader will just peep in at the entrance of a well regulated hunter's camp, he will see at a glance how the disciples of Nimrod live in their wilderness, womenless home. He will observe that excitement renders them not only contented but comparatively happy, in a little hut, destitute of a chair, table, or bed. Should the visitor accept an invitation to step in and dine, he may expect to receive a liberal slice of meat, scorched upon one side and nearly raw on the other, with a reasonable allowance of salt and a morsel of stale bread, if not too late in the hunt, served with a hearty welcome upon the inner side of a clean piece of bark; while he is seated upon a large stone, or block of wood. If he tarried over night, for an evening's entertainment, he would listen to not a few perilous adventures in unexpected encounters with wild animals, or novelties attending the chase; and at early bed-time, he would find himself stretched upon a hurdle of hemlock boughs in one corner of the lodge, gathering himself into as small a heap as possible; with a secret prayer that no hungry wolf would thrust its nose beneath the blanket or pelt that covered him, while midnight visions of squaws and beaver-skins haunted his brain.

Out of provisions and almost out of their reckoning, Stoner and his friend, having hung up their fur in some safe place which they could again find, were making their way to one of the nearest white settlements, when suddenly they came upon an Indian in the forest, whom the major mistaking for some other animal, *possibly a bear*, was about to fire upon. The Indian, whose name was Anderly, proved to be one of the Caughnawaga tribe, from Grand river in Canada. He had with him a little daughter, his wife having died in the forest. The sudden appearance of two white men greatly terrified this little forest flower; but her fears were quieted with an assurance of friendship, and the white hunters shared the hospitality of their dusky friends over night. This Indian first communicated to the Johnstown trappers the fact, that hostilities had commenced between England and the United States. Knowing this fact, and thinking that possibly the whites were either spies or foes, was what at first caused the fear of the young wood-nymph. Parting with their new friends, with whom they were much pleased, Stoner and Mason journeyed on, and finally came out in Norway, Herkimer county; where they obtained provisions, and where too, they saw several families that were removing from the Black river country to the Mohawk valley. They also came in contact with a body of United States drafts marching to the line between New York and Canada.

Trappers in their excursions seldom take shaving utensils with them, and not unfrequently on their return home, they might have been mistaken for the prototype of Lorenzo Dow, of long-beard memory. The Johnstown friends had wandered so long in the forest, that their clothes were much worn; and Mason, whose appearance was perhaps the most ragged, was arrested on suspicion of being a *spy*, and his gun taken from him. Stoner having been a hero of the preceding war, was fortunately known to some of the soldiery, and succeeded in effecting the liberation of his comrade and the restoration of his gun; and after liberally replenishing their larder, they again buried themselves in the moaning wilderness. In this hunt, Stoner car-

ried his rifle and Mason a fowling-gun with which to
shoot small game for food.   On their way back to the
place where they had secreted their fur, and when in
a gloomy, mountain-encompassed dell, they accident-
ally fell in with two Indians, who were there on the
same errand as themselves.   It seems to be a pretty
true, though stale maxim, that two of a trade can not
agree.   The strangers were Canadian hunters, having
very little fur, one of whom was armed with a rifle.
Scarcely had the parties met, when the one last alluded
to commenced a fierce quarrel with Stoner.   He took
the latter for Green White, another bold trapper, and
accused him of plundering and then burning their
camp some two years before.   Stoner, enraged at the
false charge, retorting the harsh epithets of his accuser,
denied being White; or having stolen the fur of any
one.   The other Indian, who said he had seen White,
told his companion that he was not the hunter before
them, but this the passionate savage would not admit,
and the dispute continued.

Observing that his partner would not be appeased,
and that the quarrel must prove a serious one, the Indian without a rifle approached Mason, who, as we
have seen, was a little timorous in such an emergency,
and desired to look at his gun.   His object undoubtedly was to arm himself.   This seemingly small favor
would possibly have been indulged, had not a caution
from Stoner, in the Low Dutch tongue, reached his
friend, to beware of a treacherous design.   The master-

hunter could not only understand, but spoke the Indian dialect very well. Determined to possess himself of Mason's gun, his antagonist grappled with him to wrest it from his hands. A shrill rifle-shot now rang among the towering hemlocks, followed by a yell so loud and death-like, as to startle the wolf and panther in their mountain lair. A moment after and the figure of an Indian was seen receding in the forest with the fleetness of an antelope, and the click of a gun-lock fell on the ear; but its priming having been lost in his scuffle with Mason, it missed fire, and the dark form vanished in safety and *alone*.

After this adventure, the Johnstown trappers pursued their way, without further molestation, to their fur and their traps, and ere long they returned home, to the great joy of their friends; bearing a most valuable lot of fur, and *a spare rifle*. It is not improbable that their store of fur was augmented some in that lone spot, where they had left a human carcass to return to its earthly affinity.

Major Stoner was gone so long that a rumor prejudicial to his character was put in circulation in Johnstown just before his return. It was reported, and perhaps by some believed, that he had been engaged in the contraband trade of smuggling goods from Canada to that village, for Cornelius Herring and Amaziah Rust. He says the accusation was false, and although he saw goods carrying in the wilderness at this time, which may have been destined for Johnstown; they were in the hands of individuals who were strangers to him. Squaws generally started with the merchandise from Canada, and at some designated place they met and gave it over to men employed to run it through.

It is not unlikely that Green White, to whom allusion is made in these pages, who was a celebrated and successful trapper, traversing the wilderness from Otsego county to the shores of the St. Lawrence, had numerous and sometimes fatal quarrels with rival hunters. John G. Seely informed the writer that he once playfully, though ironically, remarked to White, *" he did not like it that he was killing off all his nation."* The hunter replied, *" D—n them, they must not search my traps then. The last one I saw was peeking over the bushes to look into one of my traps, and soon after my dog was shaking his old blanket !"* Some further account of this hunter, with his melancholy fate, is given in another part of this volume.

CHAPTER X

White hunters as well as Indians wore moccasons on their long hunts; usually making their own from the pelts of wild animals. Aaron Griswold hunted with Maj. Stoner on one occasion, and having killed a bear, as his boots chafed his ancles, he was not long in making himself moccasons from the raw hide, with the fur inside; and hanging up his boots in some secure place, they journeyed on some fifteen miles. Stoner had a favorite dog with him at the time, and in the night the animal ate up one of the newly made moccasons. Griswold was very angry next morning, and swore he would shoot the dog; but Stoner appeased his wrath by cutting the needed garment from his own blanket, which lasted until the return of Griswold to his boots; about which time the major shot a deer, and the breach in his companion's wardrobe was repaired from its skin.

Maj. Stoner was on a deer-hunt many years ago to the Sacondaga vlaie, in company with Captain Henry Shew. At a suitable place to camp out, he collected some dry wood and struck up a fire for their comfort, his companion in the meanwhile, visiting a favorite crossing place of the deer. Having started his fire, he crossed the low ground to the bank of the creek which courses through it. He had scarcely reached the stream, when he saw the tall grass covering the bog on the opposite shore bending towards him. He at once recognized in the undulatory motion of the grass, the probable presence of some wild animal; which he thought hardly lofty enough in its carriage for a deer. He remained quiet, and soon the object made its appearance near the creek. At first sight he thought it a hunter's dog, but its wild appearance undeceived him, and he shot it. This was near night, and the following morning they made a raft of drift-wood, on which Capt. Shew crossed the stream to see what Stoner had killed. It proved to be a large she wolf, and a young cub which had just been trying to obtain nourishment from it, fled on the hunter's approach, (as he had not taken his gun along,) and secreted its famishing form in the rank grass. Shew skinned the wolf, and Judge Simon Veeder paid them twenty shillings, the then legal bounty, for its scalp.

Maj. Stoner shot but one other wolf while hunting, although he trapped them often. He never killed a panther, as none were so reckless of life as to cross his path; but he very often heard their startling scream from their mountain haunts. He killed no less than seventeen bears in two seasons.

The celebrated Nathaniel Foster and Maj. Stoner were hunting together one fall, when they trapped a large eagle. They set the trap beside the carcase of a deer the wolves had killed on the ice upon

Round lake; and the national bird, as a reward for the low company it kept, was caught in a wolf-trap, and flew off with it; a heavy clog being attached to its chain. The following spring one Barrington visited the place with Stoner, and in searching they found the trap in the bush beside the lake, where the clog had become entangled, else the majestic bird would possibly have soared away to its eyry with its vast load. It was dead when discovered, and the trap, which was Foster's, was restored to him.

During the time he was a hunter, a period of forty or fifty years, Maj. Stoner hunted with very many individuals; among whom were several Indians. He was out some time with a man named Flagg, of whom we can say nothing, except that he wore a curious cap, made from the skin of a loon with its downy coat on. He hunted one season with a St. Regis Indian, named Powlus, and his acquaintances wondered that he dared to do it. With this Indian he explored the head waters of Grass river, which empties into the St. Lawrence. At this place they met with a small area of land with a fine growth of hickory and oak timber. Persons going from Canada to Johnstown in the summer season, either had to go by way of the Sacondaga river, or else far to the west of it, on account of a large territory of drowned lands in the vicinity of Grass river. The latter district was traversed with ease in the winter, however, by hunters on snow shoes, when the low lands were frozen.

Near the head of Grass river, the Johnstown trappers met a French Canadian hunter, who had a squaw for a wife. He was desirous of going as far south as Johnstown, and Stoner traced a map of the most feasible route for him, upon a piece of birch bark, to enable him to accomplish the journey. Whether he ever reached the designated point is not known.

Subsequent to Maj. Stoner's hunting with Mason, Dunn, and Jackson, who were most frequently his companions; he hunted two seasons with another St. Regis Indian, called Capt. Gill; with whom he was very successful. They caught twenty-six beavers and five otters, beside considerable other game, in one spring. Beaver usually sold for about one dollar a pound; and good skins would weigh about four pounds each. Otter skins sold from five to seven dollars the pelt. Stoner has received one hundred dollars for peltries taken in a single season.

Gill had his squaw Molly with him while hunting, and a daughter, or a Molly junior, who, the Indian said, was not his papoose. Indian women usually remained at the camp, and did the cooking for the hunters. Beavers generally built their dams across the outlets of the lakes. Gill was very successful in spearing those sagacious animals in their houses. While together, they once trapped no less than four beavers in a single night. This Indian was a catholic, and in a thunder shower would cross himself repeatedly. He was in the English service in the war of the Revolu-

13*

tion, and was present at the destruction of Stone
Arabia; but in the last war he took protection under
the authorities of New York. He entertained no little fear, and possibly harbored not much love for his
fellow countrymen; and on an emergency, would perhaps have scrupled as little as did his fearless companion, to punish their aggressions.

Eben Blakeman, who several times hunted with our
hero, was once on a hunt when the Indians disturbed
his traps; but being joined by Stoner, they left the
hunting grounds *sans ceremonie.* Obadiah Wilkins,
another lover of the chase, was more than once associated with Major Stoner in trapping excursions.
Their wives were cousins. On one occasion when
they were hunting in Bleeker, Wilkins, to replenish
their larder, took fishing tackle and seated himself on
a rock in West Stoney creek, a tributary of the Sacondaga. He had barely gained the position, when
a stout Indian came to him and inquired rather insult-
ingly, " *What doing here?* " He replied, " I am fishing." " *Have got gun?* " interrogated the visitor.
" Yes, at the camp," said Wilkins, a little disconcerted at the fierce manner of his inquirer. Observing
the advantage he had gained, the red hunter continued,
" *This Indian's hunting ground—Yankees no business
here—you must leave him!* " As Wilkins made but
little reply to the last remark, the speaker continued,
" *Has white man got partner?* " " Yes, at the camp."
" *What his name?* " " Nick Stoner."

Had the witch of Endor risen before him, the forest-son would not have been more disagreeably taken a-back, and he gave a loud guttural " *Umph!* " Observing the magic wrought by the utterance of a single name, Wilkins became reassured, and invited the blanketed hunter to go with him to the camp. " *No! Indian go to his own camp!* " he responded, and soon after disappeared in the wilderness. This Indian had frightened a hunter, named Wheeler, from these grounds not long before; but when he heard that Stoner was in the neighborhood, the air seemed to oppress his lungs; and hastily collecting his traps, he broke up his camp and sought afar off a new forest-home. The reason assigned by Wilkins to his partner for being disconcerted at the interrogatories of this savage hunter was, that the latter was armed with a hatchet, and himself only with a fishing-rod.

The last difficulty Stoner had with the Indians while trapping, occurred at Lake Pleasant. Dunning, who then lived at the Ox-Bow, four miles from Lake Pleasant, had left his traps in the wilderness where he had previously hunted, and was afraid to go after them alone at the return of the hunting season. Obadiah Wilkins left home with Stoner on this enterprise, and leaving him to hunt with Dunning's father nearer home, Stoner and Dunning set out to find and use the hidden traps. Before reaching them, and about thirty miles from the settlement, Stoner set two of his own traps for beaver, one in the stream and the other on the shore of a small lake; a little distance further **he** set another trap for an otter. Arriving at a pond which lay in their route, not far from where the last trap was set, they found a large moose in it fighting flies, which Stoner, with some twinges of conscience, drew up and shot. They skinned it and sunk the hide beneath the water, to get the hair off; and two musk-rat skins they had already secured they hung up in the vicinity. Not more than one-fourth of a mile far-ther on, they came to a deserted camp, with the appearance of having been recently occupied. Much wearied and the day far spent, they tarried over night at this hunter's lodge.

On the following morning, as the distance was not very great, Dunning went back to the place where the nearest trap was set, but could not find it; and before renewing the journey for his traps, they returned together, if possible to learn the fate of the one, and recover the other two traps. The trap set for an otter was indeed clear gone, and about it were Indians' tracks, but the other two were safe. In the one left in the creek a beaver had been caught that proved wise enough to gnaw its own leg off, and escape by leaving its foot in the trap; and in the other they found an otter.

While on their way to obtain their traps, they heard the report of a gun fired in the distance, which they thought might possibly tell what direction the lost property had taken. Recovering Dunning's traps, they now went to another stream to hunt, where they had some success. Visiting their haunts one day, they found one trap had been robbed of its game; and as it was a very heavy one, the robber not caring to take it along had left it suspended by the jaws upon a stump. On their route home, the hunters halted where the moose had been slain; and here they found fresh evidence of intrusion upon their rights. Well was it for the evil doer that he had not lingered there, else he might have been mistaken for another of Mason's bears. The moose-skin had been pulled up and some of it cut off, and the muskrat-skins had found a new owner.

Arriving at Dunning's Saturday afternoon, they learned that two Indian trappers had just come in at the lake settlement, four miles distant, with fur; at which place there was a tavern, a small grocery, store, &c. Capt. Wright kept the tavern, and one Williams the grocery; the latter dealing principally in such articles as ammunition, blankets, rum, &c., to sell to trappers and adventurers. Stoner wished to visit Lake Pleasant to see whether the hunters had not got his lost trap and stolen fur; but Wilkins declined going with him, and the younger Dunning became his companion.

On their arrival at Wright's they learned that the Indian hunters were Capt. Benedict and Francis, a large yellow-skin, and that they were encamped in the woods about one hundred yards from the inn. As it was nearly dark, they concluded to defer a visit to their place of rest until morning. Some time in the night, a sister's son of Wright awoke his uncle to inform him that the dogs of the Indian hunters were killing their sheep. Stoner got up and accompanied the young man to the field to drive the dogs from the sheep, one of which they had already slain. In the morning Stoner visited the Indians at their fire in the woods. Near it lay the dogs, and at hand were two rifles, a basket of potatoes, and a piece of pork. The rifles were resting one on each side of the basket, while between his knees Francis held a jug of whiskey, over which he was singing a *huntsman's chorus.*

Capt. Benedict, who was a pretty likely Indian, was well known to Maj. Stoner, and as the latter approached, told his companion who he was. In the group lay a bundle of traps tied together with thongs of Stoner's moose-hide, and conspicuously among them appeared his lost trap. It was known the previous evening in the neighborhood what the object was of Stoner's visit to the lakes, and when he went to the hunter's lodge early in the morning, Wright, Williams, one Peck, and perhaps others who may have taken a nap the less to enable them to, stole up behind trees as near as they could without being observed, on purpose, as they afterwards said, to witness the *fun* they anticipated would follow the interview.

After friendly salutations had passed between Stoner and Benedict, the former walked to the traps and jerked his up from the rest, enquiring sharply how it came there? He would have recognized the trap among a thousand others: it was made by William Mann, of Johnstown, and had on it Stoner's private hunter's mark. When blacksmiths made traps for hunters, they generally put some peculiar mark on them their own fancy suggested, never placing the same device upon the traps of different hunters. Seeing Stoner about to cut it loose, Francis exclaimed, "*No cut him! No cut him!*" extending his hand to prevent the act, at which interference the claimant raised the whole bundle and knocked the intruder down with it. Regaining his feet and seeing the trap already in the possession of its owner, the conscience-stricken trapper said gruffly, "*If trap yours, take him!*"

Pay was next demanded for the lost fur, and epithets were bandied between Stoner and Francis, of which passion was the parent. Benedict, who was evidently ashamed of his company, now interfered, and to some extent pacified his old acquaintance, who accepted the *jug of friendship*, and drank of its supposed healing and cooling, though very fiery waters. As readily would oil put out a flame, as alcohol have quieted the storm of human passion. After a little further conversation with Benedict, not wishing to be outdone in generosity, Stoner asked the Indians to go to the tavern and drink with him. The invitation was readily accepted, and Francis, as the partner of

Benedict, went along, although at first he pretended he would not go.

The two friends before the bar soon held each a tumbler of liquid fire, and Stoner asked Francis to pour out and drink with them. He declined in a very insolent manner, whereupon the former smashed the tumbler he held, liquor and all, against his head. The Indian, as soon as he could regain a standing position, enraged at the act, closed with his adversary, and in the short scuffle which followed, the latter proved too smart for his yellow antagonist, and pitched him neck and heels out of the bar-room door upon the ground. He had a hard fall, and when he rose up several gravel stones remained half buried in his cheek and temples. The fight would no doubt have become a deadly one, had it not been arrested at this point by the by-standers, who held the parties asunder until their ardor and passion had a little time to cool down.

When reason began to assume her throne, Stoner demanded of Francis either the furs stolen from his traps or the money for them. The parties now went to Williams's store, where they found the green beaver-skin stolen from the heavy trap, which the Indian had there sold the previous afternoon. He finally admitted having taken that skin from the trap mentioned, but denied having taken the two muskrat pelts, although several were among the fur he had sold Williams, saying that probably some young

Indians who were then hunting in the woods had
taken them. A compromise was now made, and
Francis paid Stoner a certain sum to settle their difficulties, a receipt for which was drawn up by Williams,
as dictated by Stoner. About this time the young Indians referred to, five in number, came in. They had
several marten-skins, but more fully to establish the
guilt of the accused they had not the pelt of a single
muskrat. One of the boys, a likely young Indian,
who answered to the name of Lige Ell, and who was
a son of Benedict, when told that he had been accused
by Francis of having taken Stoner's fur, seemed highly
offended by the insult. The truth was, the traps of
Francis being fastened together by strips of the moose-
skin, near which the lost pelts had been left, if it did
not prove his guilt, was at least strong evidence
against him.

Lige Ell went to the store to buy a pocket-knife,
but did not like any there. He said of all Williams
had, "*there wasn't no more fire in 'em than there was
in his nose.*" Hunters wanted a heavy knife, with
which they could not only skin large game, but one,
the back of which would elicit from flint the spark of
comfort in the wilderness. Stoner handed the lad his
own knife, with which he seemed delighted, and as
the old trapper was rather partial to the boy, he made
him a present of it. The young Indian then, to cap
the climax of his happiness, bought a quart of the
red man's exterminator, *rum*, and a cake of maple

14

sugar, got pretty drunk, and with his no less tipsy companions went to shooting at a mark.

Here is no doubt given a true picture of the manner in which the Sabbath is too often kept, or rather, broken, on the outskirts of civilization. Benedict's son told Francis, after a knowledge of all that had transpired between him and " Old Stoner," with whom by repute he was no stranger, that if he desired to *live*, he must never show his head in that region again; as, if he did return, he would certainly be killed. It is believed he never afterwards intruded on the hunt-ing grounds of the Johnstown trappers; *if he did*, he certainly was cautious not to disturb either their traps or their furs.

It was customary some twenty years ago, in the summer season, for Indian families to come down from the north and locate themselves for weeks, and some-times for months, in the neighborhood of the Mohawk river settlements and make baskets, which they ex-changed at the nearest villages for trinkets, gay calicoes, liquor, tobacco, scarlet cloth, &c. Three of a party that had taken up their residence one sum-mer to make baskets in Stoner's neighborhood, lodged in his barn. The major had a large dog at the time, and his guests a small one. One day when he was gone from home, his dog, not pleased with the In-dians' canine friend, which he considered intruding upon his rights, took him by the neck and gave him a hard shaking. The owner of the little yelper, armed with a knife, set out to revenge the insult with the death of the offender.

This incident happened when Mary Stoner was in her teens, and at the time, she and her mother were at home alone. Hearing an unusual noise, Mary opened the door, and seeing the Indian in pursuit of their dog, she called it into the house and fastened it in. Arrested at the door, he uttered numerous threats, and several times stuck his knife into it, at which moment Stoner approached. Seeing an Indian armed with a long knife, attempting to enter his dwelling, he ran up and knocked him down, and was giving him a few hasty kicks, when the other two Indians came to the rescue of their comrade. Hearing her father's voice, Miss Stoner looked out, and seeing two Indians hold of him, she feared they would kill him, and hastened to place in his hand a heavy fire-shovel for his defence. The act proved the girl " a chip of the old block," but he told her to carry back the weapon, that the Indians would not hurt him. They did not seek his injury, but to rescue their friend. The day after this dog difficulty the Indians in the neighborhood all disappeared, and one of the party who had borrowed a blanket of Stoner to go deer-hunting, forgot to return it.

Maj. Stoner was a very successful trapper, and frequently brought in such large quantities of fur that many suspected he had obtained it unfairly from other hunters, but such he declares was never the case.

CHAPTER XI.

Maj. Stoner became a widower when he had been married over forty years; after which he lived between fifteen and twenty years with Mrs. Polly Phye, and until her death. Her husband, Daniel Phye, abandoned her, for what reason is unknown. He died many years ago at the westward.

After Phye had been gone several years, and dark mystery had drawn her curtain of uncertainty around his fate; gossip sometimes made Mrs. Phye a grass, and at others, a hay-widow. At this period Maj. Stoner paid his addresses successfully, to the supposed widow; and although she considered herself absolved from all farther connection with Phye; still, as he *might* be alive and *possibly* return, prudence prevented a ceremonial marriage, which could by law consign her to the inner walls of a prison; and they resolved to unite their stock in trade, and move along cheerfully if they could, in the great wake of the human family. Thus they did pass on quietly and happily until separated by death. They had no children by this voluntary marriage. Let the stickler for a rigid adherence at all times to established laws without reference to their operation, imagine this case wholly their own, before they feel prepared to condemn the course of this couple, or brand their conduct with the title of crime.

On the 23d day of April, 1840, having been a second time a widower for several years, Maj. Stoner married his present wife; who is considerably younger than himself. Her maiden name was Hannah Houghtaling, but at the time of their marriage she was the widow Frank.

At the present time (1846), the *old trapper* resides in the town of Garoga, Fulton county; at a settlement which has recently sprung up, called Newkirk's Mills. He owns a comfortable dwelling in which he lives, draws a pension from the general government, and from keeping several boarders, who work in the mills, which the industry of a smart wife enables him to do, he passes down the evening of his life very comfortably. Garret Newkirk, the proprietor here, has an extensive tannery, and a saw-mill in which two saws are almost constantly rending asunder the trunks of the surrounding forest. The place has some fifteen or twenty dwellings, a school-house, a post-office, (called Newkirk's Mills) &c., and is situated pleasantly on the outlet of the Garoga lakes, two crystal sheets of water, each several miles in circuit, located some twelve or fifteen miles to the westward of Johnstown. Since the above was written, a public-house has been opened at this place, several new dwellings erected, and a plank-road constructed from thence to Fonda, sixteen miles distant.

14*

I have somewhere alluded to Chase's Patent. Wm.
Chase, the patentee, was in early life a sea-captain,
and in the Revolution became an American privateer.
He was captured and taken to Europe, and while
there visited France.   After the war he removed
from Providence, Rhode Island, to Hoosick, New
York.   At the latter place he built a bridge, by constructing which, ne was enabled to purchase some
12,000 acres of land in the western part of Fulton
county.   A large tract of land adjoining his, and
which Chase intended to buy, was subsequently sold
in Albany by auction, and was purchased by Barent
Bleeker, Cornelius Glen, and Abraham G. Lansing.
It was known as Bleeker and Lansing's patent. Failing to secure this tract of land, on which he seems to
have set his affections, Capt. Chase was heard to ex-
claim with an oath, "*I would rather have lost my
right in Heaven, than a title to this soil!*" People
when excited often utter expressions devoid of wit
and common sense, if not, in fact, foolishly wicked.

In most of the surveys of wild land in and adjoining Fulton county, made since the Revolution, Maj.
Stoner, who was peculiarly fitted for the task by his
familiarity with the forest, and his ability to endure
fatigue, acted as pilot for the parties.   At one time
while engaged in exploring lands with Capt. Chase,
the latter lost a gold snuff-box which had been a present in France, a gift he prized far above its real
value.   Stoner, fortunately for the old privateer's

peace of mind, for he was not a little vexed at the misfortune, seeing it glitter in the leaves, picked it up aud restored it to tbe owner, who almost waltzed for joy. This same Capt. Chase wâs not a little eccentric, and usually got up at least once in the night, to drink and take a pinch of snuff.

When the lands contiguous to Piseco* lake, known as the Ox Bow tract, were surveyed, a road, " beginning eight miles northerly from Johnstown," was laid out from thence to Ox Bow lake, a distance of 26 miles and 9 chains. Major Stoner attended the surveyor and commissioners as pilot, and was thus engaged for two seasons. Lawrence Vrooman of Schenectada was the surveyor, and Stephen Owen and James McLalin were the commissioners on the road, as appears by a map of the survey, which was filed in the county clerk's office April 1, 1811. Not a few pleasing incidents transpired in the wilderness during this time, to keep the party, which sometimes numbered nearly twenty, in good spirits. Of the number while laying out the road, who thus enjoyed a portion of the novelty attending a trapper's life, and learned how large mosquitoes will grow in the woods if well fed, were J. Watts Cady, and Marcus T. Reynolds. At

* Pi-se-co is an aboriginal word, and in their pronunciation, the Indians speak it as though spelled *Pe-sic-o ;* giving a hissing sound to the second syllable. It is derived from *pisco,* a fish, and therefore signifies fish lake.—*John Dunham.*

Piseco, says *Spafford* in his *Gazetteer of New York,* and which he spells Pezeeko, is so called after an old Indian hermit who dwelt upon its shores.

that time they were young men, possibly with some " wild oats," but since then they have become legal gentlemen of no little notoriety.

At one time when the surveying party were near the Ox Bow, a name significant of the shape of one of the lakes, and far removed from any human habitation; they got out of provisions, and the pack-men, whose duty it was to go after a supply, were unwilling to start, entertaining some doubts about ever finding their way back. In this emergency Stoner volunteered to proceed with as little delay as possible to the nearest settlement, which was Lake Pleasant, and relieve the necessities of his comrades. Arriving just at evening at the house of a pioneer, named Denny, the family baked nearly all night; and early in the morning, with a sack upon his back, containing nearly a dozen large loaves of bread, and a good sized cheese to balance, he set out on his return. Knowing the necessities of his forest friends he did not tarry to let the bread get cold, and as the weather was warm, his back was almost blistered on his arrival. Before he reached the place of destination, he met a messenger despatched by Vrooman to assist him; bringing a junk-bottle of rum.

Speaking of his experience in surveying in the Piseco country, Cady observed of Stoner, that he would kindle a fire—climb a tree—cook a dinner—empty a bottle—shoot a deer—hook a trout—or scent an Indian, quicker than any other man he ever knew.

The old trapper, as he informed the writer, took some pains to show the young men named, (who were law students at the time,) how to catch trout, and in the north branch of the Sacondaga, Cady, under his teaching, caught a bouncing one; of which exploit he was very proud, as in fact he had a right to be; for it made a meal for the whole surveying corps.

Anxious to get through as soon as possible, the party laying out a road, continued their labors in some instances on the Sabbath. Stoner usually carried a small flag, and while crossing a mountain in advance of the men on Sunday, he discovered a mass of ice between the rocks, and gave a shout that at first excited the anxiety of his comrades, lest some wild beast lingered in their path. The next day they captured a large turtle on the shore of Piseco lake, and from it took *one hundred and seventy-two eggs*, of which they made egg nogg; cooled before being served round by ice obtained by letting one of the corps down between the rocks. About twenty individuals partook of the beverage, among whom were Seth Wetmore, the state's agent for opening an intersecting road, and Obadiah Wilkins. The last named gentleman acted as master of ceremonies in dressing and cooking the turtle's meat, which afforded the party a fine repast. This was on the 4th day of July, 1810.

At some period of the survey, Stoner shot a hedgehog, which Vrooman wanted skinned; and besought several to do it, but in vain: they did not dare to handle it. The old trapper volunteered and took off the bristly pelt; which the surveyor, on his return, carried home with him.

The southerly portion of country under consideration is hilly and in many places mountainous. The soil is generally stony, though in many instances, fertile; but far better adapted to grazing, than the production of grain. The prevailing rock is of the primitive order, consequently the shores of the lakes which sparkle here and there in the glens, abound in deposites of beautiful sand; which often afford good writing sand. The timber is principally beech, birch, maple, hemlock and spruce. Much of the hemlock is sawed into fence-boards, and acres of the spruce annually wrought into shingles or sawed into floor-plank; all of which find a ready market at the nearest accessible point on the Erie canal: and since the Garoga and Fonda plank road is favorable to its re-moval, not a little will find its way to Fultonville, where considerable quantities were landed before the plank road was laid out.

Much of this country still has a primeval look, but its majestic forest lords and advantageous water powers, must in time invite in the thrifty artisan and hard-fisted yeoman, to subdue and cultivate it: indeed, the time may not be distant when this new country shall not only " bud and blossom *as* the rose," but *with* the rose. It certainly must be a healthy district; for it abounds in waters the most limpid, and breezes the most invigorating. The lakes and their tributaries are stored with an abundance of delicious trout; and if not walled castles, stately mansions may yet rear their imposing fronts in those glens; to be known in future ages as the rivals of the far-famed glens of Scotland; when some Scott or Burns shall rise up, to picture their Indian legends in story and in song.

The outlets to some of the lakes around which Maj. Stoner used to trap the sagacious, though too often confiding beaver, run off in a northerly course to swell the Hudson, while other lakes send their tribute in a southerly direction to the Mohawk. The most eastern of the latter class are the Garoga lakes, discharging in a creek of the same name, which runs into the Mohawk in the western part of Palatine. Some two or three miles to the westward of the Garogas is a larger lake, known among the early hunters as Fish lake, though often called Canada lake, because it pays tribute to the East Canada creek.

An anonymous writer in the Geneva Courier, over the signature of Harold, has thus pertinently described this sheet of water and its locality, in that paper, bearing date, Oct. 28, 1845. "Two and a half miles from Caroga [Garoga must be the aboriginal word] is a larger lake, about four miles in length, to which I gave the name of Lake Byrn. It takes exactly the form of the letter S. I think this is the most romantic spot I ever visited. The surface of the ground rising

back from the shore, is covered with large irregularly
shaped rocks, from five to forty feet in diameter, lying
entirely above ground, and often tumbling together
in mountain masses, lodged and wedged in like drift-
wood.   Many of these rocks are riven asunder and
the base of each portion thrown outward from the line
of separation, the superior parts resting against each
other, thus forming apartments with a solid stone roof
large enough to shelter a dozen or twenty men.   This
I think must have been the work of fire.   Strange as
it may seem, all this is in quite a dense forest, and
almost infinite are the shapes taken by the trees in
their turnings and twistings to avoid the numerous
rocks.   In some instances the roots of a single tree
have grown astride a huge rock, the base of the trunk
resting on its apex, six or eight feet from the ground.
The appearance is the same as if the rock were forced
up from the ground beneath, elevating the tree with it,
but not a particle of earth attaches to either; and these
are all living, healthy trees.   It is in this neighborhood that tradition says large sums of money were
buried by certain Spaniards, in the time of the American Revolution; but ' *it's sure never a bate o' it did I
find at all, at all !*'   So said a hard-fisted son of Erin,
relating the story.   Near the centre of Lake Byrn, is
a small rocky island, covered with evergreens, birch
and flowering shrubs."   This island, the reader will
remember, I have named Stoner's island.   The writer
above quoted called on Major Stoner, at the time of

his visit, and his *Chips of Travel* contained a brief summary of the old warrior's military life.

A few miles distant from Lake Byrn is a body of water of nearly the same size called Pine lake, on account of the lordly pines about its shores: it empties into the former. Two small crystal sheets above Pine lake are called Stink lakes. Their unpoetic name attached from the following incident. Stoner and De Line were there on a hunt, and discovered many bushels of dead fish, principally suckers, which had got over a beaver's dam in a freshet; and which, being unable to return, had died on the recession of the water, to the great annoyance of those hunters, who thus named the lakes. Their outlet runs into that of Pine lake. Several small lakes in the southerly part of Hamilton county, unite their waters to form the head of West Canada creek. Lake Good Luck, some ten or twelve miles in circumference, which lies only a few miles to the northward of Stink lakes, empties into the west branch of the Sacondaga, one and a half miles below Devereux's mills. This lake derived its name from the following incident. While Vrooman was surveying near it, and several of his party were making a large canoe from the trunk of a tree, John Burgess, his son-in-law, discharged his gun at a loon, off on the water. The piece burst and scattered its fragments harmlessly in every direction. The accident terminated so fortunately, that the name the lake now bears, was entered on the surveyor's field-book.

15

About two miles below the mouth of the outlet from Gook Luck, is a small lake called Trout lake. It abounds in trout, which circumstance originated its name; and not a few anglers visit it to replenish their larder. On the shore of this lake, the reader will remember, a poor Indian once lost a turtle's and his own shell. Stoner at different times, killed two moose in the edge of this lake, while the animals were fighting flies. Satterlee's mills are located on West Sacondaga, at a rapid some two miles below the outlet of Trout lake. From those mills to the outlet of Piseco lake, the stream is rapid, affording fine mill-seats. At this rapid was also a carrying place, where the Indian and other hunters carried their canoes over land to get into Piseco lake. It is some twelve miles from the inlet of Piseco lake, to where the east and west branches of the Sacondaga unite.

The Piseco is the largest of a cluster of lakes in Hamilton county, which empty into the west branch of the Sacondaga, and is some nine miles long, and in places, nearly three broad, or twenty miles in circumference. Of the lakes in the neighborhood of Piseco, are Mud lake, so called because its shores are muddy; Spy lake, so named by the surveyors, because approached so unexpectedly by them; Round lake, the name indicating its form; and Ox-Bow lake. The last mentioned is three or four miles long, though not very wide, and shaped like the bow of an ox-yoke. In the territory adjoining, and known as the Ox-bow tract, Seth Wetmore, a former sheriff of Montgomery county, owned some thousands of acres, a considerable portion of which was received from the state as compensation for opening a road, the survey of which I have alluded to, from the shore of Piseco lake to the Bleeker settlements. Lake Pleasant, another large and beautiful sheet of water, lies off to the northeast of the Piseco; and its outlet, with other streams, forms the eastern branch of the Sacondaga: to the westward of Lake Pleasant, some ten or twelve miles, is a pretty lake, called Louis's lake, after a Canadian Indian, who formerly hunted upon its shores.

The land in the Piseco country, though hilly and often mountainous, is said to be less stony and more fertile than that of the Garoga and Bleeker territory; and when New England gets her telescope upon it, it will beyond all doubt, be thickly peopled by enterprising inhabitants. Many acres of the soil are covered with a heavy growth of pine and spruce timber, which only needs an avenue to market richly to reward the pioneer for the blows of his axe and saw.

From the lakes of Hamilton county, streams run off in almost every point of compass. Besides the lakes named, there are numerous others in different parts of this county; among which are Lake Janet, named after the accomplished wife of Professor James E. De Kay, zoologist of the state in her late scientific survey; Lake Catharine, named after a multitude of good Dutch women, and *one* in particular; Racket and Long lakes. The two last named are the largest in the county, being one fourteen and the other eighteen miles in length. Hamilton county, from her isolated situation with regard to the export of her products; being too far removed to warrant a transport by land to a good market, is mostly in a wild and unsettled condition; she having only one legal voter to every twenty-six hundred square acres of her territory; but could a communication by rail road or canal be opened to some good market place, it would soon teem with a busy population. That a connected water communication is feasible, is thus hinted at by Professor Emmons, in his volume of the New York Geology. He observes, speaking of the waters of Hamilton county: " These lakes, together with their bays, inlets and outlets, and other waters which may be connected with them, are capable of forming an extended line of water communication, by which a large portion of this section of country may be traversed; and probably the time may not be far distant, when it will be thought expedient to form and perfect some of the natural channels of communication which intersect this part of the state."

In one of his annual reports during the geological survey, Dr. Emmons thus describes this region of country. " I have the pleasure of stating that it is far from being the *wet, cold, swampy*, and *barren* district which it has been represented to be. The soil is generally strong and productive; the mountains are not so elevated and steep, but that the soil is preserved of sufficient thickness to their tops to secure their cultivation, and most of the marshy lands may be reclaimed by ditching; by this means they will become more valuable than the uplands for producing hay. In fine, it will be found an excellent country for grazing, raising stock, and producing butter and cheese. The strength of the soil is sufficiently tested by the heavy growth of timber, which is principally of hard wood, as beech, maple, yellow-birch, butternut and elm. The evergreens or pines, are confined mostly to the lower ranges of mountains. Some of them are of the largest growth of any in the state, and are suitable for the main shafts of the largest of the cotton mills. In the main, the county resembles the mountainous districts of New England, and like these produces the same intermixture of forest trees, and has about the same adaptation for the production of the different kinds of grain, as wheat, rye, oats, peas, barley, together with fine crops of potatoes."

Comparatively little is yet known of northern New York, indeed, a great part of what has heretofore been known, was only so in error; this is my apology, for saying so much about it.

In a hunting excursion accompanied by Lieut. Wallace and one Coffin, Major Stoner went down to Jessup's river, some fifteen miles below Fish House; and in the woods between that river and the Sacondaga, they found the body of a white man they supposed

15*

had possibly been insane; and had strayed into the wilderness and there died: but he may have been a hunter and crossed the track of one of like craft, who revenged with death a real or supposed injury.

The local Indian names Garoga, and Kennyetto, I have sought in vain to get the English definition of. If any individual can give the signification of either of them, they will confer a favor by communicating the same to my address. It is not only important that Indian names be preserved, but that their true meaning be handed down to future generations, which, divested of the prejudices that influence the present, will drop a tear of pity over the wrongs and injuries done this brave, indeed once noble but now degraded race; and cherish the significant and purely American names they once gave to our lakes, rivers, and mountains, as they would their household gods.

CHAPTER XII.

Nathaniel Foster, justly celebrated as a hunter and trapper of northern New York, was a native of Hinsdale, Windham county, Vermont; the town is now called Vernon. He was named after his father, and was born about the year 1767. At the age of three or four and twenty he married Miss Jemima, daughter of Amos Streeter, of New Hampshire; a year or two after which, and nine or ten years subsequent to the close of the Revolution, he removed to the town of Salisbury, Herkimer county, New York; at which time the country around his new home was mostly a wilderness.

In person he was nearly six feet high, erect and strongly built, with a large muscular frame that seemed well fitted for fatigue. His features were commanding, though not finely marked, and when cheerfulness lit up his countenance through his keen dark eye, they were rather prepossessing. His complexion was sallow, his hair was a sandy brown, but not very gray to the hour of his death, although he grew bald in the latter part of his life.

At the time of Foster's emigration to New York, wild game was so abundant in the northerly part of Herkimer county, that, with his fondness for the ex-

citement attending a hunter's life, circumstances com-
bined to make him a perfect Nimrod.   To adopt the
language of a correspondent, " *He was a Leatherstocking of an original stamp, and devoted to a wild-wood
life.*"   He began his pioneer residence in the winter,
and the following spring he took a sufficient quantity
of fur, principally beaver, to purchase a cow and
many articles necessary in housekeeping.   He afterwards obtained yearly large quantities of valuable
fur, such as beaver, otter, musk-rat, marten, &c.   He
has been known to have three or four hundred musk-
rat traps set in a single season, employing at times
several men to help him tend them.

Deer, bears and wolves were so numerous for years
after Foster made his home on the borders of the
forest, that he slaughtered them in great numbers.
Indeed, it is believed, that he has killed more of
those animals collectively, than any other individual
in the state during the same period; having slain no
less than seventy-six deer in one season, and ninety-
six bears in three seasons.   He has also been known
to kill twenty-five wolves in one year; having a line
of traps set for them from Salisbury to the St. Lawrence.   These animals were so great a pest among
the sheep-folds when the country was new, that a
liberal bounty was paid for their destruction by the
state; increased at times by the liberality of certain
counties and towns in which they were the most numerous.   The avails of his hunting and trapping

amounted in one year, when a liberal price was set upon wolves, to the sum of *twelve hundred and fifty dollars.* He occasionally killed a panther.

The bounties paid for the destruction of wild animals, often made the taxes of frontier towns a burthen; and a wealthy farmer in the neighborhood of Foster, took a stand one season which prevented the paying of such a reward for the destruction of wolves as hunters thought they deserved. The consequence was, that all the old and young Nimrods in the vicinity turned their attention to other game, and purposely let the wolves alone; which in a year or two more were greatly on the increase. Foster told his farmer friend at the election, he would be sorry for the manner in which he had voted, and after the animals had had time to increase, he was not much surprised, one morning, to hear a most pitiful story from him, about the injuries he had sustained the night before by wolves; they had been into his sheepfold and destroyed more property in a single night, than his tax, when the highest bounty was paid for their scalps, had amounted to in several years. He soon found, to use a hunter's phrase, he was barking up the wrong tree for sympathy. " Well," said Leatherstocking, with not a little manifest indifference, " I don't know as I can pity you *much.* If you are unwilling to pay *me* for protecting your sheep, you must buy traps and take care of them *yourself.*" It is perhaps unnecessary to add, the penurious far-

mer was ready to vote a more liberal bounty than
ever for the destruction of wolves, at the next proper
election.

Some winters Foster turned his attention almost
wholly to the killing of deer, disposing of their sad-
dles and skins for the eastern market.   The visitor to
the Albany Museum will there see the skin of a large
moose which was shot by this hunter, and for which he
received from the proprietor some *fifty dollars*.   There
is the skin of another large moose in a New York or
Philadelphia museum, also killed by this hunter.
The following incident attended the death of one of
those animals.   Foster had a favorite dog, as fond of
hunting as was his master.   The bay of this sagacious animal one day called its owner to a retired
spot in the forest, where he discovered Watch
holding a moose by the nose; keeping his own body
between the fore-legs of his adversary, to avoid the
heavy blows aimed at him with the antlers of the
enraged animal, which formidable weapons weighed
together nearly thirty pounds.

On nearing the spot Foster sent a bullet through
the heart of the moose, which in its death-struggle
dashed the dog off with a terrible blow.   The print
of the dog's teeth remained upon the nose of the
moose, but both animals appeared to be dead.   Foster
took off his coat and laid his canine friend upon it,
at which time a partner in the hunt arrived upon the
ground.   With a heavy heart Foster prepared to skin

the game, when his comrade observed a moving of
the muscles about the dog's neck, and told the former
it would recover, but the old hunter shook his head
doubtingly. After a while Watch raised his head
slowly from the ground to receive the caress of his
master; but as soon as his eye rested upon his fallen
antagonist, he sprang to his feet and seized the life-
less moose by the throat, from which he was with no
little difficulty removed. The restoration of his favorite dog to life, caused Foster more real joy than could
possibly the killing of a dozen moose.

One or two years after Nathaniel Foster settled in
Salisbury, his father removed from the east with his
family, and located in the same town. He, too, was
something of a sportsman. Nathaniel had two brothers younger than himself, who, as they attained
sufficient age, indulged occasionally in hunting deer.
The following incident will show how providentially
the elder brother was once saved from harm. His
brother Elisha having on some occasion borrowed his
gun, sent it home by a young son. The lad as he
neared the dwelling saw his uncle going in at the
door, and to be very smart, as boys sometimes are, he
drew up the piece and snapped it at him. On entering the house he told his kinsman what he had done;
when the old hunter took the piece from the hand of
his nephew, walked to the door and snapped it,
and a bullet whizzed through the air from its muzzle.
He remarked as he went to set it away, that he had

shot *seventy-six deer* with his rifle that season, *and it had not before missed fire in a single instance during the whole time.*

The rifle with which Foster usually hunted would carry two balls as well as one; and when he desired to render the death of large game doubly sure, he loaded with two bullets. Foster and Stoner had each a rifle at one time made after the same pattern, by Willis Avery, of Salisbury, and called *double shotters.* They were made with a single barrel with two locks, one placed above the other far enough to admit of two charges, and have the upper charge of powder rest upon the lower bullet. The locks were made for percussion pills, and when the pick which crushed the pill at the first lock was down, there was no danger to be apprehended in firing the lower charge. These rifles cost about seventy dollars each. That of Stoner was borne by a soldier into the late Florida war.

The following incident will serve to show one of the numberless perils to which hunters are exposed in the forest. Nathaniel Foster and his brother, Shubael, were on a deer hunt many years ago in St. Lawrence county, when the former came suddenly upon two noble bucks trying titles to the soil. To end the dispute, he drew up and shot one, and as it fell the other bounded off a few rods, and halted to witness a more novel engagement than its own recent one. The fallen deer was not killed, but was badly stunned by the ball striking it near the back-bone, and as the hunter ran up to cut its throat, the animal sprang upon its haunches, and in its own defence struck furiously at him with its antlers. Quick as thought, this modern Leatherstocking placed the knife between his teeth, and grappled the weapons of his unexpected foe. The struggle for the mastery was long and fierce, the hunter not daring to let go his hold; but, as good luck would have it, he got the head of the deer between two trees, against one of which a horn was broken, and the worried animal thrown down. Before it could recover, the hunter dealt it a blow upon the head with a club fortune had placed at his command, when he succeeded in cutting its throat. The tussle lasted more than thirty minutes; and when his brother arrived upon the ground, he found the grass and bushes trampled down for several rods around. The strength of the hunter was nearly exhausted in the engagement; while his tattered garments gave evidence, that a visit to his wardrobe would alone restore his outward man to the condition it was in an hour before

On a certain occasion, Shubael Foster visited a wolf-trap, in company with his brother, Nathaniel, in which a wolf was caught by one of its hind legs. It crawled under a log on their approach; and the senior hunter conceiving it would make him a fine pet, resolved to take the snarler home alive. With a forked stick he fixed a kind of halter upon its

16

nose, and loosening it from the trap, he thus led the
captive home. It would go ten or fifteen rods as
quietly as a dog, and then spring at their faces with
all its might. He kept it muzzled and fasting about
the house for several days, much of which time it
concealed itself under a bed. It was finally slain and
a bounty taken for its scalp.

Nathaniel Foster was familiarly called Uncle Nat,
among his intimate friends. His early advantages at
school were limited, as were those of many of the
hardy pioneers of western and northern New York,
who chanced to be boys in the great American contest for *liberty*. When he settled in Salisbury, he
could neither read nor write; but, about the year
1810, William Waterman, then a merchant in Salisbury, learned him to write at his store, as he informed
the author.

The northerly part of Herkimer county was not only
a wilderness when Foster began the life of a hunter,
but much of it is still in a state of nature. It is dotted
with numerous crystal lakes and rivulets, to the shores
of which Foster was invited in his hunting excursions,
as wild game grew scarce nearer his home. About
the year 1793, or 1794, John Brown, a capitalist of
Rhode Island, purchased a tract of *two hundred and
ten thousand acres* of wild lands about the head waters
of Moose river, a tributary to the Black river. Lying
in the north-east part of Herkimer and the western
part of Hamilton counties, is a connected chain of

eight small lakes, and their outlet forms one branch of
Moose river. It is known there, however, as the Mill
stream. These lakes, which lie in a line running
nearly east and west, are called in Gordon's Gazetteer,
the *Fulton lakes,* but why they are so called, does not
appear.

Brown did not purchase this land of the government, as I am informed, but got it of some individual
in payment for a debt, and soon after opened a road
from Remsen to it. It is said to have cost Brown
some thirty cents an acre. He visited the tract in the
winter of 1798 and 1799, and had then, or previously,
several log dwellings, a grist-mill and a saw-mill erected upon it, with the view of bringing it into market.
He spent very little time upon the tract, however, and
had not accomplished much in the way of subduing
those wild lands at the time of his death, which took
place in 1806.

Charles F. Herreshoff having married the widow
Francis, a daughter of John Brown, resolved upon
making a permanent settlement upon Brown's tract
(so called since his purchase), and went on to it with
that intent about the year 1812. He has generally
been regarded as a German, but in answer to an inquiry, he assured Darius Hawkins, he was a Prussian
by birth. He had a commanding appearance, being
over six feet high and well formed. He was very
gentlemanly in his deportment, though extremely
proud and aristocratic. He is said to have been a

finished scholar.   On entering the forest he declared
with an oath, that *he would settle the tract, or settle
himself*.

Herreshoff spent the greater part of his time on the
tract for several years, but his wife, it is believed, was
never there: she disapproved of his seemingly visionary operations.   Although he was not as well calculated as some men of a less enterprising spirit are to
settle a new country, still, considering the great difficulties he had to encounter, which are of a magnitude
people living at ease in cities can hardly conceive, he
had accomplished much towards the fulfilment of his
purpose.   He repaired the mills Brown had erected,
and in the course of a few years he had cleared up
nearly two thousand acres of land, the greater part of
which had been heavily timbered, and erected thereon
some thirty or forty buildings.   The mills were nearly
three miles from the most westerly lake of the Fulton
chain, and at that place he built a forge for the smelt-
ing of iron ore.   He also opened several roads to the
nearest settlements.

He had expended, it is said, more than *fifteen thousand dollars* (some persons have named a much larger
sum), with as yet the prospect of its paying little or
no interest, and made a call on his Providence friends
for more money.   But alas! for his peace of mind—
the draft was dishonored.   Unwilling to survive the
mortification attendant on a failure of his schemes,
and unable to prosecute them any further for the want

of means, he became disheartened, loaded a pistol, went into the yard in front of his dwelling, and blew out his brains; thus effectually *settling himself.* The report of the pistol instantly brought out the inmates of the house, who found the victim of ambition sitting upon the ground, where, in a few moments he lay a gory corpse.

Such was the melancholy and tragic fate of one of the most enterprising men that ever entered the wild lands of New York, to subdue them. It would almost seem as though he had lived before his time. Large sums of the money he had expended, were exhausted in searching for *iron,* where it is very possible, with the knowledge modern science has at her beck, little or no expense would have been incurred. That iron and perhaps other valuable ores abound in that part of the state in large quantities, is not unlikely; and some more fortunate, though less enterprising man than the first active settler upon Brown's tract, may yet reap a rich harvest there for his labors.

The death of Herreshoff took place December 19, 1819, at which time he was boarding with Gardner Vincent, whose family resided on the tract. Herreshoff took three hundred merino sheep on to his clearing, where he also kept a span of horses. The body of Herreshoff, after his death, was carried out to Russia Corners, a distance of nearly fifty miles, where an inquest was held upon it by Henry S. Whiting as coroner. Several citizens of Boonville were there at

16*

the time, who requested to take the body to that place, after the inquest, for burial, and they were permitted to take it.   Says Mr. Henry Graves of Boonville, N. Y., in a communication to the writer: " At this place I examined the wound of Herreshoff.   The ball entered the right temple and passed through the head."   A few years after his death Herreshoff's friends placed at his grave, which is near one corner of the village grave-yard in Boonville, a marble slab with the following inscription:

CHARLES
FREDERICK
HERRESHOFF,

Obiit Dec. 19th,

1819,

Ætat   50.

Herreshoff is said, on good authority, to have manufactured just a ton of iron at his forge, from ore obtained on Brown's tract.   It was of the very best quality, and cost, when ready for use, just *one dollar a pound*.   Says a correspondent, " Black sand found upon the lake shore, and separated by magnets, was principally used in making his iron.   He, however, expected to find mountain or rock ore, and in one case he followed a small vein in the rocks some 200 feet, at an enormous expense."   Some have stated that the quantity of iron made by Herreshoff was less than is named above, and a friend writes that " every pound of iron he made cost him more than an ounce of gold."

The cost of his iron gives a principal reason why he committed suicide. The taxes upon the tract were also heavy for unproductive property. The assessor's valuation was *one shilling* an acre. Samuel Giles went in from Russia two seasons (believed in 1813 and 1814), and collected the tax, which was sixty dollars each year.

Stephen Smith, 2d, of Russia, was engaged as a surveyor on Brown's tract, in the years 1815, 16 and 17. He was employed by John Brown Francis, a step-son of Herreshoff, who has since been governor of Rhode Island. The tract was divided into eight townships, numbering from one to eight. Names are said to have been given to those paper towns, two of which are believed to have been Economy and Frugality: names very proper for any of those townships, and indicative of the virtues it would be necessary to practice, in order to live there.

In 1817, Smith was engaged in laying out a public road through the tract. It began two miles east of Boonville, and striking the tract it ran through townships number 1, 2, part of 3, and all of 7. From Herreshoff's mills it ran up on the north side of the lakes, terminating at the Sacondaga state road, leading from Russel, St. Lawrence county, to Lake Pleasant, in Hamilton county, then being surveyed by Judge Atwater, of St. Lawrence county, and located by John Fay, Esq., of Fish House, as commissioner. This road extended southerly to the town of Wells, as I have elsewhere shown. The greater part of it is now overgrown with trees. The road opened by Smith was forty miles long, and intersected the Sacondaga road twenty-seven miles from Lake Pleasant. Smith was engaged on his road, of which he was also a commissioner, sixty days, with nine hands. Bridges and cross-ways were not made by the surveying party.

Moose lake, after which Moose river is called, is one of the largest and purest lakes on the tract, being several miles in extent, and very deep. It lies a few miles south of the western end of the Fulton chain. Southerly from Moose lake, and farther to the eastward, heads what is called the South branch of Moose river. It is three miles from Moose lake to the South branch; on which stream, and nearly opposite Moose lake is a small clearing of several acres, called *Canashagala*, an Indian name. Some suppose this clearing was made by the Indians, and others that the timber was destroyed by fire. The stream at this point is a remarkable spot for fishermen.

The survey for the road was first extended up on the south side of the Fulton chain, and north side of Moose lake, to Fifth lake; but as the route was found impracticable for a good road, on account of the difficulties to be overcome in the make of the land, it was located on the opposite side of the lakes. The road laid out by Smith, struck the Black river ten miles from the starting point: from thence to Moose river, was six and a half miles; from which place to the middle settlement, or the Herreshoff dwelling, it was nearly five miles more, making the whole distance from Boonville nearly twenty-four miles. The land on each side of the road was taxed to defray the expenses of its survey. Going in from the Remsen road, Moose river is crossed about one mile south of the clearing. Near the road from the middle settlement (on the right in entering), is a little lake of several acres, called Huckleberry lake, those berries growing on its shore The outlet of this pond runs into the Mill stream.

Few incidents attending the survey of Brown's tract are now remembered. A porcupine, one day, claimed a preëmption right to the soil, and evinced a disposition to dispute the surveyor's title, planting itself in a bristling posture directly in the road. It was an ugly customer to handle without mittens, or rather tongs, and surveyor Smith, acting upon the forest hunter's rule, that *might* makes *right*, wilfully and maliciously slew the *varmint* with his compass staff.

Herreshoff was a good feeling man, and at times rather jovial, liking a little fun withal. On some occasion, Smith, accompanied by Herreshoff, Vincent and Silas Thomas, went in a boat to the head of Fourth lake, to select some pine timber. Passing one of the islands in the lake, probably Bear island, Herreshoff desired to be set ashore on a bluff extending some rods into the lake. As is generally the case with foreigners, who find tobacco very cheap in this country, he was a great smoker, and having lit his pipe, he concluded to increase the fumigation by also lighting the grass and dry brush around him. A few minutes only sufficed, with the breeze then puffing, to spread the flame over the bluff. The wind drove the heat toward him, and calling for the boat to come to his assistance, he gained the extreme point of land, in the hope of escaping the fire. Before the boat could get to him, however, the flame drove him out upon a tree which extended horizontally over the water.

The craft seemed to him to move like a snail, as the heat and smoke—of which latter commodity he for once had enough—became more and more insufferable. He held on to his footing until he saw a sheet of flame coming directly in his face, when he sprang off into the water, among the trout. He did not glide along as noiselessly though as they did in that element, for he floundered like a porpoise; and for once, if we mistake not, quit smoking with tobacco still in his pipe. He was finally rescued by his companions, though half drowned and half frozen, as he took the unexpected bath in September, and shivered for hours to pay for it. This, it is said, was not the only time he came near being scorched by his great passion for fire and smoke.

CHAPTER XIII.

Mr. W. S. Benchley, of Newport, N. Y., who was well acquainted with *Uncle Nat*, and who has often been on Brown's tract with Foster and since his day; has at my request kindly furnished me by letter with several incidents in the old *trapper's* life, and a description of the tract, or a portion of it, which letter I shall do my readers a favor to present in his own words; notwithstanding he tells me at the outset he is " entirely unused to writing other than common business transactions." I trust he will pardon me for the liberty I have taken with his name and letter.

" I have long been acquainted with a part of that region of country called *Brown's Tract.* At an enormous expense, Brown has opened three roads on to his tract.* The route now taken to approach it from this direction is, to leave the northern turnpike at Boonville, Oneida county. Taking a north-easterly direction, you pass the last improvement some eight miles from Boonville, beyond which the road is impassable for carriages. Pack-horses, or what we call drays are used for carrying our provisions, &c., in our

---

* The road from Boonville surveyed by Smith, in the employ of Gov. Francis, I suppose to be one of the roads here alluded to.

hunting and fishing excursions; last September [1848] I went in with a dray.

"On reaching Moose river, about five miles from the last settlement, we have to scow our luggage over; and frequently to swim our horses. Moose river at this point is twice as large as the West Canada creek, and quite rapid. In fact, the entire length of the river is one continued fall, or succession of rapids; making sufficient water-power, if improved, for the use of the whole state of New York. From Moose river to the first clearing we reach on Brown's tract, is eleven miles, over a most horribly rocky, stony, cold region; though very well covered with timber, such as spruce, balsam, beech, birch, some maple and hemlock.*

"The first clearing you enter is called Coal hill, from the fact, I believe, that most of the timber from this clearing was made into coal for the use of the iron-works erected by Herreshoff, son-in-law to Brown. A short distance from this you enter a large improvement with one framed house, where Herreshoff used to live. [This is in township number 7.] In this clearing he expended a large amount of money in searching for iron ore; blasting and digging at the base of a rocky hill or mountain running through this

* That much of this tract in an agricultural point of view has a most forbidding aspect, there can be but little doubt. Judge Stow, of Lewis county, once observed of it, "that it was so poor it would make a crow shed tears of blood to fly over it."

improvement. Failing to accomplish what he expected, he became discouraged: his friends at the same time refusing to advance him any more funds, and left alone as he was, to bear the blame of a failure; disheartened and spirit-broken, he died, ' as the fool dieth,' by blowing out his brains with a pistol.

"Since Herreshoff's death, the improvements made by him have been mostly abandoned, except by hunters and fishermen. There is still one settler residing there, however, a Mr. Arnold, who has a large family. He accommodates fishermen with boats. He keeps several cows, horses, &c., and raises a large quantity of oats yearly, which he draws to market in the winter. On leaving this clearing you cross one branch of Moose river, which is the outlet of eight small lakes, of which I shall speak hereafter. Passing through several improvements for two and a half miles, you reach the spot where once stood the forge, a saw-mill and grist-mill, with several dwellings; but now entirely gone with the exception of one barn-frame with the roof on, otherwise entirely stripped of covering.

" All the improvements at one time must have covered some *two thousand acres*, with about *forty* families upon them. All the buildings now remaining are two dwellings, one barn, and two frames of barns, divested of covering. When Foster left the tract [1833], some remains of the forge, mills, &c., were still standing. Iron was manufactured at this forge

17

of a good quality, though said to be at a cost of one dollar per pound. I have no doubt iron ore abounds in this region, in inexhaustible quantities, with other valuable ores, waiting for enterprise to develope them, after the gold fever has subsided. Where Herreshoff erected his mills, is one of the best water powers in the world. A dam some forty feet long is still standing, and when first constructed, raised the water in the Fourth lake about two feet. This dam is about three miles below the First lake. [The lake usually denominated the First lake in this chain, is, in truth, the last, or Eighth lake; but approached as they generally are from Moose river, the last is recognized as the first, and the reader will understand when the relative numbers of those lakes are given, that they number upward, or from west to east.] After this dam was built, it was three months before the water flowed over it; in fact, search was made supposing the water had found some other outlet.

" At Herreshoff's dam we take boats for fishing excursions, and three miles up the stream we enter the First lake, a beautiful pond, say one mile by one and-a-half miles in extent, containing one small island, called Dog island; a dog having been found upon it by an early visitor. About half a mile down the outlet, and near a point of land now called Indian's point, Uncle Nat shot the Indian. Leaving this lake you pass into the Second lake, separated from the First by sand-bars, with a narrow channel some twenty feet wide. This lake is some longer than the First, but is not as wide, and has no islands. Along the north shore of Second lake, rises a most grand and sublime mountain, presenting a front of naked rock for nearly one mile, at a height of several hundred feet. On its summit Uncle Nat told me he had often been, ' that from it he could see numbers of lakes; and that there he could enjoy himself, and not be troubled by the d—d Indians.' [This bold promontory I shall take the liberty to call *Foster's Observatory.*]

"From the Second you enter the Third lake by passing through a strait of some ten rods. It is a pretty, pure, deep pond, about the size of the First and Second. In this lake is a small island, called Grass island, because it is well covered with grass, and has few trees or bushes upon it. Leaving the Third you pass up a stream some fifty or sixty rods, and enter the Fourth lake, which is seven miles long, and from one to two miles wide. It has four islands, the first of which in ascending is called Deer island, containing about 100 acres of well timbered land."

Desirous of permanently fastening the names of the most celebrated Nimrods of this region upon its scenery, I shall take the liberty to call this island Benchley's island, after George Benchley; who shantied at the head of Third lake, but a short distance from the island, and who perished in the wilderness while following the fortunes of a trapper.

George and Joseph Benchley (brothers of my correspondent), were engaged in trapping in the fall of 1819, in the region of country under consideration. George, who was the oldest, possessed a roving and very romantic disposition. For a while he was engaged in a sea-faring life, but tiring of its monotony, he severed the halliards which bound him to the " rolling deep," and returned to the home of his childhood. The pursuit of a forest-hunter seemed well suited, from its excitement, to his danger-daring temperament.

The brothers had a line of marten traps, extending from the Fulton lakes to some point on the State road, running from Wells to Russel, not far from Racket lake, where they had a shantee. The line of traps extended thirty or forty miles, with several hunters' cabins on the route. They were engaged in their pursuits until the last of November, having two men employed to assist them. They took turns in traversing the route, and George was alone on the eastern end of it, when a heavy fall of snow suspended their operations. Joseph and the assistants were at the main shantee, at the head of Third lake, where they remained several days anxiously awaiting the return of the senior hunter. As he did not come in, two unsuccessful attempts were made to seek for him; but the great depth of snow in that direction prevented the possibility of reaching him without snow-shoes, and they had not a pair with them.

While in a feverish state of anxiety about their absent friend, not caring or perhaps not daring to return home without some tidings of him, an old hunter, named Morgan, arrived at their lodge on snow-shoes. He had come, he said, directly from their eastern shantee on the State road, and assured Joseph *that his brother was well, and had gone out to Lake Pleasant to obtain food.* Giving full credit to Morgan's statement, Joseph and his men returned home.

The winter wore away, and nothing further was heard from the absent hunter by his friends at Newport; but, as he was a single man, and well weaned from home, little anxiety was felt about him, as they supposed him safe at the house of some back-woodsman in Hamilton county. In the spring a message reached Newport, that the body of a man had been found by Indian hunters, in a shantee near Racket lake. The probability was, that Benchley's shantee was indicated, and his brothers Jenks and William, anxious to know his fate, made a journey out there, in company with two other persons. The body, which had been buried, was exhumed, and their worst fears were realized—the remains were those of their kinsman.

Dark mystery has ever hung over the last moments of this unfortunate hunter, and suspicion over the character of Morgan, who was doubtless the last individual who saw him alive. That hunter was not very

scrupulous of his acts, as was well known, and it has
ever since been surmised that he seriously injured
Benchley in some manner, took his fur, if he had any,
and left him to perish.   The Indians found his gun in
the shantee, but no fur; and, as he had gone over the
whole line of traps, it seemed impossible that he
should have taken none.   Morgan had considerable
fur when he left the forest.   That Benchley suffered
most acutely in his last hours, there can be no doubt.
He had, with his hunter's knife, evidently cut small
pieces of wood to feed his fire, from the logs of which
part of the hut was built, while he had strength to do
so; but, how long he hungered—how keenly he suffered, in body and mind—how many cold, dark and
dreary nights he lay shivering, without an earthly
" eye to pity, or arm to relieve," is only known to
Him to whom no mortal's fate is a mystery.

Joseph Benchley was a musician; and the fall he
was hunting with his brother, he had his violin with
him, and often played it, " to drive dull care away,"
and afford a pastime for the wild animals within its
hearing.   Orpheus, a celebrated Greek musician of
lang-syne, is said to have called down the mountains
to listen to the melody he discoursed in the valleys.
It would have troubled him, we opine, to have started
any of those on Brown's tract, as their roots were too
long; and Benchley, aware of the fact, very properly
chose his position, not at their base, but upon their
summit.

The hunter Morgan, was a morose and rather petulent fellow, and not very popular among the craft. He traversed the forest for several years, on and about Brown's tract, but finally went off to Canada and died there. He was pretty successful in taking fur, and at times was accused of getting it unjustly. He was one of those devil-daring woodsmen of whom the Indians stood in awe. From this digression I return to Benchley's description of the country.

" The next island in Fourth lake [above Benchley's island], contains about one quarter of an acre, is a pile of bare rocks, and is known by the name of Elba; which name can not fail to remind the reader of the ambitious and unfortunate Buonaparte. It produced a solitary pine, which for many years was its only object of attraction. A Vandal hand has lately cut it, to the deep regret of all sentimental hunters. (App. E.)

" The third island in Fourth lake contains ten or fifteen acres of land, and is called Bear island, an early hunter having killed one of those animals upon it. Near the head of this lake, and some fifty or sixty rods from Bear island, is a small island called Dollar island, from its rotundity of shape. There is, in shoal water, between Elba and Bear island, and about a mile distant from the former a bare rock, called Gull rock. This rock is said to be on the line between Herkimer and Hamilton counties. Brown's tract extends across Herkimer, and into the counties of Lewis on the west, and Hamilton on the east.

"On the forest-bound Elba of Fourth lake, I have shantied several times with Foster.   On one occasion, when there, the Indian (whom he afterwards killed) and his squaw, came and spent the night with us, taking from the lake their bark canoe and dried moose-skin for a shelter.   I have spent several days upon this lake with Foster.   He conversed but little, and his restless, roving eye was never still.   With his rifle beside him, he seemed ever anxious to discover something on shore, worthy of his never erring aim.

"The bald-eagle, which frequents this region, he would never disturb, for he thought those noble birds were made to live unmolested by man, 'although,' as he said, 'the c—d Indians killed them.'   He seemed to feel as though he was lord of Brown's tract, and that no one else, especially an *Indian*, had as good a right there.   With the Indian he shot, I was well acquainted.   He was indeed a noble looking fellow in appearance.   He was of the St. Regis tribe, with a cross of French blood.   [Says Mr. Graves, in a communication to the author, "I have often seen the Indian Foster killed.   He was a very friendly, intelligent man, and belonged to the St. Regis tribe on the St. Lawrence."]   His wife was slender and very feminine.   She was under the most perfect subjection to her husband, and was no doubt often ill treated by him when tipsy: in fact, I believe that his and Foster's difficulties first commenced when they had both been drinking.

" Frequently, when on these waters, Foster would direct my attention to an object on some distant, grassy beach, saying, ' See! there is a deer: watch, and you will see it move.' He was never mistaken; still a man unacquainted with the wood, would very seldom suppose that any thing of the kind was in sight.

" At the head of Fourth lake was formerly a grove of white pine. [To this grove Herreshoff was going when he was compelled to take a cold bath.] *Five* distinct echoes to the human voice may be heard at this place, and here I have repeatedly discharged a gun, to hear mountain after mountain send back its tardy response, until my rifle's shrill note had been mimicked by five (as I suppose) mermaid hunters.

" Lying parallel to the Fulton chain, and mostly opposite Fourth lake, say two miles to the north of it, is a chain of three small lakes, several miles in extent, which also discharge their waters into Moose river. The stream is called the North branch, and the lakes are known in the forest by the name of North Branch lakes.

" Leaving the Fourth, you pass up the inlet some half a mile, into the Fifth lake, a small pond of eight or ten acres. From the Fifth to the Sixth lake, is a continued fall of three-fourths of a mile. Here is a carrying place; and Foster, at the age of sixty, would take his skiff upon his head and shoulders and carry it from one lake to the other, with but one stop. In fact, at that age, Foster was known to carry a deer

three miles on his back.   With a single lock between
Fifth and Sixth lakes, a water communication might
easily be obtained the whole extent of the eight lakes.

" The Sixth lake is quite small, and after wading
and pushing up a narrow, rapid stream, say one and a
half miles, you enter the ' Noble Seventh,' as Uncle
Nat called it.   The visitor on entering this lake, meets
with a grand and beautiful view.   The lake is about
four miles long and two wide, with a nameless island
near its centre, of some fifty acres, covered with rocks
and pine timber.   [I have mentioned in these pages a
forest-trapper named Green White, who was often on
the island under consideration.   With the reader's
permission, I will call this island White's island.*]
Near this island, on its south shore, we frequently get

---

*White was rather under the middling stature, with a dark
complexion, and possessing a very keen, dark eye.   He was a
man of few words, but celebrated for his shrewdness.   He learned
the blacksmith's trade at Schenectada in his early life, and always
made his own hunting-knives and hatchets.   He was a very successful hunter, was extensively known, and by Indian hunters he
was universally feared.   *The Indians*, he said to his friends, *never
stole his fur but once.*   He occasionally crossed the track of Maj.
Stoner, to whom he was well known, but as he hunted to the
westward of Stoner, they did not often meet.

Says Henry Graves, of Boonville, "I was well acquainted
with Green White, who was a great trapper on and about Brown's
tract.   He hunted some in connection with Foster, but they
generally had the separate interest.   White, however, was much
the most successful trapper.   He would sometimes bring in a
hundred dollars worth of beaver at a time—lay drunk until he

the salmon trout in 100 feet depth of water. [Another informant says they are caught here weighing fifteen or twenty pounds.]

" At the head of Seventh lake is a grove of pitch-pine timber, which timber is not elsewhere seen in the district. On entering this lake at one time with Foster, he discovered a deer feeding upon a grassy beach, nearly half a mile distant. Said he, ' B., put me on shore and I will give you some venison for dinner.' I did so, and then rowed out into the lake, far enough to see the deer. After remaining some time, I saw Foster step suddenly from the bushes upon the beach, some distance from the deer. Almost the very

had spent it all, and then back to the woods. Not so with Foster: he liked a glass, but would be called a temperate man.

" I should think White had been dead some fifteen years. He with another man was coming in from the tract; they halted by the way-side, built them a brush shantee and stopped for the night. During the night, a small stub of a tree fell across the shantee and broke White's leg. Early in the morning the man with him came to Boonville about *seventeen miles* for help. He was brought in on a litter; but before a surgeon could be obtained to amputate it, the limb mortified and he died."

In the fall of 1815, said the surveyor Smith, White came in from Brown's tract with *three hundred dollars* worth of fur, and as usual on such ocasions, he *trained* until it was all gone. While hunting, after the provisions were gone he had taken in from the settlement, he lived on wild game and fish. This was the usual fare of hunters in the forest. White is said to have been about the same age of Foster, and is believed to have followed trapping about the Fulton lakes a few years earlier than did Foster. There was a hunter named Williams, on and about Brown's tract in 1815.

instant the deer raised its head from feeding, I saw
the flash of his rifle and the deer fall. At Foster's
call I went ashore, he not knowing that I had seen
the deer fall. Well, Uncle Nat, said I, have you
killed him? He straightened up like a soldier, with
his head erect, and eyes glistening; and grasping his
rifle in his right hand and holding it above his head,
he said, ' B., he never told a lie. When you hear
him speak, he always tells the truth.' I stepped on
shore and found he had put his ball precisely in the
centre of the deer's forehead. He must have been
full twenty-five rods from the animal, and fired the
instant it raised its head. In a very few minutes he
had a fine piece of venison roasting before a good fire,
and ere long we had a sweet morsel to dine upon.

"At another time, while we sat fishing from our boat,
he discovered an old doe with two fawns, the latter
about as large as lambs at two months old. They
were feeding and playing upon the beach, perhaps a
quarter of a mile distant. Foster was on fire immediately. If he could kill the old doe, he said, he could
kill the fawns, and their runnets would bring him fifty
cents each. I remonstrated against killing the little
fellows for so small a gain, and proposed to pay him
the dollar and let them go. But no; nothing would
satisfy him short of a shot. I then rather refused to
row him within shot; but one *look* from him satisfied
me that I might as well comply. However, I managed
in the operation to make noise enough to frighten the

old doe; but not without strong suspicions on his part, that it was done intentionally.

" From the Seventh to the Eighth lake is three or four miles, and the lake is some four or five miles long. From these eight lakes runs the stream on which the mills on Brown's tract were erected. A carrying place from the Eighth lake, some two miles, brings you to what is called the Racket inlet, running easterly, down which you can go in a skiff into Racket lake, and from thence down Racket river to the St. Lawrence.

" The poor Indian Foster killed, was buried on a point near where the mill dam now stands, and a rude cross was erected at his head by his friends. Last September [1848], I looked for the grave, but it was so overgrown with grass and bushes I could not find it. When he shot the Indian, he went about five miles to gain Indian Point before his victim arrived."

The Indian here alluded to, is said to have been quite successful in killing deer. He often *floated* for them. This was done in the night time. In his bark canoe, behind a few green boughs, he would proceed as silently as possible along the shore of a lake, and shoot the timid deer there feeding on grass, or standing in the water's edge to cool, as they gazed in wonder at the torch light in the bow of the craft, which seemed at times to fascinate them. This mode of killing deer much displeased Foster, and is believed to have been one cause of difficulty between them.

18

Besides the lakes already named in the region of country under consideration, there are several others of greater or less importance. The Jerseyfield lake, a handsome sheet of water some two miles long, and around the shores of which Foster, in his earlier days, used to hunt, lies in the easterly part of Salisbury. Black creek, which is one of the tributaries of West Canada creek, has its source in the Jerseyfield lake.

Jock's lake, so called after Jock (Jonathan) Wright, an early trapper upon its shores, is a very pretty lake, five or six miles long, though not very wide; and is situated in the north-eastern or wilderness portion of Herkimer county, some ten miles from a place called Noblesborough. Its outlet is one of the sources of the west branch of West Canada creek. Some four miles south of Jock's lake is a small sheet of water called Little Salmon lake, and about two miles to the westward of Jock's lake, is another trout inhabiting pond, called Black River South lake. Around those lakes, and along their streams, were favorite haunts of the trapper Wright.

Of the physical outline of Hamilton county and the northerly part of Herkimer, Prof. Lardner Vanuxem, thus remarks in his volume of the Geology of New York. "The most interesting feature of the wilderness region is its chain of lakes, placed so nearly upon a level that but little labor from man is required to connect those of three counties together. The lakes of Herkimer and Hamilton are arranged upon a line which is parallel with the St. Lawrence river and Ontario lake, and with the Ohio, &c.; appearing not to be accident merely, but the result of a law whose operations were in their direction, and on several parallels. These lakes, were a communication opened from east to west, would be much resorted to. The beauty of their waters, their elevation, and the wild scenery which surrounds them, would not fail to attract visitors."

CHAPTER XIV

With the death of its proprietor, the Herreshoff settlement on Brown's tract became tenantless, and in a short time all the improvements were going to waste and destruction. Hunters occasionally visited the place, and when there, camped in the deserted dwellings. In May, 1830, the premises were leased for a small sum, and in February 1832, Nathaniel Foster, who had for years traversed this region, purchased an assignment of the lease and moved his family there; that he might with greater convenience follow his favorite avocation of a wilderness trapper. His family, consisting of himself and wife and his son David and wife, occupied the Herreshoff dwelling nearest the forge. In a hut not far from Foster dwelt an Indian hunter named Peter Waters, familiarly known in the forest by the name of Drid; and in another house erected by the original proprietor, resided three old bachelors, William S. Wood, David Chase, and Willard Johnson. Johnson first entered the forest with Herreshoff, to work at his forge. Some part of the time there were three or four other persons on the clearing, increasing the population to some fifteen inhabitants, all of whom depended principally upon hunting and fishing for their support. Johnson, who was a man somewhat advanced in life, often hunted with Foster; and Wood, of whom we know but little else, would have frozen to death on one occasion, but for the attentions of Foster.

The condition of the other settlers at this period on Brown's tract, was rendered the more comfortable by the family of Foster, whose women were able and ready to dispense the numerous little comforts the sex can command. A difficulty arose between Foster and his Indian neighbor, which, from one of a trifling nature, assumed a most serious aspect. A feeling not the most friendly began to gain a place between them, and some person, either from motives of mischief or terror, took occasion to tell Drid *that Foster was unfriendly to him—that he did not like other hunters—was a dead shot*, and the like. It was a person or persons, no doubt, who had had some misunderstanding with the Indian, and adopted this method to excite his fears without intending Foster any injury; possibly the informer was merely desirous of intimidating him, by making him feel conscious that one man, at least, who did not fear him, had the ability to punish him; whatever the motive was is unknown, but the red hunter's worst passions were now aroused, and ere long he resolved to destroy a supposed foe, at whatever hazard. On several occasions, when intoxicated, he threatened the life of Foster, and to such a state of feverish excitement had he arrived, that he only seemed desirous of an oppor-

18*

tunity for executing his diabolical threat. The hunter Johnson, on several occasions, accompanied Foster to prevent a surprise from his avowed enemy.

The Foster family had always been very kind to that of Drid, and when the latter was gone on a long hunt, his squaw depended almost entirely upon the former for the support of herself and children. As Foster kept a cow, the family of the Indian neighbor was supplied with milk free of charge; while not a few necessaries dealt out to them when Drid was from home, had been carried into the clearing by Foster, upon his back. Of the latter articles he made a charge, and embracing some favorable opportunity, he asked the Indian to pay the account, in amount about seventeen shillings; the latter promised to pay a part of it. Foster now told the Indian that he had heard of his having threatened his life; this he admitted, said they lived there retired from any settlement, *where there was no law,* and added, "*If I kill you, I kill you ; and if you kill me, you kill me!*" Foster told him he would make no such agreement, that he did not wish or design to injure him, and he must not harbor such feelings.

One of the earliest causes of difficulty between these hunters originated as follows; nearly a year before his death, Drid took Foster's boat without permission and left it in the river a mile below where he had taken it. He was admonished that he must not repeat such an act if he would not be punished for his temerity, at which just reproof he was very indignant; and soon after was heard by several persons to say, "*Me got a bad heart, me put a bullet through old Foster.*" It was about the time of the boat disturbance, that certain individuals attempted to terrify Drid by threats of Foster's vengeance.

In July, and about two months before his death, Drid was returning to the tract in company with a man named John Carpenter, when, as he drew near his home, he fired off his rifle, reloaded and carefully primed it. His companion inquired why he did it? saying they would then find no game. The Indian replied, "*Me going to old Foster's, me shoot him else he shoot me!*" He did go to Foster's dwelling, and standing at a little distance from the door, he hailed several times, to draw the object of search to an exposed situation. Mrs. Foster came to the door, and was alarmed to see the threatening attitude of her neighbor. He inquired for her husband, and being told that he was not at home, he exclaimed as he turned to go away, "*Me shoot him if he had been!*" Next morning the family of Drid being out of provisions, applied as usual to Foster's family for food. Informed of the Indian's conduct by his wife and Carpenter, Foster took some flour and in company with Carpenter, sought the red man's cabin to relieve the wants of the family. In the presence of the witness he asked Drid if he had not called at his door intending to shoot him? He admitted that he had, and assigned as a reason, that he had been told that Foster had threatened to kill him for taking his boat. *"I made no such threat,"* said the old trapper, *" I said it would not be well for you or any one else, to take my boat a second time and fasten it a mile from my landing."*

In August following the above incident, Drid returned from Racket lake with furs, and halted at Foster's door, at which were several neighbors; when the old trapper very civilly asked him to pay his account. *" You are d—d liar! "* said the Indian, *" me don't owe you cent! "* He raised his tomahawk to strike the old man, who sprang into the house. He opened the door with his rifle in hand, when his foe sullenly fell back and exclaimed, *" If you ever go to Seventh lake, or to Racket lake, me kill you ! "* Foster threatened to complain of him before a justice of the peace, and he replied, *" I'll get there soon as you do—haint no law in woods here ! "* The Indian with many threats then went off to his cabin.

Soon after this encounter with his adversary, Foster went before Joshua Harris, a justice of the peace in Brantingham, Lewis county, *twenty miles* from his own residence, although the nearest one, and complained that this Indian had then a third time sought his life, on which account he demanded his arrest. The magistrate declined issuing a process against Drid, saying that if he proceeded against him, the latter would be as likely to kill him as complainant.

Failing to get a precept against his dusky antagonist, some of his acquaintances advised Foster to remove his family from the forest, but he declared " *he would not be frightened off by an Indian.*" He was very malicious, so much so that Aleck Thompson, an Indian hunter, who had a shantee near his, would have nothing to do with him, at least, so say the friends of Foster. The apprehensions of the Foster family were such all the latter part of the summer, that they seldom lit a candle in the evening, from fear that Drid would fire in at their windows. Indeed, he had threatened to enter the house in the night time, and stab him in his bed. He had even inquired on which side of the bed Foster slept, that he might make sure of his victim. When told that so rash an act would endanger the life of Mrs. Foster, he replied, " *She good woman—me no care to hurt her—but rather kill 'em both, than not kill him!*"

On the morning of Drid's death, Foster was, agreeably to an arrangement made the evening before, to accompany Wood and Chase on a hunting excursion to Fourth lake. The Indian had left his traps and rifle at Racket lake, some twelve miles beyond the intended destination of the party, but concluded to go up with them as far as they went. Foster called in the morning to see if the bachelors were ready for a start, and the Indian being present, renewed his quarrel with the former and attempted his life. He was a stout young man, between twenty-five and

thirty years of age, and Foster was upwards of sixty.
He succeeded in getting the old man down upon the
floor, but was foiled in taking his life by the inter-
cession of the by-standers, who drew them apart, not
however until the Indian had cut his arm, in the
attempt to thrust a knife into his heart. Thwarted
when he thought his victim sure, he threatened vengeance, and declared at the end of a horrid oath,
" *you no live till Christmas!*" Foster, whose worst
passions were now excited, retorted, " *you'll do d——
well if you see another moon!*"

Foster retired after the difficulty with the Indian,
and did not join the party, increased on its setting
out by several others, who were going a few miles on
a fishing excursion; but well satisfied that his foe
would return and lurk about his dwelling to shoot
him, as soon as he had obtained his rifle, he at once
resolved to destroy the Indian, and thus prevent the
possibility of a future surprise. He accordingly proceeded up the river nearly to the First lake, where,
upon its northern shore, a point of land projected into
the river, now known among hunters and fishermen
as Indian's point. With his rifle carefully loaded
with two balls, Foster obtained a commanding position on the point, to await the arrival of the party.
After some delay in getting ready they left the dam
at the forge, Drid in a light bark canoe, Wood and
Chase in a large bark canoe, and the fishing party,
consisting of four persons, in a boat.

DEATH OF THE INDIAN TRAPPER.

See page 215.

The Indian, fearing no doubt from the morning's encounter and Foster's threat, that his personal safety was in jeopardy, kept his little craft near that of Wood and Chase. At length the party neared the point, at which its present occupant knew the white hunters must land to get some concealed traps. The fishing party rowed on as the canoes put in for the shore, and passing the point they discovered the old trapper in the bushes, and pointing in the direction of the bushes, they said to the hunters, *" there's old Foster !"* This announcement caused the Indian, who was then between the other canoe and the shore, to change his position, and take the lake side of his companions. The object of Foster's visiting the point was rightly divined by the white trappers, who landed and obtained their traps without loss of time, and put off from the shore, when Drid placed his canoe along side of theirs, so as to bring himself about midway between them, if possible to endanger their lives should a shot be attempted at himself.

Although Foster was several rods distant from the canoes, still the position of his foe did not secure his safety. The Indian's eye caught a glimpse of the fearful figure in the bushes just as the rifle was poised, and he threw up his arms in terror at the moment of the explosion. Both bullets entered his left side near the arm pit, passed through his heart and went out just below the right arm. They entered in the same spot, but left two places of egress opposite. The

Indian fell backwards, with his head and shoulders in the water, his feet and legs remaining in the canoe. He fell so dead that his position continued unchanged, the fairy craft preserving the cradling motion communicated to it by his fall, for some length of time after the spirit of its owner had winged its flight,

"To range the circuit of the sky."

The party in company with the Indian at the time of his death, either from fear or some other motive, did not offer to touch the body, but returned as speedily as possible to the place of starting. Leaving their boats, several proceeded directly to Foster's house, where they found him lying on a bed. The distance from the dam to Indian's point by water is greater than by land, and the old trapper having finished his morning's work, had gained his own dwelling, wiped out his rifle and prepared it for other game, ere the messengers arrived there. Foster expressed some surprise at seeing the party return so soon, and enquired what brought them back. He was answered, that a dead man was up the lake, the Indian Drid, and they desired him to go up and aid in getting him down. Agreeably to the request, Foster went up with the party to get the body, and himself took it into the boat, as the rest seemed afraid to touch it. He also aided in burying it, near the Indian's former residence. For killing this Indian, Foster was arrested soon after, by the authorities of

Lewis county; but when it was ascertained that the scene of blood was not within the jurisdiction of that county, he was removed from Martinsburg to Herkimer, where he gave bail for his appearance when required, and returned to his family.

NOTE, *explanatory of the engraving.* A friend who made a little drawing of the Fulton chain of lakes, to give the writer an idea of the position of the parties, inadvertently placed the point on the south side of the lake, which led to an error in the cut representing this scene, as the point is on the north side. The cut, though an ideal one, is said (by persons who have been on the ground) to give a very striking representation of the point, as Foster came out between two trees. A row of fir trees are seen in the distance, said to be more numerous than are here represented. The cut is rather a spirited one, and if the reader will imagine the point transposed to the opposite shore, and the position of the parties changed accordingly, he will get a good idea of the tragic scene.

CHAPTER XV

Having been indicted for murder, at a court of general sessions, in Herkimer county, on the third day of February, 1834, for killing the Indian Drid, or, as called in the indictment, Peter Waters; Nathaniel Foster was arraigned for trial at the circuit court held in that county on the fifteenth day of September following. The trial, which lasted nearly two days, was one of very great interest, and drew together an immense crowd of anxious spectators. Several individuals, some of whom were hunters, were subpœnaed to prove the quarrelsome disposition of the Indian killed by Foster; but they were not called upon the stand.

The court consisted of his honor, Hiram Denio, circuit judge, and Jonas Cleland, John B. Dygert, Abijah Osborn, and Richard Herendeen, judges of the bench of common pleas. After setting aside *eleven* jurors, who were challenged on the ground of having prejudged the cause, the following jurors were impanneled: Jacob Davis, John Harder, Henry Ostrander, James F. Fox, William Bouck, Peter Rickert, William Shoemaker, James Shoemaker, Lester Green, Nicholas A. Staring, Earl Trumbull, and Peter Bell. From the fact that so great a number of jurors were disqualified for the reason assigned, we may properly infer that the circumstances which induced Foster to take the Indian's life, were generally known; and it may be questioned whether any twelve freeholders, called promiscuously from the county, would have rendered a different verdict from that given by the jury impanneled.

James B. Hunt (district attorney), and Simeon Ford, were counsel for the prosecution. The prisoner was defended by E. P. Hurlbut, with whom were associated J. A. Spencer, A. Hackley and Lauren Ford Mr. Hunt opened the cause by observing that the prisoner was arraigned for murder, a rare crime in that county; stating in a brief and pertinent manner, the facts he expected to show in the progress of the trial. Having cited from the statute laws what would and what would not be justifiable homicide, he adduced the following testimony:

DAVID CHASE, sworn.—Was at West Brunswick on the 17th of September last; there saw Peter Waters; knows the prisoner; saw him also that morning. Jonathan Tyler, William Tyler, Hiram Thomas, and Nelson Stimpson, started together in one boat to go up the lake; Wood and witness were in a bark canoe; Waters was in a canoe [of bark] alone; they started from the forge in company, and kept up the pond, east, until they came to a point of land about two miles from the forge, when they stopped to get their traps; witness and Wood were going to trap with the Indian in partnership; Waters's boat was six feet from wit-

ness and along side; the other boat was opposite four
or five rods. At this point of land, First lake commenced; as Wood stepped out to get the traps, witness heard a rattling in the bushes and looked up the
lake, thinking it was birds; turned his head and kept
watch; saw Foster, he was bent over a little, ap-
parently, going sideways; saw him while passing, a
distance of six or eight feet; had no doubt as to the
person. Wood took up a load of traps and brought
them to the canoe; does not know but he went again;
thinks he brought them in two loads; went back out
of sight half a minute; came out very quick; clenched
up the traps and threw them in the boat in a hurry,
and then moved off; Indian, as he heard a rattling in
the bushes, shoved his boat close up to witness; they
shoved off from shore and brought the Indian between
witness and Wood, in his own canoe; the gun then
was heard to go off upon the shore on the point; witness turned and Indian was falling backwards from
his canoe; made two motions with his hands; his
legs stuck in canoe and thus he died. Witness turned
to shore and saw Foster on shore in the direction of
the report, and where he saw him before; witness and
Wood had each a rifle; neither of their rifles were
discharged. Witness called to his companions and
said ' *here is a dead man.*' Waters had no fire-arms;
an hour from leaving forge to that time, he thinks,
but is not certain. Witness examined the body; under the left arm, about two inches, the balls entered,

and came out about six inches below the right arm; these killed him; gun was very heavily loaded; saw no other person on shore but Foster; Wood was in the boat before gun was fired.

Cross-examined.—It was two or three rods from their boat to where Foster stood; after report saw him in the same open spot again; did not see any gun in his hand either way he passed; did not notice any smoke; was pretty badly frightened.

NELSON STIMPSON sworn.—Was present 17th Sept. last; saw Waters and prisoner; mentions same party in boat named by previous witness; Wood and Chase were in one canoe and the Indian in another alone; went up two miles; is not acquainted there; thinks it may have been an hour before the catastrophe; saw a wake in the bushes; boat passed along but Wood's boat had stopped; witness saw Foster pass ten feet partly bent over (lurking) in the bushes; witness and his party were hallooed to at a distance of thirty rods from this, and after the report of a gun, came back and found Indian's head and part of his body lying in the water, and his legs in the canoe; did not see any gun in Foster's hands; did not examine body; Chase fired off his gun two charges; it was a *double shotter*, and appeared to have been loaded sometime; Wood discharged his gun; did not see Foster after report of gun; saw no smoke there.

WILLISTON TYLER, sworn.—Saw Foster on the 17th of Sept. last at Foster's house; saw Waters at the

19*

forge same day; went up from forge with party
spoken of; they went up to the point (say two miles)
in company; Wood and Chase together; Waters
alone; all making to this point of land; W. and C.
went a-shore; Stimpson spoke "There goes Foster;"
witness looked and saw a man there that he (witness)
called Foster; they rowed round the point out of
sight of the rest; Foster was walking a little stooped
and sideways; rowed thirty yards, heard report of a
gun; heard Wood or Chase hallo "come back as
quick as you can;" they went back, and Chase said
they had a dead man there; Waters's head and
shoulders were in the water and his legs in the canoe;
did not examine his body; two holes in the shirt under one arm; examined guns of the others and found
them charged as stated by the other witnesses; saw
no gun in Foster's hands; bushes two feet high; was
five or six rods distant when he saw him; witness
and Wood went to Foster's house; found Johnson on
the hill after this in a house occupied by Wood and
Chase carrying in some hay; Johnson lived with
Foster; this was four miles from the place of execution; did not see Foster after report of gun until
at Foster's house same day, four miles from point.

Cross-examined.—Went to Foster's house on the
way from point; found him there lying on the bed;
did not know Foster until the night before; he was a
stranger until then; Foster may have passed eight or
ten feet in witness's sight while they were going

along in the boat; there were bushes there but not so high as elsewhere; some were ten feet high; saw side of his face; judge of him partly from his general appearance; he was without a hat; was bald-headed; he was leaning the same way they were passing; stooped; did not see his hands; Foster was between two and three rods from the point which was to the left; when they found Foster he was lying on a bed; saw his gun in a corner of the room; does not know whether it was loaded or not; was nothing peculiar in Foster's dress; witness was not rowing when he saw Foster in the space; neither saw him before nor after he was at that point.

Direct testimony resumed.—Foster discharged and reloaded his gun before he started; this was about one quarter of a mile from Wood's house; Foster's house is on the right-hand side of outlet; and he saw him at the other side of the outlet; the nearest way to get to that place from Foster's house was to cross the bridge at the forge; had a conversation with Foster after he fired the gun and reloaded; witness inquired " have you shot the deer? " " No, that d—d Indian," showing on his wrist a scratch and blood; " have had a squabble with the Indian and he cut this spot; and if it had not been for Mr. Wood and Chase the Indian would have killed me; go either forward or behind; I shall not go fishing."

Cross-examined.—The place called the forge has not been used in many years; this is about eighteen

miles from any settlers; the outlet is from ten to fifteen rods wide; they talked of going to the Fourth
lake; lives in Leyden, Lewis county; the houses were
dwelling-houses erected by some past settlers.

WILLIAM S. WOOD sworn. — Knows the prisoner;
knew the Indian killed; was with Chase; did not see
Foster there [on the point] that day; went ashore to
get traps; heard the report of a gun; the Indian was
killed; saw no person in the bushes; heard no noise;
was very busy; got into the boat about as quick as
usual; was about three or four yards from Waters
when shot; Waters's boat lying still; witness was in
his boat when the gun was fired; did not see Foster
at all up there; saw him at home lying on his bed
after the killing; also before that at my house in the
morning; it was three fourths of an hour from the
time Foster left my house in the morning to the gun
report; not far from 9 A.M. when gun was fired;
about four miles from my house to the point.

For the prisoner.—The counsel for the defence here
offered to show that the premises where the Indian
was killed, were leased on the 4th of May, 1830, by
Caleb Lyon, for himself and as agent, to David and
Solomon Maybee; that the Maybee's went in and occupied under the lease, until the 26th of February,
1832; at which time David Maybee assigned the lease
for the sum of ten dollars, to the defendant, who took
possession and occupied under said lease until the
alleged murder was committed; at which time his

right had not expired. Judge Denio said that the defendant was presumed to occupy in his own right; and rejected the evidence offered as conventional.

WILLIAM S. WOOD recalled.—Has known the Indian eighteen months; was twenty-eight years old as he said; was a short able-bodied Indian; have hunted with him.

Counsel.—Did you ever hear this Indian threaten to kill Foster?

Counsel for prosecution.—Objected to, on the ground of irrelevancy.

Counsel for defence.—We urge the evidence, because it is competent, and goes to establish the fact of " imminent danger," to the life of Foster; and whether it sufficently establishes that fact is for the jury to determine.

Judge Denio said the testimony was inadmissible, and Judge Dygert was of his opinion; but when the whole Bench was appealed to, behold! the other three judges were for admitting it; and for the first time and probably the last time in his official station, his Honor found himself over-ruled by the Common Pleas judges.

Witness.—Has heard Indian at different times threaten to kill Foster. " He said ·Foster was calking his boat (this was in July) and he had a mind to go up and tomahawk Foster and throw him into the the river; but his squaw took hold of his coat and persuaded him to go to his shantee;" he said he had

a notion to go back; "If I can not do it now," said
he, "the first time I catch him alone I'll be the death
of him." This was a year ago last July; Foster
came to witness's house the morning of Sept. 17, to
see how long before witness would be ready to start
up the lakes; witness lives on south side of outlet,
and Foster on the north side; a mile from witness's
to Foster's; one and three-fourths miles from witness's
house to the forge; Foster came to the door, (Chase
and witness were eating breakfast). "How long before you will be ready to go?" asked Foster. "In an
hour or perhaps less," we answered. Foster turned
round to go out; Indian was standing at the fire-place
and said, "What you call me d—m rascal, d—m
Indian, so much for?" "Because I am a mind to,"
he answered; the Indian sprung upon Foster, took
him by the neck and drew his knife upon him, which
Foster knocked out of his hand upon the floor; Indian
said, "You old devil, I got you now, I kill you;"
witness then sprang and grabbed the Indian, and
Chase secured Foster's rifle; then witness relieved
Foster, who stepped to the door, saying, "Where's
my rifle." Indian said, "Where's my tomahawk?
d—m old cuss!" Witness said, "You want no tomahawk; be peaceable;" said Indian after Foster went
out, "Now Foster wont live to see another Christmas!
I'll kill him, d—m old cuss!" It was an Indian
hunting knife which he carried by his side; in a
sheath in his belt; knife looked as if it had been a

case-knife, ground off to a peak and pointed; Foster
was cut across his wrist and face in the flesh; Indian
belonged to the St. Regis tribe, a Canada Indian;
British Indian stout and athletic; after Foster went
out Indian said, " I should have killed him then if it
had not been for Chase and witness;" three-fourths
of an hour after this, Indian was killed; witness was
with Indian about six weeks, and left him.

Cross-examined.—Did not tell Foster the last threat
at witness's house; about a quarter of an hour after
this they started; were about half an hour in walking
up to forge; Waters went with witness and Chase;
were not long at forge; found others at forge; about
twenty or thirty minutes at forge, can't say precisely;
took perhaps twenty or thirty minutes to go to point;
never told Foster of any of the threats; witness and
Chase and Indian were going trapping together;
Chase was not in first partnership of witness and
Indian.

Counsel for defence.—Object to evidence of defendant's confessions, as opening the case anew after
the prosecution had rested; overruled; witness went
to Foster's house, and Foster went back with them
[to the lake to get the body]; did not hear Foster
say any thing.

Judah C. Marsh sworn.—Was at Foster's between
the 15th and 20th of August, a year ago; Foster
asked Indian for seventeen shillings, pay for sundry
articles; Indian offered to pay a part but not all;

Foster said, "I've let you have articles to keep you from starving; Indian meal and potatoes which I have carried on my back seventeen miles;" Indian offered to pay a part; "why not pay the whole? I've dealt with you like a brother; I've heard you threatened to take my life; you came once where I was fixing a boat (I've been informed) on purpose to kill me; you came once to my house with your rifle loaded and called me to the door to kill me;" "yes;" "why do you want to hurt me? I never wanted to hurt you; I would as soon kill a white man as an Indian; I would not kill you for a million of worlds;" Indian asked how soon he would come to the Seventh lake; said "You must never come there; if you do you never come back again alive; we're now on Brown's tract and out of the way of all law; if you kill me you kill me; if I kill you I kill you;" Foster said, "I agree to no such thing; am afraid of your sly Indian way of fighting; I have heard that you threatened to kill several at Lake Pleasant; and a man by the name of Lyon; I shall complain of you and have you taken care of; I am afraid of my life;" Indian said, "Complain and be d—d, me meet you;" Indian threatened to kill David Foster (son of defendant) if he came to the Racket lake; Indian started to the door, took up his tomahawk; prisoner stepped into the house, and Indian let his tomahawk drop after prisoner was out of sight.

Cross-examined.—Is a son-in-law of defendant;

resides at Auburn; went there last July; don't recollect the amount of flour, &c., that Foster called over; when items were mentioned once he said it was cheap enough; Indian spoke tolerably good English; some broken; witness staid but eight or ten days on tract after this; David left after October; witness advised defendant to come away; he said he should come as soon as he possibly could; for he considered his life in danger every moment; Seventh lake is some fifteen miles from Foster's; Indian had a squaw and two children: squaw went back to St. Regis; defendant and wife, son and son's wife, witness and his wife, and Johnson were in the house, and three children, two of David's and one of witness's.

Direct testimony resumed.—Foster said, " as soon as I can get the old lady away, I shall go;" she was rather feeble; she was not able to go with witness; wanted to wait till sleighing; David's wife was unwell; a numb palsy affection.

ABNER BLACKMAN, sworn.—Knew the Indian named and Foster; Foster was narrating a story about Indian's coming to his house; he said the " Indian had loaded his rifle and come to his door to shoot him; Indian said it was well for him that he was not at home, as he came to shoot him; he would have put a bullet through him; he (Foster) would have seen his God in two minutes;" witness told him that the Indian had told him the same thing, as to his coming

to his house to shoot him; has heard the Indian
threaten the life of Foster.

Cross examined.—Had a conversation with Foster;
he said the Indian had threatened to kill him a good
many times; and in different ways; he had spoke of
not being afraid of Indian, but he was really afraid,
and looked behind every old log and bush expecting
the Indian ready to kill him; he trembled as he
walked; said he would have been glad to have got
away, if he could conveniently; but his property and
family were there; his son's wife unwell, and could
not be moved then; he said like this, " he had a gun
that had always told him the truth, and he had pushed
a bull off the bridge;" he said they came down to his
house for him to go up; he went, and found Waters
in the canoe; no one dared to take hold of him; he
took hold of him and pulled him up; did not tell him
how the Indian got killed, nor that he killed him;
was talking about hunting and killing deer when he
said he pushed the bull off the bridge; and, perhaps,
about the Indian also; were not talking about the
Indian when he said his gun always told the truth;
has seen Indian at witness's house; heard Indian say
he belonged to St. Regis tribe; witness lives in Greig,
Lewis county; conversation in that town on witness's
way to and from Herreshoff's; Greig is nineteen or
twenty miles from Herreshoff place.

JOSHUA HARRIS, sworn.—Lives in Grieg, Lewis
county; was a magistrate in September last. The

defence offered to prove by this witness that Foster applied to him to get a warrant, and complained that he was in fear of losing his life; that the Indian had threatened to kill him repeatedly; had intimated several times that Indian had threatened to kill him.

Witness.—Has conversed with Indian; has heard him say repeatedly, he would kill Foster; " if Foster goes up to Fourth, Fifth, Sixth or Seventh lake again, he will never return alive if I can catch him there;" the Indian roused up, " Foster, how many deer you kill ?" " Don't know." " D—m him, I'll pile him up with my deer by-and-by;" at another time in harvest, he said, " I'll serve Foster, d——d old cuss, as I have a number of the d——d Yankees, I will take his life, or butcher him;" the threats were often repeated; he would rave against Foster.

Cross examined.—Indian was there a year ago last October, and often, until killed, shantied [lived in a shantee or hut] on witness's farm, forty rods from house, about two months; was about twenty-eight years of age; has conversed with Foster since the death; he intimated as much as though he had killed the Indian; said " he was not guilty of shedding innocent blood; what he had done was done in his own defence;" he was talking about his being taken for killing the Indian, and his trial.

ASA BROWN, sworn.—Knows Foster; knew Indian; has heard the Indian threaten the life of Foster; Indian came to witness's house in Greig, Lewis county, in the fore part of August, a year ago; between the first and twentieth; he said he did not want to say much about old Foster; he d——d old cuss; Mrs. Foster good old woman; he went on and stated how well she had used him, and squaw, and little pappooses; then he said, after the favors, "old Foster, d—m old cuss, want to make me pay for it;" he said he should not; he meant to kill old Foster; "me get good rifle; me shoot straight; me put ball right through the heart." I said, "Peter, you must not talk such language as that, for you are liable to be had up and confined." "Me care not a d—m for that; no law on Brown's tract." Said I, if there is no law on the tract, there is here, and will put you where the dogs wont bite you. "Me no care for dat; me kill d—m old cuss." Witness advised him to peace with Foster. "Mrs. Foster use me well; good woman; Foster d—m old cuss; put ball through his heart." Never saw him alive after that.

Cross examined.—Saw Foster about two weeks after this, and told him what the Indian said; Foster replied, "If the Indian would come in sight, and shoot quicker than he did, then he (Foster) would be killed; if not, not; he had a rifle that never told a lie; and said he had heard a great many such threats from the Indian, and felt in danger of losing his life when traversing the forest for his traps; he said his eyes were continually on the watch, for fear the Indian was skulking about to shoot him;" has seen Foster

but once since the Indian's death; heard no confession
of killing.

WILLARD JOHNSON, sworn.—Knew Foster and Indian; resided on Brown's tract; has heard Indian
threaten Foster to kill him; the first difficulty was
about a boat; Foster said, " you should not do so; if
you want a boat, ask for it." Indian said, " d—m
old Foster, I'll put the ball there," pointing his finger
in center of his forehead. The next, Foster had let
him have things, and Peter refused to pay; about two
or three months after, can't say exactly, Foster said,
" this is the usage I get, I backed in these things and
paid my money for them." Waters flourished his
hatchet; Foster went in quick, and if he had not, he
would have struck the hatchet between Foster's
shoulders. Again, the morning before Waters was
shot, witness was at his own place, a mile from Foster's, when he saw Waters; talked with him; said
" go along with me and make peace with Foster;"
" old Foster I will kill, if I can get him out to shoot
him. I'll butcher him in his bed; I know which side
of the bed he lays; and if you hear anything there,
don't you come nigh, you may get hurt; old woman
is good; I wont hurt her; but you must not come nigh
me." [The Indian requested Johnson to tell Mrs.
Foster to keep her own side in the bed.]

Cross examined.—Thinks he told it to Foster the
night before the killing; every time witness saw Waters, he would enquire when he was going home; and

witness did not know what to make of it; an Indian
is an Indian; Foster went to swear the peace; Indian
was a crabbed sort of a fellow; had no conversation
with Foster since Indian was killed.

The counsel for the prisoner offered to prove threats
of the Indian to kill Foster, by several other persons,
but was overruled, and the defence rested.

For the prosecution.

WILLISTON TYLER, sworn.—Was at Foster's the
evening before killing; he said the Indian had threatened his life; but he was not afraid of the d——d
black blood, unless it were by secret revenge; he said
if he could catch him out any where, he would put
him where the dogs would not bite him; they were
talking about his complaining against Indian; he said
it would be of no use: he would go into the woods
before they could take him; but if he should catch
him out, he would put him where the dogs wouldn't
bite him; in going back up to the point where killed,
witness asked the question whether he was standing
or sitting the moment he was shot; Foster replied,
" Sitting down; why I say he was sitting down is,
that they always did sit down, and never stand up in
a bark canoe;" Foster went to the place where Indian was killed; they covered up Indian; went back
next morning and re-covered it [the grave]; might
have been four hours from time witness saw Foster
last to killing.

Cross examined.—Wood told Foster, " I've bad

news to tell you; Peter's dead;" Foster asked, " Did
he die in a fit ?" Wood informed Foster that he was
shot and at what place, in answer to his inquiry; pre-
sumes they generally sit in a bark canoe.

DAVID CHASE, sworn.—Don't remember every item
of the scuffle; they were fixing to go away that morning; Foster came in his house; said " Good morning;"
witness was busy packing up things to go away;
Foster was eight feet from a small fire place; witness
about ten feet away, packing; Indian spoke, but don't
know what he said; Foster answered, but don't remember what; Indian pitched upon him and grabbed
Foster; witness rose up and took Foster's rifle and
set it up side of the house, about twelve feet from
where they clenched; got back and Indian had thrown
Foster; witness got his right hand, and Wood his
left hand, and told Indian to let loose; Indian rose up;
one called for his tomahawk and the other for his
rifle; Foster went out, and witness said stay and get
your things; he did so; witness went into the house,
got his hat and rifle, and gave them to him; after this
Foster said, " How long before you will be along ?"
As witness turned to go back, he saw blood on his
own hand; this was pretty early in the morning; it
was near noon when the shooting happened; between
three and four hours; Indian, Wood and witness were
going trapping.

Cross examined.—Did not see a knife; as they took
them apart, Indian was talking fast; and when he

came back he was cooled down; Wood got to Indian and Foster first; had no conversation with Foster since.

NELSON STIMPSON, sworn.—Saw the Indian clench Foster; Foster went into the house and spoke to Chase and Wood; asked them what time they would be up the lake; Indian " How many times more will you call me d——d liar ?" Foster, " Do you want to pick a quarrel with me this morning, you black son of a bitch ?" The Indian sprang and clenched him, and jammed the door too, and witness saw no more of it; saw Foster as he came out; he told witness to go down to the forge; four hours from time of scuffle to killing; had some conversation with Foster coming from tract next day.

FRANCIS E. SPINNER, sworn. There was some conversation when Foster came down from Martinsburg; he said something; don't think he said he killed him; witness advised him to say nothing; he said there would probably be no dispute about the facts; there would be proof enough; thinks he said the Indian suspected something, and put up his hands; he said he examined the body, and in examination found he was shot with two balls; he said his rifle never told a lie; don't know whether this latter observation was in that conversation; he said they were afraid to take care of the body, and he went up; found it was a centre shot; a hole under one arm, close up, and two on the opposite side; is not clear, but he may have said that his arm must have been thrown up, or the ball could not have entered there.

The testimony having closed, Mr. HURLBUT opened the defence to the jury, and his associates, SPENCER and HACKLEY, summed up. The cause is said, by spectators, to have been very ably conducted on both sides.

Judge DENIO, who was from another county, a stranger to the parties and unbiased by the prejudices which made either for or against the prisoner, determined to try him fairly and impartially. There can be no greater virtue in any tribunal, than that of *impartiality* in the administration of justice. Indeed, when other motives influence judicial decisions than those of equity, and power is warped to favor, rapine and anarchy stalk the earth unbridled, honesty wears weeds, and disinterested benevolence folds herself up in a garment of sackcloth.

The following is a brief memorandum made by Mr. Hurlbut, of Judge Denio's charge to the jury.

" The court advise the jury, that the law applies to the region of country where the offence was committed. The law pervades every section of the country. There is no place where crime is not cognizable.

" In regard to the race of men to which the deceased belonged, when the question is, *what will authorize the taking of the life of such an one?* we answer, no one can take such life without such reasons as would authorize the taking of the life of any other human being.

" There are two cases of killing which is not murder. *First,* when there is killing in a sudden affray:
it is manslaughter. If, at the time of the rencontre
in the morning, before his passion cooled, the prisoner
had shot the Indian, it would have been manslaughter
only. But if his passion cooled, and contrivance or
malice was aroused, it would have been murder.
Second, a man has a right to kill another in self defence. The court would not abridge that privilege.
If Wood's account be true, if the Indian came with
his knife drawn and offered a fatal blow, and Foster
had not time to retreat, he would have been author-
ized to shoot him dead. That would have been a
legitimate case of self defence. The law of this
country is not, when a man is out of immediate danger, but has a secret enemy, that he has a right to
kill him. This would not be a good code of laws if
that were so. In a state of nature, it would have
been morally right to have taken the Indian's life in
this case. The principle of self defence applies only
to the case of present attack upon the accused. If
Foster seriously believed he was right and justified,
it makes no difference in law, morally it does.

" These views you have a right to overlook. You
are not bound to pay any further regard to this
opinion, than the superior means of the court of possessing information may entitle it to."

The jury retired.

Before the trial commenced, Mr. Hurlburt received

from Foster the most urgent instructions to convict him of murder or acquit him altogether. He protested against being found guilty of manslaughter, as he dreaded imprisonment, even for the shortest term, worse than death.

The jury, after a deliberation of two hours, returned into court with a verdict of *acquittal*. As they entered and took their seats, the " cloud of witnesses " became hushed; the moment was one of intense interest; and to so great a tension had the feelings of the old gentleman been drawn by the excitement his precarious fate had invoked, that his spirit seemed hovering between life and death. Says Mr. Hurlbut, " When the jury came in with their verdict, he was insensible; and it was with some difficulty he was roused to consciousness, so as to understand the verdict. When the words *not guilty*, after being two or three times repeated to him by his counsel, struck his senses fairly, he rose up, stretched out both hands wide over the heads of the spectators, and exclaiming, ' *God bless you all ! God bless the people !* ' rushed out of the court room, and strode home his well known hunter's pony."

A murmur of applause ran through the crowd, the sympathies of which were nearly all enlisted in his favor, as the *old trapper* left the court room for the street, to which he was followed by scores of people of all ages, anxious to offer their congratulations. At Little Falls, great was the rejoicing and clapping of hands, when the news reached that place that Foster was free; indeed his enlargement met with one universal burst of approbation throughout the county. Not because he had killed a poor Indian, and been acquitted; but because he was not to be hung for having killed a man in his own defense, *as they viewed it.* There can remain little doubt, when it is known as a characteristic of the red man that he *never forgives* a known or imagined injury, and seldom a grudge, especially one he has determined to punish with death, but that he would have killed Foster " before Christmas," if Foster had not slain him.* But we leave this case to HIM who set his own mark on the first murderer, *Cain;* and to whose mercy *Moses* was subjected, when he slew and concealed his man in the sands of Egypt.

* The celebrated Joseph Brant, once found it necessary to kill his own son. The latter had taken umbrage at his parent for some cause, and on an occasion, pursued him with a knife, bent on his destruction. Brant retreated to the corner of a room, armed with a tomahawk; and satisfied the son would execute his threats, as he rushed upon him, the father sunk the fatal tomahawk in his head.—*Isaac H. Tiffany.*

CHAPTER XVI

About the time of Foster's trial, to an interrogatory from the Hon. Charles Gray, whether he did not consider the lives of the white hunters as greatly endangered, when he directed the balls between them only a few feet apart, which penetrated the heart of his victim? he replied, " No, not at all! my old rifle never made so great a miss as that! "

Remarking to Maj. Stoner my surprise, that Foster should have dared. to fire between two white men in a changing position at a third person, the old Natty Bumpo replied, " Poh! Foster would have shot the Indian's eye out had he desired to! The truth is, either of us could send a bullet just about where we chose to." At an inanimate and fixed target they were not so remarkably celebrated as marksmen, but give them game moving sufficiently to excite their anxiety, and these two modern Nimrods may be said to have been *a dead shot.* At a reasonable distance they would have driven an apple every time from the head of some young Tell, and scarcely displaced a hair, provided the head was moving.

When a sufficient length of time had transpired after this Indian's death for intelligence of it to go to his friends near the river St. Lawrence, a brother-in-

21

law of his, who was a chief of the St. Regis tribe, and a very likely man, came down to Brown's tract to remove his sister. He said the deceased was at times a bad fellow, and had been expelled from their tribe for some misdemeanor. He had even threatened the life of this chief more than once; and he did not express any regret that he was killed; on the contrary, he said he thought Foster was justifiable in taking his life under the peculiar circumstances. Drid's squaw was present when the body was brought down, but instead of manifesting sorrow she smiled, and with a pair of scissors she cut out a piece of his blanket or shirt, having in it a ball hole, and placed it carefully away in a work-pocket. Her brother had the body taken up and interred in Indian style; and before its reburial he cut out that part of the blanket having the remaining bullet holes in it; which he carried home with him. Foster had been sent to Martinsburg before this Indian arrived; but previous to leaving the tract, he advised the members of the Foster family still living there, to leave the place, as they were innocent of Drid's death; and it was possible some of his blood might attempt to revenge his death. He took his sister and her children back with him, that he might provide for their wants.

After the death of Drid, Foster visited Brown's tract but once. He feared the Indians might catch him napping; indeed it was said that several were there in wait for him, but a correspondent who says he was there the next season, saw no Indians. Foster removed with his family to Boonville, Oneida county. From thence he went to reside for several years in the north part of Pennsylvania, where he again followed his favorite pursuits. *His mind seemed never at rest after killing this Indian,* says a friend, *and he would not,* after his return to Boonville from Pennsylvania, *venture out of doors in the dark.* He died at the house of Mr. Edgerton, his son-in-law, in the western part of Boonville (now Ava), Oneida county, in March, 1841; at the age of about 74 years. His widow died at the residence of her son, Amos Foster, in Palatine (near Stone Arabia), Montgomery county, in December, 1844.

It is the belief of very many of Foster's acquaintances, that Drid was not the only Indian with whom he had had a fatal rencontre. The following story furnished the author by Mr. Frederick Petrie, comes so well authenticated and corroborated, that there can be very little doubt of its truth.

Before the American Revolution there dwelt about two miles from the present village of Little Falls, an Indian named Hess, who took an active part in that contest as a hireling of Britain; and who undoubtedly was one of the most cruel and blood thirsty of his race. Some ten or twelve years after the war, this Indian returned to his former hunting grounds, to prosecute his favorite employment. A country inn at this period was, for the spread of knowledge to be

smoked in and watered, a kind of "circulating me-
dium," a place where in the absence of our now
thousands of newspapers, the people of the surrounding country met to learn news from quidnuncs; and
as Little Falls, with possibly her dozen (much scattered) insignificant dwellings, was then a place of
some notoriety, on account of her *new* inland locks,
and *old* moss-clad rocks, the bar-roon of the village
one-story tavern became the place where all the classic events of olden time, and all the improvements of
modern days, particularly those which aided the river
sailor in navigating the far famed Mohawk, were,
sans parliamentary forms, freely discussed.

On a certain occasion Foster met the Indian Hess
in the bar-room of the Little Falls tavern, and observing that his dress a-la-mode was that of a hunter, he
attempted to engage him in a conversation. He
feigned ignorance of the English language, however,
until his white competitor in beaver skins oiled his
tongue freely at the bar, when lo! the seal upon his
lips was broken, and he spoke English tolerably well.
The two hunters soon after left the village and tra-
veled some distance together, when the conversation
turned upon Revolutionary scenes: boasting of his
individual exploits on the frontiers of New York,
the Indian exhibited a tobacco pouch. "This,"
said the crafty warrior, "me got in the war. Me
kill white woman; rip open belly; find young pap-
poose; skin him some; make pouch!" He also

opened the box in the breech of his rifle, and exhibited some evidence he there carried of the number of prisoners and human scalps taken by him in the war; the tally ran up to the almost incredible number of *forty-two.* Just before parting, the Indian inquired of Foster his name, and on hearing it he exclaimed, " *Ha! Nat Foster! you bad man; you kill Indians!*"

On the Indian's making the recognition of him, Foster thought he detected in his look and manner a lurking devil that seemed to say, " if ever you fall in my power you will feel it;" and hearing himself called an *Indian killer*, he believed the old hunter, if opportunity presented, would not scruple to take his life. The boast of murdered innocence drew a frown across the sunburnt brow and stern features of the young hunter, that seemed to send back defiance to the red man's look of meditated death. They parted soon after, and if not as friends, certainly not as avowed enemies; but each no doubt felt apprehensive, that a second interview might not terminate so fortunately for them both; and certain it is, that one at least resolved not to be over-reached by the other.

Not long after the above incidents transpired, Foster was threading the forest alone, in the northerly part of Herkimer county, in the pursuit of game. In a secluded spot, he came unexpectedly upon and shot a moose cow. While securing the noble game, its mate, a most ferocious bull, attracted to the spot by the bellowing of the dam, attacked him with great

21*

fury. In a dodging fight, the hunter was obliged to
make some half a dozen shots in rapid succession.
Foster reloaded his rifle before he ventured to approach an animal that had been so tenacious of life,
although dying (he seldom changed his position in
the woods without a charge in his gun); and while
advancing to it, he was startled to hear a footstep
within pistol shot distance of him, and was possibly
not less surprised to find in the person of his new
visitant, the muscular form of the Indian Hess.

Supposing, as is presumed, that Foster's rifle was
unloaded, his recent acquaintance, who now experienced no difficulty in " murdering the King's English," at the end of a whoop that told credibly for his
lungs and the absence of balsams, shouted aloud,
" *Now Foster me got you! me kill you now!* " Between Hess and his intended victim there was a
marsh, over which was a fallen tree. Mounting the
log to approach the white hunter, with uplifted tomahawk and death-boding mien, the report of a rifle
again echoed amid the fir-tops of the forest, and up
sprang the Indian high in air from the log. A bullet
had plowed its way through his heart, and with a
guttural groan, the dark warrior fell dead upon the
marsh. Lest Hess might not be unattended in the
forest, the eagle-eyed marksman, whose rifle had not
only been quickly loaded but quickly discharged,
stamped the carcase of his victim deep into the mud.
Dark mystery hung over the fate of this lone hunter

for years. Many remembered that his disappearance was sudden and unexpected; and others that they had heard Foster say, shortly after his interview with him at Little Falls, *that he had met him once, and only once after that time.* He confidentially communicated, many years after, to Jacob I. Christman, with whom he was hunting, the fate of this unfortunate savage, for whom

> No solemn bell's metallic tongue
>   E'er toll'd its death note on the breeze :
> Zephyrs alone his requiem rung,
>   Where ivy green her mantle hung
>   Mid plumed and bowing trees.

Foster, although a man of undoubted veracity, when speaking of his own exploits, made use of aphorisms, or such unexplained expressions, as left them a mystery to his auditors. This was particularly the case where legal advantage could be taken of his sayings and doings; hence, it is impossible to arrive with positive certainty, as is believed, at some of the most interesting incidents in his life. On this point, says a correspondent, " Foster would occasionally tell some of his exploits, but in such a way you could hardly guess his meaning. For instance, " The best shot I ever made, I got two beaver, one otter, and fifteen martin skins; but I took the filling out of a blanket to do it !' And again, ' I was once in the woods, and saw an Indian lay down to drink at a brook; something was the matter; he dropped his face into the water and drowned; I thought I might as well take his fur, gun, blanket, &c., as leave them there to spoil.' "

Says the same correspondent, " On his way to jail, I saw Foster; he said to me, 'Brother B., *I am the man that pushed the bull off the bridge ; I never liked Indians !*' While confined at Herkimer, he was asked how he fared? He replied, " O, very well, only I don't like to be stall fed among *gentlemen !* "

About the time of Foster's trial, while some friends were speaking of his success as a hunter and extraordinary skill as a marksman, he said the greatest shot he ever made was at otters, securing *eighteen* of their valuable pelts at a single shot. Although the fame of the (then) old hunter was very great, this story seemed to stagger the faith of his most confidential auditors; and when one ventured to express a doubt as to the truth of the assertion, he explained as follows. In a hunting excursion he had once fallen in with an Indian, who carried upon his back eighteen otter skins; that he had no intention of harming the Indian; did not know that he had killed him; but that he never let an otter skin escape him *alive*. He fired; they all fell; he picked them up and came away.

In the latter part of his life, Foster's sight began to fail him. His brother, *Shubael Foster*, who is many years younger than Nathaniel, says he was deer hunting with the latter, not many years before his death, in St. Lawrence county, on the Oswegatchie,* in which excursion they killed *twenty.* Informant shot several before his brother got any; when they came together, the latter procured a good slice of venison, saying that *if he could get a piece of deer into him, he could see to shoot them.* During this hunt, they one day cornered a flock between them and a ledge, exposing the innocent creatures to their cross-fire. They drove the terrified animals from one to the other until they secured five of their number, four of which fell before the old rifle of the senior hunter. So much for eating a good steak of venison.

•Foster and Stoner were both remarkably expert at loading their rifles, but the former most so, at least if it became necessary to make several shots in hot haste, and at a short distance. Foster has been known repeatedly, upon a wager, to commence with his rifle unloaded and fire it off *six times in one minute.* This, to the reader, if a modern marksman and unaccustomed to taking game upon foot, seems incredible, but it is nevertheless true. While hunting he usually wore three rifle balls between the fingers of each hand, and invariably thus in the left hand, if he had

* *Os-we-gatchie* or *Ogh-swa-gatchie,* an Indian name, the historian JAMES MACAULEY, informed the author, which signifies *going* or *coming round a hill.* The great bend in the Oswegatchie river (or the necessity of it), on the borders of Lewis county, originated its significant name. An Indian tribe, bearing the name of the river, once lived upon its banks; but its fate, like that of many sister tribes, has been, to melt away before the progressive step of the Anglo-Saxon.

that number of balls with him.   He had a large bony hand, and having worn such jewels a long time, they had made for themselves cavities in the flesh, which concealed them almost as effectually as they were, when hid in the moulds in which they were run from the fused lead.   The superficial observer would not have noticed them.

Foster's quick shooting was in the days of flint locks.   He had a powder flask with a charger, and with six well pared balls between his fingers, he would pour in the powder, drop in a ball that would just roll down without a patch, and striking the breech of his gun with his hand, it was primed; soon after which the bullet was speeding to its mark. These rapid discharges could only be made at a short distance, as to make long shots it became necessary to patch the balls and drive them down with a rod, the latter being dispensed with in the former case.

Foster would make his six shots, so as to kill so many men, within one minute, at a distance not exceeding ten rods.   A regiment of such riflemen, in close action, would soon decide the fate of a battle.

In the second American war with Great Britain, the following incident, says *Shubael Foster*, took place in Manheim, Herkimer county.   A company of riflemen, under Capt. FORSYTH, passed through that town on their way from the Mohawk valley to the military lines between New-York and Canada, and encamped there over night to wash their clothes.

The celebrity of Foster, as a marksman, coming to the ears of Capt. Forsyth, as the hunter was in the vicinity, he had him called to the camp. The most expert rifleman in the company was a man named Robinson, from South Carolina. The Captain was desirous of seeing whether Foster or Robinson could make the most effective shots in a minute, at a target ten rods off, each commencing with unloaded rifles. They began to load at a given signal, and Foster sent six bullets into the target within the minute; his competitor putting the sixth bullet into his piece, as that of his own rifle sped to the mark. The whole company was astonished to see their fellow member—able, as was supposed, to make the most shots in a given time of any man in the world—fairly beaten by a New-York trapper. A murmur of applause ran through the ranks, and Foster at once became a *lion* in the camp. Surprised at the unexpected skill of a New-York woodsman, and anxious to secure his services, Capt. Forsyth offered Foster *thirty dollars* a month to join his company with the complimentary assurance *that he should eat at his own table;* but as Foster did not approve of the war, he could not be prevailed upon to adopt the life of a soldier.

When hunting, Foster would make his camp in forty-five minutes, where the snow was a foot deep. He usually set up two crotches, laid a pole across them, and others from thence to the ground upon the sides and one end; covering the whole with hemlock boughs. In front of the open end, for his own comfort and security against wild beasts, he built a good fire. Provisions placed under his head for a pillow at night, were often frozen hard in the morning. In cold weather, he carried a blanket, strapped upon his shoulders as a knapsack. He usually wore a hat, but at times a cap, and uniformly a coat when hunting; over his shoulders were strapped a powder horn and bullet pouch, of sufficient dimensions to warrant a lengthy hunt. He was always very careful to have a pocket compass with him when in the forest.

CHAPTER XVII.

Since the preceding chapters were written, Col. DANIEL C. HENDERSON, of Norway, has kindly furnished me with some interesting memoranda in the life of Jonathan Wright, a hunter previously named; and several incidents worthy of notice, of several others of like craft, who followed trapping many years ago on and contiguous to Brown's tract. From Henderson's manuscript I glean the following facts.

Jonathan Wright, or Jock, as he was called in the wilderness, was a native of Hinsdale, Cheshire county, New Hampshire; and of respectable parentage. He was about five feet ten inches in height, rather stoutly built, with a sallow complexion. In the latter part of his life, and when known to my correspondent, he had a very stooping gait, and a walk peculiarly his own; lifting his feet high as though treading upon something light. His peculiarity of motion was no doubt acquired by carrying, as silently as possible, heavy burthens upon his shoulders in the forest, such as traps, wild game, provisions, canoes, &c. He had a keen eye shaded by heavy brows; and upon the whole was rather good looking. He was a man of few words, but they were pithy and uttered with energy. His education was such as the common schools of New England afforded at that early day, he being a school-boy just before the Revolution.

But little is known of Wright's youthful days, except that he was rather eccentric; and early evinced a disposition to be alone in the woods, with his dog and gun. At the age of eighteen he had, in the pursuit of wild game and fur, reconnoitred the northerly part of his native state, knowing more, doubtless, of its topography than of its improvements. When our Revolutionary difficulties began, he was found among the champions of liberty; and five days before the Bunker Hill battle he arrived at the American camp near Boston, accompanied by a neighbor named Moffatt; both armed cap-a-pie for action. He was a volunteer under the brave Prescott, to aid in fortifying Bunker hill the night before the battle, in which he took an active part. When Wright got back to his quarters in the evening, almost exhausted, he heard a call for a guard to prevent surprise from the enemy, " There 's no danger of that," he exclaimed, " the rascals have enough to do to dress their shins and wrap up their fingers for the next twelve hours, without beating up our quarters. I shall sleep for the next ten hours without fear."

The reveille and tattoo savored too much of restraint for the tameless spirit of a hunter, and tiring of camp monotony Wright returned home, and did not again join the army until Arnold's retreat from

Quebec to Ticonderoga; when he there enlisted under
Capt. Whitcomb; preferring to perform scouting or
other hazardous duty. Capt. W. had been accused
of shooting Major Gordon, a British officer, and rifling
his pockets; of which act General Carlton complained, and demanded his trial for *murder.* The American officer in command did not think the act, which
was one of daring, demanded such a title; but viewed
it as a consequence of war, and soon the matter was
hushed.

While on duty at Fort Ticonderoga, Wright and
his captain went on a scout toward the lower end of
lake Champlain, where they unexpectedly fell in with
and captured two British officers well mounted. They
proved to be a pay-master and lieutenant; who, not
expecting a foe so far from the American camp, were
off their guard, and easily secured by their rifle-poised
captors. The horses could not be taken along, and
they were set free in the road, to return to their mas-
ters' former quarters. After the prisoners were dis-
mounted and disarmed, they inquired the names of
their more fortunate companions. At hearing the
name of Whitcomb the pay-master turned deadly
pale, and inquired with evident agitation, " Are you
the man who shot Major Gordon? "

" I suppose that I am; " replied the captain.
Wright, who witnessed the effect of this announcement, divined that a desperate effort might be made
by the prisoners to escape, and advanced with a

ready rifle to a commanding position; when he assured them they should have good quarters, and not
be injured unless they tried to escape; in which event
they would be sent to oblivion in a hurry! This assurance tended to quiet their fears, and soon the party
were threading a circuitous route for Ticonderoga.
The pay-master chanced to have no funds on his person, on which account he may have felt the more
secure. When the captures were made, the scout
were just out of provisions, and early the next morning, as Wright was the best runner, it was settled
that he should proceed to the fort with all possible
dispatch; obtain food, and return to succor the party,
which was to proceed up the lake shore. The adventure was carried out as anticipated, and in a few days
all arrived safely at Ticonderoga. Soon after, the
captives were exchanged.

Wright ever spoke highly of this lieutenant, whose
name is now forgotten. Just before they parted, the
latter addressed him as follows, " Wright, you have
been kind to us, and I shall always retain grateful
feelings toward you. We shall be down the next
campaign, and then you may rely on my friendship,
as you must and will be subjugated! "

" You go to the devil! " replied Wright. " If you
come again, death is your portion. You talk of subduing the States; *when you come again, you fetch
your coffins with you, for you 'll surely want them!* "

He continued with the northern army, acting much

of the time either as a scout or a spy, until after the surrender of Burgoyne. Some few days before that event, being on a scout in the vicinity of the British army, a violent rain-storm came on, and he sought a temporary shelter beneath the trunk of a leaning tree; with his blanket over his shoulders, and his rifle in a position to be kept dry. While thus situated, his quick ear detected amid the roaring elements, an approaching footstep; and looking up, he saw a large wolf just ready to spring upon him. He carefully raised his piece, and without bringing it to his shoulder, discharged it, the muzzle being within a few feet of the animal's head, which was literally blown off. Thus did he scalp one English ally.

Recollecting his former friend, the British lieutenant, Wright sought for him among the vanquished, and found him an object of commiseration. He had been wounded, and what with his sufferings and privations, had grown dejected; sick in body and mind; and did not readily recognize his former captor. When he did he saluted him with great emotion. Indeed, the meeting was such as caused the better feelings of both to mingle in a flow of tears. Wright was the first to regain his self-possession, and broke forth in a strain between seriousness and jesting much as follows:—" By ——! you are a lucky devil though. I supposed you long since dead, as I told you you would be at the end of this campaign; but I rejoice to find you still alive, and hope you may live to repent of

22*

your sins; but by the heavens, if I ever find you in arms against the States again, I will surely blow your brains to the four winds!"

Wright with no little trouble got his friend in a wagon and conveyed him to a place of security, where he was well cared for, and soon after they parted, as they supposed, for ever. The winter following, the lieutenant was retained with many other prisoners in Boston; and having occasion to visit that city in the mean time, Wright and his British friend again met; the latter then in good health and fine spirits. After several days of social intercourse the friends finally parted, but not until the lieutenant had pressed upon the acceptance of his guest numerous presents; with an assurance that no consideration would ever induce him to be found in arms again, against so brave and generous a people. Wright said in the latter part of his life, that of all the friends he ever met, this military foeman gave him the *heartiest welcome.*"

Wright took no active part in the war after 1777, but followed his favorite avocation of a hunter in the northerly part of New Hampshire and Vermont; which the neutrality of the latter state, then a territory in dispute, enabled him to do. Soon after the war, he, and a cousin of his, named Belden, who was usually called the *Rattle-snake hunter,* began to frequent the shores of lakes Champlain and George, and their inlets; as also the sources of the Hudson, in quest of fur. Belden bore a deadly hatred to rattle-snakes, and when near their haunts was continually warring with them; hence his significant appellation. The following incident attending his snake-killing, I shall give very nearly in my correspondent's own words.

" One day in early spring, as they were on the west shore of the lake near fort Ty., and upon a ledge of rocks; they came to a den just as the snakes had crawled from their winter slumber, and lay basking in the warm noon-day sun. Belden was dressed for hunting, having on a loose woolen frock retiring below the knee, with shoes and leggins to match. Armed with a long stick in one hand, and a short one in the other, Belden led the way to the snakes; and Wright followed with his companion's dog and gun. Belden's eyes flashed fire at the sight before him, and a smile on his lips betrayed that their snakeships' quarters would surely be beaten up. He began the onset striking and dealing death at every blow, jumping and springing from one to the other, in fear that some might take shelter in the rocks.

" In his eagerness, his foot slipped as he was aiming a blow at a monster that lay in a fighting attitude, and he fell forward. He tried to keep himself off from the dangerous reptile, but without effect, and it struck his frock near his chin, and hung fast by its fangs. Both fell down together, rolled off the ledge and down a declivity, some twelve feet, tumbling

over and over; the snake coming up at the last roll.
Belden bounded up, seized the snake round the neck,
loosened its fangs, and whipped it to death against
the rocks; as his sticks had been lost in the fight.
Wright often said this was the only time he ever saw
Belden either scared or even started by danger; but
the snakes had rest the remainder of the day."

The two friends followed trapping for several seasons in the region of country under consideration,
and until beaver began to grow scarce; for the reader
must not suppose that they were sole monarchs there;
Indian hunters were continually crossing their tracks.
As game grew scarce, however, they occasionally
hunted for a season as far eastward as the present
state of Maine.   While hunting in the neighborhood
of lake Champlain they u,ed a light skiff to coast
with, and navigate streams.   On one occasion when
they had moored their little barque in some safe nook,
they set off to visit their traps in different directions;
to meet at night at the starting point.   Wright returned just at sunset much fatigued, and as his comrade was not there, he deposited his game, laid down
in the boat, and was soon in a sound slumber; from
which he did not awake until it was quite dark.

He was then aroused by what he supposed the
halloo of his companion, and while listening to hear
the voice again, Belden made his appearance, loaded
down with a deer and other game, which he deposited
in the boat.   Wright asked him if he had heard a

human voice, or any thing resembling it, and was answered in the negative. Wright stepped to the bow of the boat to loosen it, when he was met by a loud scream and the glaring eye-balls of a monstrous panther directly before him. " Well Belden," he exclaimed starting back, you have brought a fine friend to supper!" " Yes," replied the latter, " and just wait until I give him a polite reception." Snatching up his rifle he discharged it, almost scorching the animal's head; still it was not hurt or frightened from its purpose; but stood at the bow and prevented them from untying. Wright then fired also without effect. Belden had soon reloaded, and with a piece of chalk carried for the purpose, he whitened the barrel of his rifle, took a more deliberate aim at the glaring target and fired again; when a scream and a few scratches followed, and all was still. Belden then hauled the animal into the boat, cast it off; and away they steered for their camp. The panther proved an exceedingly large and old one; its teeth were mostly gone, and it appeared to have been in the last stage of starvation.

When the hunting of fur in his former haunts would no longer pay, Wright removed to the westward. About the year 1796, he settled in the present town of Norway, N. Y., at which time he was some forty-five or fifty years of age. He then had a family, which consisted of his wife, whom he invariably called Nabby, a son, named Jonathan, and three

daughters. He wore, when hunting, a coat, called
at that time a French coat, which fastened tightly
round the waist, and moccasons, or shoe packs, as
then denominated. He was never known to wear
boots or shoes in hunting. When he left home on
a hunt, he was laden with his traps, about fifty pounds
of corn-meal, and his gun; with possibly some few
other *fixins*. Thus provided he would enter the
forest, and at times be gone for months, subsisting on
his meal and what his gun and traps could provide
him; with the addition of now and then a trout. He
had, as all men of his craft have, to eat many scanty
meals; but on returning to the settlements he made
ample amends for all privations in eating and drinking. He became known soon after his arrival in
Norway, by the familiar title of Uncle Jock. Most
people at that day were fond of liquor, and our hero
among the rest.

"Uncle Jock," said a friend one day, " —— has
stolen your jug!" A man who could scent a beaver
in the water, could easily find the course his jug had
taken, and soon he overtook the thief; not, however,
until he had secreted the stolen treasure. He refused
to disclose where it was, and old Nimrod clenched
and threw him upon the ground, where he struggled
manfully, but to little purpose; as his hands were
soon secured, and his conqueror had one to spare.
With an uplifted fist shouted the victor, "Now tell
me what you have done with the rum, or to heaven

or hell in a moment!" The brief time alloted for repentance, instantly disclosed the whereabouts of the jug, and a promise to pay all demands.

Some four or five years before Uncle Jock pitched his tent in Norway, a singular individual named Nichols began the life of a hunter in the forests contiguous to Norway. He was from some place in New Hampshire, upon the Connecticut river. He was to appearance some forty years of age, of middling stature, mild disposition; and in his deportment was simple, honest and obliging. He lived the most of his time in the wilderness by hunting and trapping. He was something of a musician, and kept a fiddle in his camp, with which to cheer his hermitage. The only living object of his care was a favorite hound, imported by Arthur Noble, from Ireland; " Which," as my correspondent observes, " was one of no vulgar blood; but a real Johnny Bull pup!" His fiddle, hound, rifle and traps, constituted the principal stock in trade of this secluded hunter.

Nichols was at first an unpracticed hunter, took but little fur, and as supposed made a poor living; for which reason it was thought by the few who now and then saw him; that he must have some resources to lean upon, besides the avails of his avocation; as he was always in funds to pay down for his plain wearing apparel, and things needed in his isolated camp. For a long time he avoided society, and was disinclined to speak of his former residence or pursuits; but before his death it became known that he was a good mathematician, and a mill-wright of the first order. From him the carpenters in that part of Herkimer county first learned to frame by the square rule, casting aside for ever their scribe rule. He was looked upon as a man of superior abilities, and what could have induced him to adopt a wilderness life was a mystery then, indeed, is to the present day.

When Uncle Jock moved into his neighborhood, Nichols, to whom he was previously known, became his partner in the chase, and under his teaching afterwards proved a very successful trapper. It was not known in Norway until Uncle Jock settled there, that Nichols had left a good property in land and mills on the Connecticut river, to which he never returned, or even looked after. Although it was never satisfactorily known what induced Nichols to abandon his property and friends, still it was believed to be solely attributable to *disappointment in love*. But whether some fair daughter of Yankeedom sighed her gentle spirit away with " hope deferred," or whether Nichols plodded his weary way through the wilderness in fruitless attempts to forget some maiden,

> With raven locks and lily skin,
> And cheeks with dimples deep within,

can not be told, as the secret died with him.

Uncle Jock and Nichols, together in their trapping excursions for beaver and other game, became familiar with nearly every source of the East and West

Canada creeks, Black, Racket, and Sacondaga rivers. They were as familiar with the lakes and water-courses on and contiguous to Brown's tract, as is a hen with her own chickens. Nichols, in tracing a small stream that is tributary to the West Canada creek, obtained upon or near it, a fine specimen of lead ore; but its locality has been sought for since, as yet in vain. In the latter part of his life Nichols renewed his avocation of a mill-wright, and only hunted in the fall and winter. He was drowned while repairing a mill, in 1803

In one of his rambles after his partner's death, Uncle Jock discovered a lake that is now called Jock's lake, to which I have elsewhere alluded. It has for years been a great resort for trout fishing. He said that when he first visited it, it appeared to be alive with fish, and for several years it became known to him alone. From it he would take loads of trout at almost any season of the year to the settlements.

Many individuals not hunters, but who were anxious to have a hunt, if it were only to be able to say that they had been in the *woods* and *camped* out with a *master hunter;* used to urge their company upon Uncle Jock; indeed, not a few of this sort received the tuition of Stoner and Foster. In a few of his trapping seasons Uncle Jock was accompanied by a stout able-bodied man, named Simmons, who was usually called Crookneck, probably from some peculiar inclination of his head. They were on snow-

23

shoes in the month of March, hunting marten; or as called by hunters wan-pur-noc-er. The bait used for those animals, which are a variety of weasel, is fresh meat; and as the hunters had taken no gun along, they had to depend on a dog to run down deer for marten-bait and their own food; which the crusted snow enabled them to do.

Their dog one day got a large buck at bay, and the hunters approached to kill it. Crookneck came up first, and hurried on thinking to seize the animal by its antlers and throw it down. As he approached the worried deer, it made a furious plunge at him. Falling short of its aim, it drove a hoof through one of his snow-shoes as Crookneck fell backwards! and not being familiar with the use of such broad " un- derstandings," it turned a somerset and fell upon the top of its antagonist. The newly initiated hunter, by his loud yells for help, gave evidence that his lungs were in good condition; and soon the master hunter was on hand, who drew his hunting knife, cut the deer's hamstrings, and then easily dispatched him. As the liberated hunter regained his feet, Uncle Jock dryly remarked, " Well Simmons, you are older than you might have been! If the buck had not fallen a little short, you would have been in oblivion now!"

At another time during the hunt, the dog started a large moose, and as the crust cut its legs, it stopped and kept the dog at bay until the hunters approached. Uncle Jock wanted his companion to kill it, but nothing could induce him to approach very near it. The senior hunter then initiated Crookneck into a new degree in game killing. He cut a pole, tied his knife to the end of it, and gaining the cover of a tree sufficiently near, he very dexterously wielded his pole and hamstrung the animal, when it was easily destroyed. To give his comrade a third degree in the mysterious art of slaughtering large animals in the forest, without a gun; when the dog called them to another moose, Uncle Jock fastened his knife to a long pole, stole up behind a large tree, and plunged the blade into the heart of his victim.

Uncle Jock was ever a firm believer in a Supreme Being, and also that *earnest* and *sincere prayer*, if consistent with our circumstances, would readily be answered by Divine Providence. One day after hearing an over-zealous, ignorant preacher pray at great length, a friend inquired *how he liked the prayer?* " How fortunate it was for him," he replied, " that he was addressing a Being that knew better than he did what he wanted, or he would have been in h— in a minute ! and at all events if he told the truth, he is deserving of a halter or state prison for life ! But though a *fool*, I think he is not quite as wicked as he represents himself."

His own prayers were remarkably brief, and delivered with great earnestness. They could hardly be repeated by another, however, without seeming very profane; and yet there was so much apparent sincerity

in their utterance by him, as to divest them of the
levity they might create when repeated by another.
One of them, which tradition has preserved entire, I
will insert. He was trapping marten in the month
of March, with Crookneck Simmons again for a partner, and was severely attacked with pleurisy. Crookneck soon became alarmed and wanted to go to the
nearest settlement, some twenty miles off, for assistance; much of which distance it would be necessary
to travel upon snow-shoes; but to this proposition
Uncle Jock would not consent. It was in vain for
him to remonstrate, however. In vain he told Crookneck, that it would take him two days to accomplish
the journey, in which time he must perish with cold,
if not by disease, as he could not keep his own fire
going; but go he would, and start he did.

Simmons had been gone but a few minutes, when
the invalid, conscious that he must soon die, unless
relieved immediately, uttered with great earnestness
the following prayer. "*Great God, Jehovah, Jesus
Christ, our Lord! if it is expedient that I should come
in and see Nabby and Jonathan again, let it be brought
to a crisis d—— quick !!* "

After the utterance of this laconic and eccentric
petition, the sick man said he not only felt greatly
relieved in mind, but also a consciousness that it would
be answered; and in about half an hour Crookneck
returned. " The more haste the less speed," is an
old adage, was verified in his case; for in attempting

to proceed as fast as possible, he got an improper angle into his neck, and down he went, breaking one of his snow-shoes; and not having ingenuity enough to repair it, he returned to their wigwam, where his sick friend was still lying upon a hurdle of hemlock boughs. The latter got him to sharpen his hunting knife, and also to cord his arm; when *he took the knife and bled himself.* Simmons fainted and fell, and Uncle Jock said " *he really thought the d—— fool would die first !* "

After a copious flow of blood, the invalid stopped it by thrusting a pin through the orifice, and winding it with a lock of his own hair. In a little while Simmons got about again, and in their camp-kettle made a strong decoction of hemlock boughs, of which Uncle Jock drank freely and laid down, when he experienced, as he said, the greatest relief he ever did in so short a space of time. He fell into a slumber which lasted several hours, and when he awoke he was entirely free from pain. The third day after he reached a settlement, and the fourth his prayer was answered, by again embracing his dear *Nabby* and little *Jonathan.*

Uncle Jock, it is believed, never had any serious difficulty with either Indian or white hunters. He often spoke of the hind quarters of a beaver, as affording the most dainty morsel an epicure could obtain; being preferable, as he said, to any other meat or fish, because *it possessed the virtues of both.* This wilderness-explorer seldom said bitter things of any one; but if insulted, the offender was pretty sure sooner or later, to feel his dry sarcasm. He received a pension from our government for Revolutionary services, under the first pension act; which might with proper economy have kept him and his Nabby from want, without the necessity of his hunting, as his children were grown up and married; but it only tended to make him the more independent of the settlements, and bury himself still deeper among the ever-greens of the forest, from which he could not be weaned.

It was his usual custom to look up suitable locations for fall hunting in June, when trees would peel the best; at which time he would build himself comfortable bark huts for fall and winter use. Hunting seemed to have become with him a second nature, and he followed it to the last. When his eye grew dim and his arm unsteady, so that he could no longer use his trusty rifle, he would still venture, unattended even by a dog into the far-off wilderness; and there, armed only with a hatchet, follow his avocation for weeks. He often said, that " the howling of the wolf, growling of the bear, screaming of the panther, and nightly concert of owls, kept him from being lonesome, and was music to his ears." Such is man of the woods ! The comforts of social life afford no enjoyment for him.

After a hunt, he came into the settlement with beaver and other furs, took them to market, returned home, sat down at the table to eat, and fell dead upon the floor without a struggle or groan, we believe in the seventy-fifth year of his age. He died about the year 1826.

The following brief notice of a hunter of northern New York, appeared in the newspapers, in January, 1850.

Death of a Nimrod.— The St. Lawrence Mercury says that Mr. Thomas Meacham, of the town of Hopkinton, St. Lawrence county, who died a few weeks ago, and who, for several years, was a resident of the North West Bay road, of what they then called township No. 10, in Franklin county, on Eastbrook, near the bounds of Hopkinton, was something of a hunter. He kept an exact account of the game killed by him, which amounts to the following: number of wolves, 214; panthers 77; bears 219; deer 2,550.

CHAPTER XVIII

Believing that the reader who has followed the footsteps of our trappers, would be interested in knowing something more of the animals they sought for fur, and of their habits, I here insert a portion of their history. The full grown Beaver will weigh from fifty to sixty pounds, and is about four feet in length from the snout to the end of the tail. The tail is a foot long, five or six inches wide, by one inch in thickness; and what is peculiar, although the body of the animal is so well covered with fur and hair, the tail is without either, except at its insertion, and is covered with scales. The fore part of the beaver has the taste and consistency of land animals, while the hind legs and tail have not only the smell, but the savor and nearly all the qualities of fish.

This peculiarity is thought by some to be accounted for by the habits of the animal, as when in the water its hind legs and tail are submerged and never seen; but it appears rather to be a connecting link between the inhabitants of land and water, its singularity in this respect being placed by nature beyond the control of mere circumstance. The beaver, when captured young, may easily be domesticated, and when hungry will ask by a plaintive cry for food. It is not

very particular about its food, if of some green vege-
table kind; but it generally refuses meat.

The bait used to entice beaver to a hunter's trap is
castoreum, as I have elsewhere remarked. This sub-
stance is obtained from the glandulous pouches of the
male animal, and is often called by hunters *barkstone*.
It is squeezed by hand into some vessel such as a cup
or bottle; a full grown animal affording several
ounces. Beaver *castor* is sometimes used by physi-
cians in medical practice. Oil, extracted from the
tail of the beaver, is used medicinally by the Indians.
The beaver is found only in cold or northern latitudes.
Its senses are acute. In its habits it is very neat, and
will allow no filth near its habitation.

In its natural or forest life, where undisturbed by
man, the beaver is social in its habits, often numbering twenty or more habitations in a single community, containing from two to twenty members each at
some seasons of the year, as circumstances warrant.
The following account of the manner in which those
sagacious animals construct their dams and dwellings,
is from Godman's Natural History.

" They are not particular in the site they select for
the establishment of their dwellings, but if in a lake
or pond, where a dam is not required, they are careful to build where the water is sufficiently deep. In
standing waters, however, they have not the advantage afforded by a current for the transportation of
their supplies of wood; which, when they build on a

running stream, is always cut higher up than the place of their residence, and floated down.

" The material used for the construction of their dams, are the trunks and branches of small birch, mulberry, willow, poplar, &c. They begin to cut down their timber for building, early in the summer, but their edifices are not commenced until about the middle or latter part of August, and are not completed until the beginning of the cold season. The strength of their teeth, and their perseverance in this work, may be fairly estimated, by the size of the trees they cut down. These are cut in such a manner as to fall into the water, and then floated towards the site of the dam or dwelling. Small shrubs, &c., cut at a distance from the water, they drag with their teeth to the stream, and then launch and tow them to the place of deposit. At a short distance above a beaver dam, the number of trees which have been cut down, appears truly surprising, and the regularity of the stumps which are left, might lead persons unacquainted with the habits of the animals to believe, that the clearing was the result of human industry.

" The figure of the dam varies according to circumstances. Should the current be very gentle, the dam is carried nearly straight across; but when the stream is swiftly flowing, it is uniformly made with a considerable curve, having the convex part opposed to the current. Along with the trunks and branches of trees, they intermingle mud and stones, to give

greater security; and when dams have been long undisturbed and frequently repaired, they acquire great
solidity, and their power of resisting the pressure of
water and ice, is greatly increased by the willow,
birch, &c., occasionally taking root, and eventually
growing up into something of a regular hedge. The
materials used in constructing the dams, are secured
solely by the resting of the branches, &c., against the
bottom, and the subsequent accumulation of mud and
stones, by the force of the stream, or by the industry
of the beavers.

"The dwellings of the beaver are formed of the
same materials as their dams, and are very rude,
though strong, and adapted in size to the number of
their inhabitants. There are seldom more than four
old, and six or eight young ones. Double of that
number have been occasionally found in one of the
lodges, though it is by no means a very common
occurrence.

" When building their houses, they place most of
the wood cross-wise, and nearly horizontally, observing no other order than that of leaving a cavity in
the middle. Branches, which project inward, are cut
off with their teeth and thrown among the rest. The
houses are by no means built of sticks first, and then
plastered, but all the materials, sticks, mud and stones,
if the latter can be procured, are mixed up together,
and this composition is employed from the foundation
to the summit. The mud is obtained from the adja-

cent banks or bottom of the stream or pond, near the door of the hut. Mud and stones, the beaver always carries by holding them between his fore paws and throat.

" Their work is all performed at night, and with much expedition. When straw or grass is mingled with the mud used by them in building, it is an accidental circumstance, owing to the nature of the spot whence the latter was taken. As soon as any part of the material is placed where it is intended to remain, they turn round and give it a smart blow with the tail. The same sort of blow is struck by them, on the surface of the water when they are in the act of diving.

" The outside of the hut is covered or plastered with mud, late in the autumn, and after frost has begun to appear. By freezing it soon becomes almost as hard as stone, effectually excluding their great enemy, the wolverine, during the winter. Their habit of walking over the work frequently during its progress, has led to the absurd idea of their using their tail as a trowel. The habit of flapping with the tail is retained by them in a state of captivity, and, unless it be the acts already mentioned, appears designed to effect no particular purpose. The houses, when they have stood for some time, and been kept in repair, become so firm from the consolidation of all the materials, as to require great exertion, and the ice chisel, or other iron instruments, to be broken

open. The laborious nature of such an undertaking
may easily be conceived, when it is known that the
tops of the houses are generally from four to six feet
thick at the apex of the cone."

The tail of the beaver when swimming, serves for
a rudder to aid the animal in its changing and often
rapid movement in the water. Near their habitations,
beavers establish magazines of green bark and soft
wood for food, keeping them well replenished; and
never do the members of one family plunder from the
larder of another. A community of beavers, although
it may consist of several hundred members, is seldom
disturbed by domestic difficulties; peace and harmony
being the bond which cements their union. If an
individual is threatened with danger, it immediately
takes measures to forewarn the whole village; which
is done by striking the water furiously with its tail.
Thus apprised of an enemy's proximity, the animals
take shelter either in the water or their strong dwellings, which are very tidily kept in order. The entrance to a beaver's dwelling is by a small open door
towards the water. The legs of a beaver are short,
the foot has four toes, and what is remarkable, the
hind feet have membranes between the toes to aid the
animal in swimming.

The Otter, which is also hunted for its valuable fur,
resembles the beaver somewhat in size, but very little
in its general habits. It lives a more solitary life,
often changing its habitation, especially in the winter;

24

when seeking to find unfrozen water. It often travels a great distance at such times, and if threatened by danger on the snow, it slides on its belly rapidly, leaving a furrow behind it. Some suppose it is done by the animal in an attempt to bury itself in the snow. This is not the case, but rather a necessity arising from the shortness of its legs, as proportioned to its body. The animal has been known, not unfrequently, to get upon a hill near its own residence, when covered with snow, and with its fore feet bent back, slide down the hill for several rods, with great rapidity. This feat is evidently performed for a pastime.

The otter usually feeds upon fish, frogs, and other small animals; and when they can not be obtained, it will eat the tender branches and bark growing in or near the water, and sometimes grass. They are bad economists of food, and often annoy a community of beavers, by destroying their husbanded store of growing eatables. The otter is less numerous than the beaver, and its fur more valuable. The foot of the otter has five toes, connected by webs, like the toes of a duck. It displays considerable sagacity in preparing its burrow, which it makes upward under a bank, the entrance being beneath the water, and that in a freshet it shall not be drowned, it opens a small vent to the surface, often concealed by leaves and bushes. The otter taken young has been tamed, and taught to fish for its master.

The Musk-rat in its habits much resembles the beaver, but is small as compared with that animal, being scarcely one-third as large. It is called the musk-rat, because it is furnished with a peculiar matter, of a strong musky odor. The entrance to its burrow like that of the beaver, is usually made under a bank beneath the water. Its food, which is similar to that of the beaver, is usually sought in the night. Although the latter animal entirely disappears as the country becomes settled, it is not so with the musk-rat, it continues its proximity to man's abode, occupying marshy lands along the shore of some river or pond, long after the lands are cleared up and cultivated to the water's edge. It is an excellent swimmer, and dives with great celerity. The flesh of the musk-rat is seldom eaten unless in cases of great hunger, because of its powerful odor. It is still quite numerous in and about the Mohawk river, where the country has been settled for more than a century, and is destroyed every spring in great numbers, when driven from its burrows by heavy freshets, at the breaking up of winter. On such occasions the banks of the Mohawk are lined with men and boys, watching with eagle-eye to shoot the terrified animals, which are often slain in the very villages contiguous to the river. Not unfrequently they are, by freshets, driven up drains into cellars, where they make great havoc among cabbage and other vegetables there stored.

The Pine Marten, or forest weasel, is so called, because of its preference to forests of pine, in the lofty tops of which it resides. It lives upon small quadrupeds and birds, obtained in the forest, and seldom approaches the habitation of man. It sometimes lives in the hollow of a tree, and not unfrequently takes forcible possession of a squirrel's nest, which it enlarges and occupies to rear its young. The fur of the marten is often used in the manufacture of hats, and in ornamenting winter dresses. The animal is about eighteen inches in length to the tail, the latter appendage being about ten inches long. The male is nearly one-third larger than the female. Trappers have often found the taking of the marten profitable.

The Wolverine, which annoys the hunter by stealing game from his traps, resembles the skunk somewhat in appearance. It is about two feet two inches long from the end of the nose to the origin of the tail, and the latter, which is quite bushy, is some eight inches long to the end of the hair. The animal is very strong for its size, having very sharp claws and teeth. It is covered with fur, but not of fine quality. It is said to be able to defend itself against the attacks of much larger animals, not unfrequently overpowering and destroying them.

APPENDIX.

A.— (page 23).— What finally became of "*Billy the Musician,*" on the breaking up of the Johnson family, is not known with certainty. Mr. Shew seems confident he did not remove to Canada with the Johnstown royalists. He probably went to New York city.

B.— (page 23).— Sir William Johnson's *Gardener*, who answered to the name of "*Old Daddy Savage,*" was very old at the time of the Baronet's death. He had long been faithful to his trust, and doubtless deserved a better finale to mortality. He remained with Sir John Johnson until his flight to Canada, when he was left at the mercy of the winds, or if not, with a pittance that soon placed him there. He was for several years supported by the charity of the district until his death, which occurred back of Johnstown about the year 1780. He died at the age of nearly one hundred years.

C.—(page 23).—As suggested to the writer by an antiquarian friend, the name of *Pontiac* was probably given to his waiter by Sir William Johnson, as a compliment to the distinguished Ottawa chieftain of that name. At the termination of the French war in 1763, which ended in the conquest of Canada by Great Britain, several western tribes of Indians who had been in the French interest, and often engaged with the French against the English and Iroquois, were unreconciled to British dominion; and, instigated by Pontiac, their master spirit, they leagued " in a confederacy, the design of which was to expel the English, and restore French ascendency."* Under the direction of Pontiac, the confederates captured several British posts on the western frontier, and by their bold and atrocious acts were filling the country with alarm, when Gen. Bradstreet was sent against them in 1765, with a force sufficient to subdue and bring them to terms. Sir William Johnson accompanied the expedition to Niagara, where he held a treaty, in July, " with the Shawanese, Delawares and Mingos;" as intimated in a letter from him to Commissary General Leake, under date of July 13, 1765.† Pontiac and other chiefs in his confidence, not present at the Niagara treaty, met Sir William Johnson on behalf of the British government at Ontario, in July 1766; when the war hatchet was buried, and peace restored.‡ This latter meeting is barely hinted at on page 861, Vol. 2 of the Documentary History of New-

* Turner's *History of the Holland Purchase* in Western N. Y.
† Documentary History, Vol. 2, p. 820.
‡ Correspondence of *Lyman C. Draper*, of Leverington, Pa.

York, in a letter from the Baronet to Gen. Gage ; but what seems passing strange, the wary chieftain Pontiac is not named in the Broadhead papers.

———

D. — (page 29). — Samuel Olmsted and Zadock Sherwood, natives of Ridgfield, Connecticut, located at Northville about the year 1786, going up the Sacondaga from Fish-House in a canoe, containing a few necessary articles ; and after constructing a rude hut, they began to clear up the forest. Nearly four years after the two named took up their abode in the wilderness, Caleb and Daniel Lobdell, brothers, removed thither from Danbury, Connecticut. Between the advent of the Lobdells, and the year 1794, the Sacondaga settlement had been increased by the arrival of Joseph Olmsted, Abraham Van Aernam, Paul Hammond, John Shoecraft, Aaron Olmsted, Samuel Price, and possibly one or two others. The settlers, who had gone through the hardships and experienced the thousand and one difficulties attending the settling of all new countries, were at this time living very comfortably on the lands, not a few acres of which, on both sides of the river, were under improvement ; yielding, in their virgin strength, a rich compensation to the husbandman.

Indian hunters were very frequent guests among the pioneer settlers of Northville ; and as the latter spared no pains to cultivate amity with them, the reader may judge their surprise, when, on some occasion in the summer of 1794 — possibly on the eve of which intimations of savage invasion had been clandestinely put afloat, an alarm spread through the settlement, that a party of Indians hideously painted were in their vicinity, only waiting a favorable opportunity to kill the inhabitants and bear off their hard earnings. While all was bustle and confusion at the rude tenements of the settlers, peal after peal of fire-arms broke the stillness of night, interrupted occasionally with the whoops and shouts of the foe, approaching as they seemed to be on the west side of the river. Every preparation that could be made on the emergency to resist the invaders was quickly made; and the colonists, there being no chicken-hearted among them, resolved to sell their lives as dearly as possible. Hour after hour wore away until morning : the clangor of arms and lungs had ceased ; still the foeman had not crossed the river.

Some of the settlers, whose mettle had been tried in the Revolution, crossed the river in the morning, when, lo! they found greater evidence of Indian invasion than did the Windhamites, on the morning after their alarm by the frogs of their neighborhood in olden time; for in a cornfield nearly opposite the Lobdell dwelling, there were numerous mocasined tracks, and not a few half consumed gun-wads. One peculiarity was observable, however ; the footsteps did not turn in at the toes, as those of the red man invariably did. It was now recollected, that Price and Aaron Olmsted had not been among the excited inhabitants when counseling for defense ; and from some impending circumstances, suspicion rested upon them of having played possum for some purpose.

It soon leaked out that the suspicion of the inhabitants was well founded ; that the two had undertaken,
as the menials of certain land speculators, to frighten
away the earliest settlers, for which service they were
to receive *twenty-five dollars;* the land sharks to get
the improvements the hard-fisted yeomanry had made,
for a very nominal sum. Accordingly they repaired to
the cornfield with pistols and stentorian lungs, to practice the war dance. When the trick was discovered,
the Achans, who had families, were obliged to make a
hasty flight from the country, to escape the vengeance
of their enraged neighbors ; and so precipitate was their
departure, that Olmsted forgot his own, and took along
another man's wife. Thus terminated the only Indian
alarm the pioneers of Northville ever experienced.

(Facts from *Nathan P. Lobdell*, a son of one of the pioneer
settlers named above.)

E.—(page 199).—The solitary pine formerly standing on Elba island in Fourth lake, which was twelve
or fifteen inches in diameter, says John Stilwell of
Herkimer county, was cut down in the spring of 1831.
In the preceding summer, he adds, the following thrilling
incident occurred there.

A party of fishermen in several boats were engaged
on the lake near the island catching trout, when their
attention was arrested by an unusual noise upon the

lake shore nearly a mile distant. Presently a noble
deer was seen bounding along the beach, closely pursued
by a monstrous panther. The timid animal plunged
into the lake and swam for the opposite shore, followed
by its bloodthirsty foe.· One of the boats which
chanced to be directly in the deer's course, was rowed
farther out from the island, to give the panting animal
sea-room; when it came into the allotted space, and
not daring to trust itself upon the sterile island near
which it passed, it swam off to the opposite shore —
adding a second mile to its voyage — and safely disappeared in the forest. The deer could swim faster
than its pursuer; and as the latter approached the
fishermen, they closed in toward the island, upon which
they compelled it to land.

The panther, for its better security, lost no time in
ascending the pine to its branches, where it crouched
with lashing tail; evidently in no very good humor at
being thwarted in its murderous design. The fishermen, some of whom were fortunately armed with rifles,
then gave their boats positions affording a good view
of the panther, yet far enough off to ensure their own
safety, should it be wounded and resent the insult. A
rifle was poised by a marksman, and the animal fell
dead at the first fire. It was a very large one, and its
skin, I am told, is now in the Utica Museum. If another effort in nature should produce a second pine or
some other forest-tree on this western Elba, we hope
it may be allowed to remain in its sentinel position, if
only to afford a favorable place from which to shoot
panthers.

Hunters and fishermen about the lakes on Brown's tract are usually much annoyed in warm weather by musketoes and punkies. It is a fact worthy of note, however, that they are not troublesome on this Elba of Fourth lake : hence a reason why it has long been a favorite place for sportsmen to take their lunch, or remain over night. For some years, the chips of the Elba pine served the temporary occupants of the island as substitutes for plates, from which not a few hearty meals have been eaten.

www.ingramcontent.com/pod-product-compliance
Lightning Source LLC
Chambersburg PA
CBHW020852020726
47497CB00005B/1370